The Elephant Girl

Chitta Ranjan

FROG BOOKS

ISBN 978-93-52019-24-3

First published in India 2019 by Frog Books
An imprint of Leadstart Publishing Pvt Ltd

Sales Office:
Unit No.25/26, Building No.A/1,
Near Wadala RTO,
Wadala (East), Mumbai – 400037 India
Phone: +91 22 24046887
Email: info@leadstartcorp.com
www.leadstartcorp.com

Disclaimer: The Views expressed in this book are those of the Author and do not pertain to be held by the Publisher.

Editor: Abhishek James Chandran
Cover: Ashwini Jadhav
Layouts: Victor Patali

MAP OF THE REGION

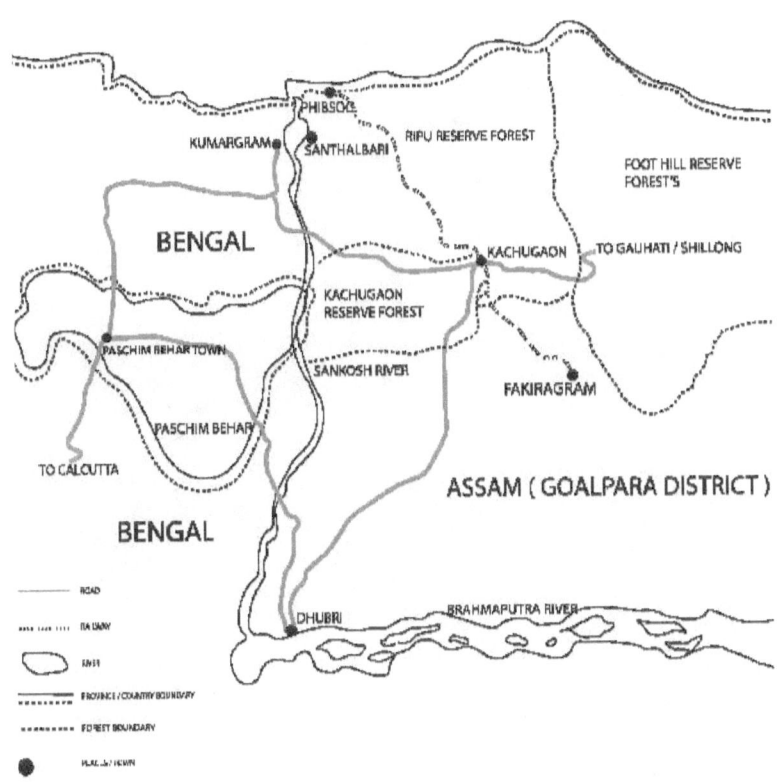

BHUTAN

PHIBSOO

KUMARGRAM
SANTHALBARI
RIPU RESERVE FOREST

FOOT HILL RESERVE
FOREST'S

BENGAL

KACHUGAON
TO GAUHATI / SHILLONG

KACHUGAON
RESERVE FOREST

PASCHIM BEHAR TOWN

SANKOSH RIVER

FAKIRAGRAM

PASCHIM BEHAR

TO CALCUTTA

ASSAM (GOALPARA DISTRICT)

BENGAL

ROAD

RAILWAY

RIVER

PROVINCE / COUNTRY BOUNDARY

FOREST BOUNDARY

PLACE / TOWN

DHUBRI
BRAHMAPUTRA RIVER

Dedication

In fragrant memories of my parents who raised me in the land of the elephant girl.

Contents

About the Author

Chitta Ranjan is a chemical engineer who lives in Perth, Western Australia, with his wife and two children. His childhood spent in the verdant north-eastern corner of India sparked his fascination for nature and wildlife. He has lived in Delhi, Kuala Lumpur, Abu Dhabi and Paris before migrating to Australia in the 2000s. He loves to visit India regularly to meet up with his family and soak up the culture and history; and to seek those corners of Eastern Himalayas, which are still green, wet and wild. His hobbies include bird watching, photography, reading and endlessly arranging the books in his book case.

His love for the jungles of India coupled with his interest in the history of the princely states under British India have culminated in his first novel: *The Elephant Girl*.

Acknowledgements

I have to start by thanking my soul mate, Manjuri, for accepting, very naively, what seemed like an anniversary gift, but in reality, was the colossal task of reading a rough-cut draft of the manuscript. If my murder mystery loving wife wouldn't have liked, the elephant girl would not have seen the light of the day. I have this book for you because of her. To her, I owe my special thanks for being my first reader and for her patience—two years is a long time.

And to my curious daughter Jiri who kept on asking; Is the book finished? Can I read it? She has grown two years older in the process.

My son, Joor, hasn't read a page—I don't think he has any intention to read it—but he randomly picks up a character and says 'I like him a lot.' Thank you for your encouragement in your own special way and for designing the chapter head logos.

To my sister, Nandini; for her support, sincere best wishes and unconditional love.

I want to thank Asmita, Anthea, Aparna, Bindiya, Leanne and Bhaskar J Barua of Agoratoli Resort for their constant encouragement, reading of the draft and providing me with valuable feedback.

I am grateful to my friends for their constant loving encouragement and to Leadstart for publishing my debut novel.

Chapter 1

Prince Raj Narayan gazed nostalgically at the portrait adorning the reception of the Calcutta Hotel. A majestic Bengal Tiger, over twelve feet long and lifeless, lay at the feet of his father, *Maharaja* Bichitra Narayan. The *Maharaja* was flanked by his assistants, and little Raj knelt on the ground, his hand resting on the tiger's forehead. Raj turned to look out at the expanse of the Calcutta Maidan, the overnight summer rain gave it a brilliant sheen. The lushness suddenly made him miss the peace and tranquillity of home; he wondered if the trip was really necessary. He thought about the invitation he'd received a week ago from the Calcutta Tram Company, commemorating the fifty-fifth year of its establishment. He was not even sure he would attend, yet here he was. The morning break was in full swing, and the sound of clinking crockery and the delegate's chatter drove Raj to shift his gaze out to the skyline, but the turbid streets below seemed to further amplify the noise from the hall.

The fragrant aroma of Makaibari wafted out to him on the balcony, enticing him inside for a cup of tea. As he poured the amber liquid through the silver strainer, he caught sight of the mounted head of a sambar stag. Such a big sambar, it must be from the forests of North Bengal or Assam, he thought, taking himself back to the balcony. The brightness of the morning sun made the interior of the hall seem dark, but Raj involuntarily scanned the crowd of delegates. It didn't take him long to notice a young man of English appearance, presumably taking up his first job as a bureaucrat in British India. He was tall, and his face had a sense of openness about it. Yet Raj noticed he looked a bit lost like he was searching for someone. As Raj surveyed him, he realised the young man was walking toward him.

'Your Highness, I am Bert Jenkins from Assam,' the young man said. 'Divisional Forest Officer of Kachugaon forest division, in the Goalpara district. It's next to your state. Originally I am from Chesterfield, England.' The sudden detailed introduction unnerved Raj. Most of the delegates didn't know much about Paschim Behar, one of almost five hundred princely states of British India.

'What is a DFO doing at a tramways seminar?' He didn't hide his bemusement; he was convinced the officer was much younger than he.

'My superiors thought it could be a useful seminar for me,' Jenkins said. 'They perhaps thought there would be a discussion on forest tramways. My division has India's only forest tramway.' The chairperson rang a bell to announce the commencement of the next session, the sound breaking through the din of the conversing delegates. But Jenkins' mention of the forest tramway made Raj furrow his eyebrows; he used to visit the Kachugaon forests near his state when he was a child.

'Kachugaon ... I know the place,' Raj said, experiencing his second pang of nostalgia for the morning. 'So, there is a forest tramway in Kachugaon? Next to Paschim Behar?'

'Your Highness, there is. Its journey reveals the myriad wealth of the Himalayan foothill forest unlike anything you've seen,' Jenkins said. The second bell rang. Raj looked at Jenkins, lifting his eyebrows as an inquiry of whether he was willing to forego the pre-lunch session. Jenkins nodded.

'Tell me about this tramway. I have been to that region many times, but I don't remember seeing it.'

'Your Highness, the Goalpara Forest Tramway is a unique property of the Assam forest department. The four-hour ride takes you into the wilderness of the Ripu reserve from the small township of Fakiragram. It traverses all the way to the Bhutan border, at the extreme north of the reserve. The track length is forty miles, and everyone's favourite stop is the township of Kachugaon, the hub of all forestry-related activities of Western Assam. Most of my junior officers are based there as it is the gateway to the great wilderness of Assam's forest. The tram passes through terai grasslands, dense sal tracts, riverine and deciduous forests, and ultimately a patch of tropical forest before it reaches the base of the Himalayas in the kingdom of Bhutan.' Raj was so engrossed he completely forgot about the session going on in the hall. 'When was the last time you visited those forests?' Jenkins asked.

'A long time ago,' Raj said, shaking his head. 'I went there as a child, with the royal hunting parties. However, I attended high school in Mayo and later moved to London, so my connection to the forests has been somewhat lost.'

'But what brings you here?' Jenkins asked.

'Well,' Raj said with a smile, 'I don't own a tramway or railway, but I have always loved trains and trams. The fond memories of train trips from my childhood cemented my love for the railways, which grew ever more so during my stay in London.'

'Why don't you come to Kachugaon to ride the forest train? I am planning a trip in a week's time and my deputy there is organising for me to travel to the Bhutan border. It would be an honour if you were to join me,' Jenkins said.

'I would love to join you,' Raj said, though he sounded somewhat hesitant. 'By the way, how did you end up in the Goalpara forests?' He was surprised to find his curiosity had not abated.

'Five years ago, I was in England, unsure of what to do with my life. I applied to the Indian Civil Services,' Jenkins said, then added with a smile, 'unsuccessfully though. A year later, I applied to the Imperial Forestry Service and succeeded in being sent straight to the Forestry Research Institute at Dehradun. I completed my two years of training in forestry and lumbering techniques by which time I was ready to be posted to one of the nine provinces of British India.'

'You chose Assam?'

'Yes, I chose Assam cadre,' Jenkins said and gave a small sigh. 'There was a reason, and it was a pretty good decision. I quickly fell in love with the scenic wilderness of my division, which encompasses Ripu and Kachugaon. You must have heard of them. They are two very large reserved forests with extremely dense vegetation and rich timber wealth.' Raj nodded. 'Ripu and Kachugaon have the finest plantations of sal, the principal tree of the railway sleeper industry of this country. The irony of the imperial forest department is that all this protection is for the sake of exploitation,' Jenkins said with a smile tinged with both sadness and sarcasm.

Raj nodded again. 'I presume the main function of the tramway is hauling timber from the interiors?'

'Yes, that is correct. My role is to plan and execute the felling operations. But we are facing problems from poachers and illegal loggers. The boat-making industry in Bengal is encouraging a lot of illegal tree felling in our forests. The biggest threat is from the ruthless river bandits who travel upstream along the various rivers and remove timber hauls via the river route, by simply floating them downstream.'

By now the morning session had concluded, and the delegates were dispersing for lunch. A few curious delegates were heading towards the balcony.

'Alright young man, it was nice meeting and talking to you,' Raj said, as he shook hands with Jenkins, resting his left hand on the man's shoulder. 'I shall take my leave now, and I wish you a pleasant stay in Calcutta.'

Jenkins hesitated, as though deciding what to do. Finally, he extended his invitation again. 'Your Highness, would you not like to ride our forest tramway before it stops plying, as forecasted by the experts here?'

Raj sensed the earnestness about the young man. He was beginning to like the young forest officer, but wondered whether he had the official authority to invite a crown prince to his division. He remembered all the protocol issues when members of the princely states visited the Indian provinces. Politely declining the invitation again, he stepped away to talk to some other acquaintances present at the event.

Two days later, Raj was back at the palace in his bedroom with Princess Divya. The bejewelled Princess was dressed in a Bandhani saree and looked even more stunning than in the large picture of her adorning the wall. Raj realised how much he had missed his wife. He could see, despite her effort to dress her best, she didn't look well. The pregnancy was taking its toll.

'Your Highness, you will have to stay with me until the baby comes. I was feeling very lonely and scared while you were away,' Divya said, as Raj eyed her swollen belly.

'There's still a few weeks until the baby arrives. I will surely be with you from now onwards,' Raj said, moving closer to her and sitting at the edge of her bed. Divya rested her head on his head and wrapped one arm around his. As he stroked Divya's honey-like smooth, yet slightly wet hair, Raj's thoughts drifted to the second meeting he'd had with Jenkins whilst in Calcutta. He had run into Jenkins in the foyer of the Calcutta Hotel and they had agreed to have dinner at Raj's hotel. Over the dinner, they talked again of the forest and wildlife. After dinner and two glasses of sherry, with a sense of finality Raj had suddenly said, 'Alright, I will come. Let's be discreet about this trip. I don't want your district officials or Shillong's to know about the trip.' Now, as he lay with his wife in the luxuriant comfort of his room, his hand caressing the smoothness of her tummy, he wondered what on earth had gotten into him.

Chapter 2

Raj was walking down the hall toward his study when he saw a familiar figure in white shorts and a polo shirt walking briskly towards him. Trailing behind him was a short man and two orderlies carrying racquets and towels.

'I hear you are going to Assam.' It was his brother Indra Narayan.

'Yes,' Raj hesitated. 'I want to see the Goalpara Forest Tramway. I will be back in a day or two. But how did you come to know?'

'Someone was talking about it. By the way, mother was enquiring as to whether you were back from Calcutta.'

Raj nodded, feeling amused that Indra addressed their stepmother, who was only a few years older than they, as 'mother.'

'Where is the *Maharaja*?' Raj realised that he had not seen his father since his return. 'Father is down with a fever, so I played with *Diwan Sahib* today. I'm going to see him now.' Raj then acknowledged the presence of the small bespectacled man, the Prime Minister of the state, who looked quite odd in his tennis shorts. He looked at his athletic brother, shook his head, and couldn't but appreciate Indra's patience.

As Indra went ahead towards the *Maharaja's* chamber, Raj retreated to his study. The room was spacious and bright, with a large mahogany table in the centre and book cases lining the walls on three sides. An expanse of the window took up much of the remaining side of the room. Attendants had already laid out his breakfast on the table.

He looked at the spread—how much he had started enjoying taking these solitary breakfasts in his study with its magnificent view. The interior rooms of the palace didn't afford such a vista. He looked out the window towards the ornate palace gates; there were no visitors yet. Flowering *golmohur* trees lined the long driveway from the gates to the palace entrance. It was a typical bright summer morning that had not yet revealed how hot the day would become. He looked toward the sky. There were no rain clouds.

Taking a bite of the French toast, he paced across the room, wondering again about his decision to visit the Assam forest. And that too with an Englishman he had met only once. A feeling of unease descended upon him as he realised that the forest official would be arriving at any moment. He picked up yesterday's copy of *The Star of India* and started browsing through the headlines, as his mind went into an overdrive trying to think of an excuse to cancel the trip and somehow make it up to the officer who had taken the trouble to drive all the way up to the palace. His thoughts were broken by a quiet knock on the door.

'Your Highness, where shall we put these?' It was his personal attendant carrying his Winchester rifle, along with bullets, binoculars, and a book titled *Wild Animals of British India*. Raj looked at Tapash, a mild-mannered man in his thirties. His well-oiled hair was neatly parted in the centre, his clothes starched and spotless. He exuded his usual aura of efficiency. Raj gestured to Tapash, asking him to wait. An orderly arrived, carrying a big tiffin box for his lunch that he would eat on the way to Assam, evidence of Tapash's meticulous instructions. Raj calculated that if they started at around ten in the morning, by the time they reached the Sankosh River which separated Bengal from Assam, it would be well past lunch time. Was he doing the right thing by planning to start out today? His new friend would arrive already quite exhausted. Perhaps it would be wise to postpone the trip by a day. The officer might be interested in seeing the royal elephant stable, which housed several prized elephants captured in the section of Assam Forest that was under his jurisdiction.

'Tapash, take all these inside,' he said walking to the window. 'I am not going anywhere today.'

No, this trip is not right. I hardly know the man. Father is unwell. Divya is unwell.

Tapash looked surprised, he couldn't hide his unhappiness either. But Raj had now convinced himself that there was many a reason to cancel the trip. He would apologise to his guest and make up for the last-minute change by entertaining him in the palace for a day or two. Though he had found the description of the Goalpara Forest Tramway fascinating enough to say yes to Jenkins' invitation, it now occurred to him, it may have been extended only out of courtesy.

Raj relaxed a bit, sinking into the plush cushioning of his office chair, but there was something else bothering him too. How did Indra know that he was going to Assam? He had decided about the trip while in Calcutta and after returning to the palace he had not told anyone except Tapash. He had, of course, mentioned it to Divya whose relief on seeing her husband after a week of being away disappeared on hearing about yet another trip. He sank further into his chair with his hands locked behind his head and legs outstretched. To distract himself, he scanned the numerous bookshelves lining the walls, but his eyes somehow fell upon a book that fascinated him as a child. Seeing the book, *Mysterious Animals of the World,* his mind flashed back to his childhood days when a loathsome image, a black monkey face with a golden mane, used to haunt him at night.

'He has arrived.' It was Tapash, craning his neck, still standing in the doorway. Raj looked out the window to see a Ford Model A making its way along the driveway towards the portico of the palace. The study was on the upper level of the double-storey palace. Raj moved closer to the window and saw Jenkins alight from the car.

'You go and receive him,' he said to Tapash. Tapash rushed out to greet the visitor. Raj heard him say, '*Sahib,* please follow me to His Highness' office.'

'I have a gift for His Highness. Can you get someone to carry the box for me?' Jenkin said.

'His Highness is waiting for you in his study. I will arrange for your box to be carried in soon.'

'No, I want it delivered to him as I see him. Now.' Jenkins

retorted in a voice that was more tired than impatient. Tapash shouted a few names and a large servant appeared from nowhere. Raj saw Jenkins leading them to the back of the car.

As Tapash ushered Jenkins into the study, Raj's warm smile came naturally. 'Jenkins, a pleasure to see you. I am sure you must be tired after the long drive,' he said.

'Thank you for asking, your Excellency, but I actually feel quite refreshed. It was drizzling in Dhubri. It was a cold, wet start for me in the morning. It became warmer as I crossed the Assam border though. But the cool interiors of your palace have revitalised me,' Jenkins said. The chirpiness in the young officer's voice after such a long trip surprised Raj. After exchanging more pleasantries, Raj said, 'Why don't you visit our elephant stable? Most of the elephants are from your forest division. Maybe after lunch, we can head off in that direction?'

'Your Highness, I have heard about the famed elephant stable of Paschim Behar. But don't you think we will be late if we stay here until lunch? In fact, I was thinking of starting for Kachugaon now if you are agreeable.' Raj hadn't expected such enthusiasm on Jenkins' part.

'Actually, my wife was complaining of unease this morning. Yesterday she ate something which didn't agree with her. She slept well, but from the early morning, she has been sweating profusely and complaining of breathlessness. I had the palace doctor call in on her. The doctor prescribed some emergency medication. She is all right now,' Raj said looking apologetically at Jenkins. He thought by now Jenkins would have realised that the long trip he'd made had been futile.

'I am really sorry to hear that,' Jenkins said. Raj couldn't detect any sullenness yet.

'In fact, the doctor has advised me to shift her to Gwalior Palace as they have better medical facilities there. It's quite strange.' Jenkins nodded sympathetically. Raj sensed that the young officer was trying to hide his confusion on being bombarded with the health issues of the Princess. 'It was ludicrous, the suggestion from our palace physician,' Raj continued, 'to send her away. Does Paschim Behar not have enough medical facilities to handle pregnancies?' Jenkins looked on, continuing to nod. 'In fact, we are expecting our first child.' Raj clarified finally.

'Congratulations, Your Highness,' Jenkins said. 'I do wish you and the Princess the very best for this momentous occasion. I can certainly understand your reluctance to leave her now.'

Raj realised that Tapash and the servants were still waiting outside with the box. He gestured for them to enter and pointing to their heavy load, he asked, 'What have you got in the box?'

Jenkins motioned for them to place the box near Raj's feet. 'This is a gift to your royal museum from the Assam forest department,' Jenkins said. 'Your Highness, if you would allow, I would like to open the box and show you the contents, which may be of interest to a wildlife enthusiast such as yourself.'

He removed the latch and lifted the cover off the box. A golden aura emulated from inside. Raj jumped in fright, as inside was a grotesque black face looking straight up at him with all the teeth including canines fiercely bared.

'Your Highness, may I present to you, the most elusive, the rarest primate in the whole world: the Sankosh langur. Also known as the golden langur, this elusive creature is found only in my forest division,' he explained. 'Very few people have ever seen this creature. My intent of the tram journey with you was to investigate the presence of this monkey. Some of my men have reported sightings of this creature on the tram tracks, but I wanted to see it for myself,' Jenkins said. 'Maybe some other time, Your Highness.'

Raj was staring at the stuffed langur, which was a fully-grown adult. 'Where was this collected?' Raj asked, his voice was low and trembled a little.

'Not far from one of the stations of our tramway. A place called Phibsoo, near the Indo-Bhutan border.'

'Let's leave for Kachugaon today. We can take the tram ride tomorrow and be back the day after. I need to be with my wife,' Raj said. 'Load the car,' he instructed Tapash. He saw a glint of pleasure in his attendant's eyes.

Chapter 3

Brown *Sahib* was sitting in his easy chair, rocking slowly. He heard the plaintive call of a brainfever bird, the melancholy sound almost like a foreboding of unpleasant news. He strained his eyes but could only make out the silhouettes of a few imperial pigeons sitting atop a tall silk cotton tree against the rising sun. The pigeons took off suddenly in a flurry of motion. He saw a cyclist riding towards the bungalow. He was surprised to see Amaresh Baruah, his ranger, so early in the morning.

'Jenkins *Sahib* is coming this evening,' the young ranger said as he dismounted and saluted his senior. 'He is bringing with him Prince Raj Narayan of Paschim Behar. They want to ride the tramway to Phibsoo tomorrow.' The surprise quickly turned into irritation. Imperials weren't commonly seen near the bungalow, and they looked so plump and edible. He knew his senior was arriving and had lined up a few things for the visit, including a trip into the wilderness in exactly three days. Even though there was a lull in forest activities due to the rainy season, he had planned the tramway trip for his senior for a special reason; the stated official reasons were, of course, different: bridge repairs, selecting new patrolling post locations and *sal* regeneration inspection.

'What is that you were saying about the Prince?'

'Jenkins *Sahib* is bringing Prince Raj Narayan of Paschim Behar with him today. They want to go to Phibsoo tomorrow. I have been asked to inform you.' Ranger Baruah repeated.

'They want to travel tomorrow by the tramway and you are telling me now?' A sudden rage built within him. 'Why didn't he communicate anything directly to me about bringing the Prince from Paschim Behar? When I met him in Dhubri before his Calcutta trip, he didn't tell me anything about any prince.' He stood up, his fist clenched. He didn't like surprises —especially those relating to entry into the reserved forests under his jurisdiction.

Kachugaon can't be dictated by Dhubri. This place is administered by me. I handle everything here. And I decide when the tramway runs. How quickly things change, he thought. It was only a year ago his forests were formed into a new division, to be regulated from the town of Dhubri by a young Indian Forest Service Officer called Bert Jenkins. And now this Jenkins, with only one year of service, suddenly sends instructions that he must organise a royal train trip to the foothills of Bhutan. He was baffled and irritated in equal measure. If Jenkins were to travel the next day, it would be difficult to convince him to take another trip shortly after, he thought. If the pre-arranged trip didn't take place, all his preparation would be in vain, and it would be a logistical nightmare to arrange another.

'Of all places, why does he want to go to Phibsoo? Is he

coming to hunt, or does he just want a ride?'

'No sir, he is not coming to hunt. I think they just want to ride the train.'

Brown *Sahib* thought for some time and then said, 'You proceed to the station. I will join you soon.' He threw the remaining tea out of his cup and, turning towards the back of the bungalow, shouted, 'Can someone get me a cup of hot tea?'

As Ranger Baruah left, Brown *Sahib* saw another ranger approaching the bungalow. It was Ranger Das, a sombre expression on his face. *Now what?* He wondered angrily.

An hour later, Brown *Sahib* reached the station. He found Baruah outlining the next day's trip to the junior field staff. Listening in, he took stock of the arrangements from Baruah. He wanted to send the Prince back to his palace as quickly as possible so that he could concentrate on the other trip he had planned for Jenkins. Clasping his hands behind his back he thought of Ranger Das' visit earlier to alert him to the recent spate of timber smugglers from Bengal, who had been entering the forest by river routes. Once this business with the trips was over, he would turn his attention to the river bandits. He had to wipe out this menace of timber smuggling. He had already lost quite a few members of his field staff to the smugglers.

'I have never allowed this tramway to be used for any purpose other than to carry my men, materials and logs. This is what I have ensured for the last thirty years. And tomorrow it is meant to take a prince appearing from nowhere on a joyride,' Brown *Sahib* said loudly to nobody in particular, his face reflecting the frustration and anger that had built up, receiving one bad news after another since early that morning. Trying to test his luck, he turned to Baruah. 'If the Prince is interested in a tramway ride, why not take him along the non-forest line to Fakiragram? He can see our big timber depot, and from there he can easily take a train back to Paschim Behar.' He knew he would be able to persuade Jenkins to take the trip to the forest section after seeing off the visitor.

'Well, actually,' Baruah said, 'Jenkins *Sahib* told me that he wanted to take the Prince through the forest section as the Prince is quite interested in wildlife. Also, they are thinking of going for a trek in the Phibsoo region.'

'Going for a trek in the Phibsoo area?' Brown *Sahib* felt the first stir of real panic.

By the time Brown *Sahib* had lined up everything in the station by giving out various instructions to the foreman, fireman, train guard and others, it was well past noon. Heading to his bungalow, he made up his mind; he wouldn't go to receive his senior and the royal visitor. It was summer, and the menace of mosquitoes was at its peak. Malaria! that should buy him some time to replan the special trip, the one which culminated after a long discussion. He had not thought it necessary, but his friend argued that they should do it one last time. Times were changing. There was a new DFO.

He headed to his bedroom through the massive hall of *Lal Bungalow,* passing the arms and ammunition room with its locked door. Lying on his bed, he stared at the yellow ceiling of the Assam-type bungalow. An insect caught in a cobweb on the roof caught his eye. The more it tried to wriggle free, the more wrapped up in the silk it became. As he watched the insect slowly becoming immobile, his mind drifted back to when he was a young energetic deputy ranger and had gotten caught in a web of a different kind, deep in the forest.

The afternoon sun coming through the window moved across his face. He awoke and looked once again at the ceiling. The insect was gone, gobbled up by a giant long-legged spider. He decided to delay the special trip by a few days. He would have to send additional rations to the waiting party to sustain them for a few more days. He came out of his room and went towards the back of the bungalow. He heard the cooks and the servants chatting.

'Hey, anybody there?' Brown *Sahib* shouted. One of the caretakers came running. 'Bring Dias here. Tell him I want to see him at once.'

Tough task master Brown *Sahib* had no idea that the additional task he was about to entrust to the train driver would turn out to be the catalyst for unmasking the secrets he had been keeping safely buried, deep inside the forests of Ripu for so long.

Chapter 4

Myriad calls emulated from the dense forests. The headlights of Jenkins' Ford shone fleetingly on civets and hares crossing the otherwise deserted road. Raj's thoughts drifted back to his childhood days when the royal hunting party had made a stop in Kachugaon before their foray into the wilderness. He remembered the township buzzing with all sorts of activities during the daytime.

After a few turns, the headlights shone on a typical Assam-type house, and Raj remembered it as the Forest Department Inspection Bungalow (the IB). The house had acted as a resting place for the royal family before they started out for hunting camps deep inside the forest. As the car slowed to a halt, Raj could make out the frantic movements of shadowy personnel, while a nightjar with its distinctive call retreated into the darkness surrounding the bungalow. An owl hooted from the burrow of a nearby tree.

Raj glanced at his watch as he was helped out of the car by two attendants. It was almost eight at night. It seemed Jenkins had ensured the staff kept the IB ready for their late arrival, as they were led directly to the dining room where a modest dinner had been laid out. After dinner, he was escorted down a long dark corridor to his room. The dimness unnerved him.

Alone in his room, he felt strange thinking just that morning he had almost made up his mind not to come to Kachugaon. Yet here he was, surrounded by the forest, which made vivid so many memories. Lying on the bed, his thoughts drifted to the royal hunting party days of his childhood when they used to camp in the nearby forests. He remembered keeping a diary, where he would write the names of the ranges and forests to map out future expeditions. These plans always involved seeking out creatures that were thought to live in the forest but were rarely seen. He remembered huddling with an old *mahout,* forest guard or Nepali grass cutter, who would regale him with stories of the forests. He would ask them endless questions that would yield stories of the creatures that captured his imagination. Stories of elusive golden monkeys that would lure hunters deep into the forests of Ripu, where they disappeared forever. As the darkest part of the night descended, the stories would shift from wild animals to ghosts and spirits of the forest. There were stories about damsels in white who would lure men away into the forest to kill them when they would go to answer nature's call. The storytellers convinced young Raj that these hunting camps were also used as quick execution grounds for certain people the royal family wished to be rid of.

'Those killed during the earlier hunting trips who did not receive proper burials were doomed to wander forever as restless spirits. They are so many in the forest that you should never come out of your tent once you are inside,' one passionate storyteller had whispered to young Raj. He remembered the agonising nights he spent trying to control his bladder, not being able to muster the courage to go outside. Thankfully, his bedroom in the IB had an attached toilet.

The white curtain on one of the windows rose and fell languidly. His mind shifted to the stories of a maiden in a white saree who would sing in the middle of the night near the edge of the forest. The maiden, he was told, was the spirit of an unmarried girl who was killed during an earlier hunting trip. She was thought to be holding a vestige that could be a source of embarrassment to the royal family, and this led to her untimely death.

Raj was bemused that returning to Kachugaon after decades was bringing to mind all these tales of creatures, both living and dead. He could feel the forest breeze increasing in strength as it wound through the thick *sal* forests rattling his window as if urging him to come out to the wilderness to seek something he had always yearned for. Then he remembered Divya's sad face when she came to know of her husband's sudden decision to visit the forests of Kachugaon. Despite the exhaustion, it took a while for Raj to fall asleep.

The next morning, Raj woke up to the gentle creaking sound of the forests beyond the IB complex, last night's thoughts far from his mind. In the dining room at breakfast, Jenkins informed him that his deputy, Robert Brown, the Assistant Conservator of Forest (ACF), was waiting to take them to the station.

'He is the man who runs this place. Kachugaon lies outside the control of civil administration. It is administered by my department, and Robert Brown is in charge. He is a veteran of the Assam forest department. Apart from the normal forestry role, my department is responsible for everything from commerce to transportation, within the region,' Jenkins said. As they arose from the dining table, in almost a whisper Jenkins said to Raj, 'There are a lot of stories about his exploits. I am just getting to know the man and learning of these stories. He is waiting outside. Let's go and meet him.'

Raj saw Robert Brown as soon as he stepped out into the verandah. He was a big brawny man with bushy eyebrows and a drooping walrus moustache. Looking around the IB compound, Raj noticed that the man's presence created a sense of awe and fear amongst the caretakers. Jenkins introduced Raj to Brown *Sahib* who greeted him with a sombre expression. His puffy cheeks were red and his stare cold.

Soon they were driving through the township, which bustled with all sorts of forestry activities. Logs were being transported by buffalo cart, *mahouts* were leading elephants toward the timber depots, labourers worked under the watchful eyes of contractor bosses, food vendors sold tea and steamed rice cakes from the makeshift roadside stalls. Anybody who saw the Ford approaching, now driven by Brown *Sahib*, would stand still and raise a salute — invariably directed at Brown *Sahib*. By contrast, the residents of Kachugaon seemed indifferent to the presence of Jenkins and Raj.

The station was a whirl of activity that centred on the carriages of the Goalpara Forest Tramway standing at the platform. A steam engine was coupled to the carriages to take Raj and the party all the way to Phibsoo, near the Bhutan border, a distance of almost twenty-five miles.

Brown *Sahib* led the group toward the waiting train. 'Today the engine will pull two salons: the VIP salon and the

Governor salon. On normal days, the engine pulls water tanks and trailers for bringing back timber,' he said pointing to the many carriages standing idle on the parallel tracks.

'The Governor salon will carry you and the Prince,' Brown *Sahib* said to Jenkins. 'All other attendees will be travelling in the VIP salon. By the way, to take advantage of the trip, two water carriages for Phibsoo camp will also be attached to the carriage.' Brown *Sahib* then steered Jenkins away to talk to a young, enthusiastic officer who seemed to be in charge at the station.

While they held their discussion, Raj decided to take a look around the station. There were some new buildings under construction and some dilapidated ones in varying stages of disuse. Sheds housed various carriages and he could see through the open door of one shed various tram parts including many rusted axles. There were three steam locomotives in another shed and a fourth was at the platform being readied for their trip. He also saw a few trolleys that were used for inspection of the tramway track. It would be interesting to ride them through the dense forest, he thought.

Jenkins, Brown *Sahib*, and the young officer were coming towards him. 'We are ready to depart, Your Highness. Your belongings have been placed on board in the Governor's salon,' Jenkins said gesturing towards the non-pretentious carriage with an attendant waiting on either side of the door. Raj climbed into the carriage which was clean, well-kept, and airy. One of the attendants led him to a seat near the window. He was followed by Jenkins while all the others boarded into the second carriage. The young ranger and Brown *Sahib* remained on the platform.

There were a sudden jolt and a deafening whistle from the engine. Raj realised it was a short train with his carriage being only second from the powerful German engine. The frantic activities on the platform were subsiding, and he saw Brown *Sahib* giving the young officer some instructions. There was a certain amount of reluctance in the young officer's gait as he walked away; perhaps he also wanted to be a part of the trip, Raj thought. As the train slowly moved away from the platform, Raj saw Brown *Sahib* eyeing the train with his chin up high, legs apart and hands on his waist.

'Mr. Brown is not coming. He has a fever. It could be malaria. Only someone as strong as he could still be moving about in spite of such feverish temperature,' Jenkins said, inclining his head in the direction of his deputy. Raj felt that Brown *Sahib* had seemed stressed. It wasn't just his malaria; there was a certain amount of nervousness in the man's demeanour: it seemed, he simply wasn't happy about the whole train trip.

Chapter 5

The train gradually gathered speed. Leaning out of the train window, Raj savoured the sights and scents of the forests. It felt like the little train was piercing through a continuous green veil that was made to resist the intrusion of the outsiders. After some time, the forest became so dense that he started to wonder whether he was in the foothills or in a rainforest. As the train rumbled past the lush greenery, all he could see were the trunks of majestic *sal* trees moving past him, their aroma thoroughly captivating his senses.

More time passed, and the train slowed down. '*Sahib,* we are approaching the Gelgeli opening,' one of the attendants spoke for the first time. He was a short affable elderly man from the local Bodo community. He spoke in the local dialect to Jenkins.

'Gethela has been with the department for more than three decades. He knows the forest like the back of his hand,' Jenkins said to Raj as he gazed out at the wet grassy plains appearing on both sides of the track.

'How many such openings are there on this track?' Raj directed the question to the old forest guard.

'Your Highness, Gelgeli is the first.' Gethela said. 'We also have Bonda Beel and then ...' Jenkins interrupted, saying, 'we have three natural openings and two big wetlands. We also have some marvellous tall grasslands and a few barren patches where timber has been harvested. Some areas near the track have been heavily felled. All these areas are excellent for game viewing.' A large wetland came into view on Raj's right. The train slowed down; it seemed the driver was used to this routine when he had officials on board.

'Look there ...' the old guard pointed towards some grey Asiatic wild buffalo about fifty metres away from the track. Further away, on the edge of the wetland was a majestic one-horned rhinoceros.

'What is that dark thing behind the rhino?' Raj asked, looking through his binoculars. 'It is quite small and doesn't look like a civet.'

Jenkins glanced at the old guard. He couldn't clearly see what Raj was pointing to.

'Your Highness, a lot of unearthly creatures have been spotted in this forest,' the old guard started up. He was stopped by a stern look from Jenkins.

'May I borrow your binoculars?' Jenkins turned to Raj and took the binoculars. 'Your Highness, that is a hog badger,' he said as he peered at the animal. It was quite a distance away from the train on the other side of the wetland. Raj sensed that Jenkins was one of the very few forest officers of British

India who was more of a wildlife enthusiast than a forester.

'Interesting, never expected to see a badger,' Raj said marvelling at both the sighting of the rare animal and his young host's knowledge. He was jostled out of his thoughts as the train suddenly lurched forward; the driver, mindful of the length of the journey, couldn't afford a longer viewing time for his guests.

After rumbling for half an hour or so, the train came to a sudden halt. It was midday and the place was buzzing with the sound of birds and insects. Raj could hear the driver and the handyman talking. He looked quizzically at Jenkins, who shrugged and after a moment said, 'I will go and check what is going on. I didn't expect any stoppage. The train is not carrying anyone other than us.'

Raj saw a small, dark, scantily clothed old man hurriedly exiting the engine cabin, carrying two jute bags. His darting eyes spotted Jenkins at the carriage door. Jenkins jumped down and was about to accost him, but the sure-footed man vanished amongst the elephant grass sandwiching a narrow forest path.

'Hey, who was that?' Jenkins shouted towards the driver's cabin.

'Sir, that man is carrying some rations,' the train driver replied as he climbed down to join Jenkins on the ground. Gethela also got down from the train and joined them.

'Whose rations? What rations?'

'Sir, the rations are for an old man who lives around five

miles from here. The porter you saw was the brother of the man,' the driver replied.

Raj stuck his head out of his compartment. 'I saw the porter. He didn't look like one of your forest department employees,' Raj said wiping sweat from his forehead, as he peered down at the group on the ground.

Jenkins pointed to the narrow forest path and said, 'One old man vanishes carrying provisions for another old man in the forest. I will have a word with Brown *Sahib* as soon as we get back to Kachugaon. I seriously don't know what's going on.' He was irritated.

'Is he a casual employee of the department?' Raj asked, though he had noticed that the vanishing old man was wearing a soiled white loin cloth, while everyone else on the train was in forest department uniform.

'I have never seen him before,' Jenkins said, looking perplexed. Turning to the driver, he ordered, 'Now, let's get going.' The driver gestured for Gethela to join him in the engine cabin.

'Your Highness, I am sorry for this unscheduled stop.' Jenkins said as he reboarded.

Just before the train started to move, another guard entered the cabin. It seemed he was replacing Gethela. The new guard bowed slightly and asked, 'Sir, should I get the lunch as it will be quite a distance to Phibsoo?'

Raj realised he was hungry and surmised that the hot noon would not provide much in the way of wild animal viewing opportunities. He was relieved when Jenkins nodded and said, 'Yes, Biren, let's have lunch now.' Lunch was poori and potatoes cooked in a delicious tomato gravy. Biren also served lemonade and fruit cake. Raj was amazed that since his arrival in Kachugaon, all his favourite foods had been served to him. He was impressed that the ACF and the young officer reporting to him had taken the trouble of providing a decent lunch on the train. Brown *Sahib's* moodiness in the morning notwithstanding, Raj thought Jenkins was lucky to have a deputy with such skills in planning and coordination.

The train passed over a long-curved bridge that stood high over an aquamarine river and a vast expanse of silvery white river bank covered with *saccharum spontaneu*m, the tall grasses locally known as *kohua*. The Himalayas came into view for the first time.

Biren pointed outside and loudly exclaimed, 'Your Highness, the *Pagli Sahan*.' Both Raj and Jenkins could see a large herd of elephants crossing the river. From the train high above, they looked like big dark blotches on a canvas of white and green. The train moved slowly over the rickety wooden bridge, affording them a glorious panoramic view of the entire landscape with the mighty herd of elephants moving against the backdrop of the mountains.

'How many?' Raj asked.

'Around a hundred elephants, I would suspect,' Jenkins said.

'*Pagli Sahan* generally has around one fifty elephants,' Biren politely said to Jenkins.

'Why are you calling it *Pagli Sahan?* What does that mean?' Raj asked Biren. The train gathered speed as it left behind the bridge and the elephants below. The mountains of Bhutan appeared quite close until the view was again marred by tall trees.

'That particular herd of elephant moves from the border of Assam and Bengal all the way to the North Kamrup Sanctuary in the east,' Jenkins responded, ignoring Raj's question.

'Why is it called *Pagli Sahan?*' Raj asked again.

'Your Highness, *Pagli* means mad girl and *Sahan* means elephant herd. Some of the locals believe this herd is led by a beautiful girl in a white saree.' Jenkins said. 'You would have to be mad to lead a herd of a hundred and fifty wild elephants,' He forced himself to smile.

'Do you believe the story? Has anyone seen the girl?' Raj asked as an alluring vision of a celestial maiden in a white saree riding a tusker flashed in his mind.

'I have seen the herd a few times. Many other foresters have reported seeing the herd from other divisions and from the North Kamrup sanctuary. Nobody I know has seen any maiden. There have been reports of the herd being led by a female elephant with a very bad temper. I believe the name *Pagli* originated from this,' Jenkins provided an explanation. Raj wondered what Gethela would have said about *Pagli*.

The train rumbled through the last stretch of *sal* plantations, now giving way to natural evergreen forests. The canopy openings threw open vistages of the brilliant blue Himalayan sky filled with flocks of hornbills. He had heard that the females enclosed themselves in tree burrows for months attending to their chicks. Their only hope for survival was their male partner who would regularly pass food through an opening in the burrow. Suddenly, the image of a sick and emaciated Divya trapped in a small room flashed through his mind — her face despondent. She desperately wanted her husband's attention, but he pictured himself distracted by a beautiful maiden in a white saree. He was relieved to have his thoughts broken by the clang of cutlery as Biren collected the lunch plates and glasses.

Raj looked outside and hoped the wind would dry his moist eyes.

Chapter 6

The afternoon sun pierced through the tall *sal* trees; it was two o'clock in the afternoon when the train reached Phibsoo. Raj realised they were at the base of the Bhutan hills that had seemed so far away when they first started. It was noticeably cooler.

Phibsoo seemed to be a station in the middle of nowhere. Seeing the *sal* logs piled up, ready for transportation to the depot, Raj was suddenly hit by the sad realisation that all this transportation development was just to exploit and extract timber from the region. The station area was smaller than a football field and infrastructure was minimal. There were a few log cabins, but every other open space was taken up by felled logs. The area was surrounded by tall trees, and it was quite dark given the time of day.

Jenkins said something to Biren, and to Gethela who had reappeared, and at once they disappeared into the surrounding woods.

'Your Highness, are you able to take a trek into the

wilderness? There is a spot known to a local guide which may have a small population of the golden monkeys. I have sent the men to fetch the guide.'

The carcass of the golden monkey still haunted Raj. He was tired and suddenly felt like returning to Kachugaon and then to his palace, but he found himself saying, 'Yes, I would like to see the monkey.' Since his childhood, Raj had heard stories of an elusive golden monkey found solely in this part of India. He first read about the golden langur in a zoological journal which described it as a pale yellow-coloured monkey common in the adjoining district of Goalpara, but that it was of unidentified taxonomic status due to a lack of any photographic evidence or a dead specimen.

'By the way, why did you present the stuffed specimen to me? Should you not have sent it to London or the Zoological Society of India?' Raj asked, suddenly realising the scientific worth of such a specimen.

'Your Highness, to be honest with you, it was Ranger Amaresh Baruah's idea. The young officer you saw at the station assisting Brown *Sahib*. He is one of our smartest frontline staff. That specimen had been in the Kachugaon forest office for years. Brown *Sahib* didn't want to send it to any of the institutions as his logic was that it would attract unwanted attention and could impact forestry operations. I don't tend to agree with him, but he was adamant that the specimen shouldn't go to London or Calcutta. When I conveyed to him through the ranger that I wanted to keep it in the Dhubri office for gifting to seniors from Shillong, he reluctantly agreed.'

'I will arrange to have it sent to the Zoological Society of London if we see any live specimens during this trip,' Raj said.

Gethela and Biren appeared from the forest edge with an old man wearing a faded Nepali cap. 'This is Daju, our local guide. He says it's likely the troop can still be located near the river. Daju saw the troop two days ago,' Biren said excitedly to Jenkins.

'Let's get our gear; we might have a photographic opportunity today,' Jenkins said to Raj with a smile.

Within minutes, the group was on the move with Daju leading the way. They took a path through the thick *sal* forest surprisingly devoid of birds or any other wildlife. They came to a clearing dotted with hundreds of felled tree stumps. A herd of spotted deer retreated to the surrounding woodland as the group approached. The team left the clearing and re-entered the forest.

'Are we in Bhutan or India?' Raj asked.

'Not very sure, Your Highness. This is my first trek in this region,' Jenkins said. Raj could sense some trepidation in his voice.

After walking for an hour or so, they heard the sound of running water. As they drew nearer, the sound grew louder and suddenly they were out in the open. It was a stunning landscape of rushing rocky riverbed where the blue sky met a vast canopy of lush green. Daju led the group along the rocky edge and after a short distance, they reached a shallow section of water. He gestured that they would be crossing. A few forktails fluttered up, surprised at the group's intrusion.

Gethela approached Jenkins and indicating the forest behind them, said something in a low voice. 'The sal forest we left behind is the last frontier patrolled by my forestry staff. They never venture across this area of the water. The locals call it *Moronduar* — the gateway to death ,' Jenkins explained to Raj. Tired, Raj was almost regretting his decision to come on the trek, but Jenkins' explanation of the place's name suddenly excited him.

After crossing, the team started to move upstream to where the waterway widened into an expanse. They had reached the main river. They rounded a long bend and Daju stopped. Two tall trees had come into view above the lower riverine forests.

Daju pointed, and that's when the group spotted the long tails high up in one of the trees, balancing the stooped bodies of about ten langurs. Their colour was a silvery-gold, not unlike blonde hair. Jenkins and Raj swapped looks, their excitement barely contained. Raj quickly motioned for Biren to hand over his camera, but realising the langurs were too far away, he asked for the binoculars instead. And yes, he could see the golden langur of his childhood fantasies just a hundred metres from him. There was real satisfaction on the faces of Biren, Gethela and Daju at being able to show the *Sahibs* what they wanted to see. Knowing that nothing much would be captured Jenkins went ahead and took some photographs anyway.

Raj could make out five adult langurs and a number of juveniles through his binoculars. He then turned to take in the view of the forest canopy as the sun was setting, at which point he caught sight of something else. A few dark, lithe creatures moved around, higher up in some other trees. They surely weren't langurs.

'What are those?' Raj said, nudging Jenkins and handing

him the binoculars.

'Where?' Jenkins asked, a bit lost.

'Behind the langurs. Across the river, to the right of that tall tree,' pointed Raj as a flock of green pigeons took flight from the same tree. 'Look to the right of the canopy — that tree, from where the birds just flew!' he shouted excitedly. Jenkins peered through the binoculars but couldn't see anything. Gethela, his face lined with worry, whispered something to Jenkins.

Raj took the binoculars back from Jenkins and tried to detect what he had spotted moments earlier. He couldn't see anything other than the langurs.

Daju asked Jenkins if he wanted to move closer to the langurs to photograph them. Before Jenkins could reply, Daju took the photography equipment from Biren and started walking towards the river. Signalling for the others to follow, he headed to the sandbar in the middle, which was the mid-way point between the langurs and the group. Gethela became clearly agitated and called out to Daju, trying to get him to come back. He moved in front of Jenkins and Raj and waved his outstretched hands, signalling for them not to follow the guide. Daju ignored him and continued, wading through knee-deep water with the camera on his shoulder. He didn't hear the now desperate shouts from both Gethela and Biren urging him to come back. Perhaps it was the prospect of some extra money for his efforts that was urging him on.

In the very next instant, they all saw Jenkins' camera and tripod slide from Daju's shoulder and fall into the water. Daju then seemed to be collapsing, and as his body turned toward them, the group stared horrified at an arrow that sat lodged in his neck. The sounds of the river swallowed up Daju's horrified gasps. Raj and the rest of the party could do nothing more than watch, as Daju fell flat between some rocks and was swiftly swept away by the river current.

Suddenly, the *Moronduar* air felt ice cold.

Chapter 7

The solemn party made their way back to Phibsoo. It was almost four thirty in the afternoon on their return and Raj could see the anxious heads of the driver, guards and other attendants craning out of the engine cabin. They started the engine the moment Raj and the others had boarded, and the train was soon gathering speed. The wind rushed in through the open windows and the evening light at once had a soporific effect on Raj. He recalled his last look at the langurs, after Daju's body had been swept away while Jenkins' camera was still stuck between two rocks. All of them had turned their backs on him in unison and their very long tails swayed as if to say, 'Go back and never come again.' He shuddered and closed his eyes. Before long he fell asleep, his head nodding back.

It was six thirty in the evening by the time a waiting Ford delivered Raj to the Forest IB. He had a quick bath and rested on his bed, reminiscing about the day's tragic journey. *Did the langurs feel a sense of violation when the humans had intruded on their remote corner? And who had shot that arrow?* But there was something that made him want to return to the forest again.

There was a knock on the door. Reluctantly, he got up and greeted Jenkins. 'Your Highness, the dinner is at *Lal Bungalow*. Brown *Sahib* has also invited the *zamindar* of Parbatipur estate.'

'Has the *zamindar* come all the way from Parbatipur?' Raj asked, wishing he could skip the dinner if there was a choice.

'He was here in his elephant camp. He is keen to meet you.'

The *Lal Bungalow* was beautifully illuminated. Two banana trees sat near the entrance, staked with bamboo pegs holding *diyas,* and there were two guiding rows of lamps along the floor. This was the majestic headquarters of forestry operations and the ACF's official residence. It was painted all in red, hence the name *Lal Bungalow*. There was a flurry of activity as the servants hurried to finish lighting the remaining lamps.

The two of them entered a large hall that had been converted into a dining room. Several people seated at the table rose to welcome them. Brown *Sahib* greeted Raj and led him to his seat. As Raj scanned the faces in the dim light, he heard what sounded like a resounding slap on someone's face. It came from an adjacent room.

'Bastard! I am going to kill you if I see you again!' A thundering voice exploded, and Raj caught a glimpse of a man running from the room, his hand covering his cheek. Moments later, a tall, well-built older man clad in a feudal ceremonial attire came out into the hall. He walked with a slight limp and exuded aristocracy.

'Your Highness, may I introduce you to Rajah *Sahib*

Paritosh Baruah of Parbatipur estate.' Brown *Sahib* seemed visibly pleased introducing Raj to the massive frame of the man. As Raj shook hands with the elderly *zamindar*, he felt somewhat patronised. Jenkins sat next to Raj while Brown *Sahib* sat next to Rajah *Sahib*. There were a few officials from Rajah *Sahib's* estate and a few prominent forest contractors. As the dinner progressed, with the officials and the contractors busy devouring the dishes and drinking, Raj saw Rajah *Sahib* intermittently staring at him.

The drinks, he understood, were courtesy of Rajah *Sahib* as Brown *Sahib* would never have been able to arrange spirits of such superior quality in a place like Kachugaon. Raj was pleased with the meal, which was a mix of European and Indian fare. He did not normally partake of game meat and ate only chicken, so it was relieving to find that there was no meat other than chicken on the table. His favourite *Mughlai* dishes were served and so was the vegetarian pilaf, his favourite.

Rajah *Sahib* raised a toast to Raj's health and wellbeing. Nursing glasses of brandy, the men sojourned to the veranda of the bungalow. It was pitch black beyond the two planted banana trees, their lamps still burning. Raj realised there wasn't even the slightest breeze, indicating it might well be a long hot night in his stuffy room. He hoped the copious quantity of spirits he had consumed would help him fall asleep quickly.

Rajah *Sahib* approached Raj and extending his hand said, 'Your Highness, I will take my leave. I have some buyers coming to my elephant camp in the morning. We are training for our annual April hunt. In case you're staying back tomorrow, I would be delighted to host you.' Raj thanked him for the invitation but politely declined. 'I would be happy to host you some other time then,' Rajah *Sahib* said, coming nearer. He was much taller than Raj. Placing his hand lightly on Raj's shoulder, the older man asked, 'Did you bring a personal physician or any attendant with you from the palace?'

Raj responded with a puzzled look. Rajah *Sahib* then asked, 'Are you on any medication?'

'No, I am not on any medication. I didn't bring anyone with me. Why do you ask?' Raj asked. He was completely baffled.

'Well...' Rajah *Sahib* hesitated and then continued, 'I was just enquiring, Your Highness. Have a good trip back.' He extended his hand to Raj and despite the limp, briskly walked away to a waiting vehicle. 'Maybe the old man drank a bit more than he could handle,' Raj said to Jenkins, who had heard the conversation and was also puzzled.

Back in his room, Raj fell asleep as soon as he lay down. He awoke to the chirping of birds and the hollow knocking of a persistent woodpecker. He arose and pulled the curtains fully to one side, to let in the morning sunlight. He saw a herd of spotted deer moving away from the IB compound, the dappled light filtering through the tall trees forming even more complex patterns on their spotted hides.

He found Jenkins waiting for him in the dining room. As they discussed yesterday's events, the caretakers laid breakfast dishes on the table. Raj's favourites; poori, aloo bhaji, corn flakes in warm milk and a banana, tomatoes and chilli omelette (without onion) were all placed in front of him. He was amazed by the spread laid on by his host. Had Jenkins managed to have a quick discussion with one of his attendants at the palace about his food habits?

'Can I have all your forest guards and rangers meet with me for an hour or so?' Raj asked. 'I want to ask them about sightings of certain animals that I think are present in your reserves.'

'I will have all of them here soon. I am sure you will want Gethela too,' Jenkins said.

Within half an hour, Raj was surrounded by around fifteen men in the hall, some in starched uniforms, others in torn khakis and some in loin cloth. Three were forest rangers and the rest were field staff. Jenkins introduced Raj to the rangers. The young enthusiastic officer Raj had seen at the station was Ranger Baruah, who was in charge of the tramway. Ranger Miri was a quiet elderly man who seemed despondent about the whole meeting. The third ranger, Das, was an old hand in the department, and had an unfriendly demeanour. The others were deputy rangers, beat officers, game watchers, forest guards and casual workers of the department. And of course, Gethela.

Raj could sense anticipation building in the group as he opened the blue suitcase by his side and removed a large heavy book. He placed the book on the table in front of him, turned a few pages and stopped at one. Pointing to an animal on the page, he said, 'Who has seen this animal?' The group hesitantly gathered around and craned their necks to see the picture. It was of a clouded leopard. Some confident and amused murmurs passed through the group.

'Come on, everybody has seen it. It is just a leopard, too common in this part of the world,' one of the guards said.

But then there was a dissent. 'Can't you see? It doesn't have spots. The colour is also different,' somebody else shouted, scorning the others. 'It is not a leopard. I have seen it before. It doesn't come down from the trees.' It was Gethela's voice.

Raj had learned from Jenkins that before becoming an employee of the department, Gethela was a full-time hunter who grew up in the forest. Most of the rangers and other employees had come from villages and towns in various parts of Assam and had not spent nearly as many years in the forest as Gethela.

'Where did you see it?' Raj asked.

'I saw it many years ago in the treetops, in the Raimona area. In fact, I once saw it in the area where we saw the golden...' Gethela stopped suddenly as if he were about to give something away that he wasn't meant to share. He was speaking in his native language but with some assistance from Ranger Baruah, Raj managed to get the gist of it.

Raj then turned the pages to a picture of a sun bear. He had heard that along with its bigger cousins black and sloth, the sun bear, the world's smallest bear, could also be found in certain pockets of Assam. A murmur escalated into several heated discussions amongst the group as to whether the creature had been seen, despite someone pointing out that it had a very smooth coat unlike shaggy, unkempt coats of the bears they had seen. Raj had heard of the species being hunted in the Assam hills, and was hoping there might be a remnant population in the Bhutan hills, even one that might venture down to the foothill forests at some point.

'Can't you see that this bear has smooth hair all over

its body? And it's so small. Have you ever seen such a well combed bear in our forest? A stylish bear?' Gethela shouted, becoming irritated as the group burst into laughter at the sheer mention of it. Raj looked at Gethela in anticipation. 'No, I have never seen this small bear,' he said with certainty.

Raj tried his luck with a few more animal pictures. It was almost noon before he realised that most of the forest department staff were just doing their jobs and were not, in fact, discerning wildlife observers.

Raj dismissed the group and they filed out, still arguing and scoffing. Jenkins and Brown *Sahib* approached him. Jenkins asked him how he thought the session had gone. 'Well, I have a feeling some of the species can be found here. Though it seems with the exception of Gethela, none of the men has seen much. I think they are just busy with their day-to-day forestry duties.'

'Please don't believe everything Gethela says. He has a very fertile imagination,' Brown Sahib said with a smile. 'By the way, it is almost twelve thirty. Please join us for a farewell lunch. It is a long drive to the palace and I presume Mr. Jenkins would like to return to Dhubri today itself.'

'I will stay back today. I would like to visit the elephant camp.' Raj said, looking at Jenkins who seemed surprised, though he didn't say anything. Raj didn't know why he suddenly wanted to visit Rajah *Sahib's* elephant camp after declining the invitation the night before.

Maybe it was the mention of a 'farewell lunch'. It had irritated him. He was not ready to go back yet. Yes, he had seen the golden langurs. But there was still something out there he yearned to see. He would go when he wanted, and not when Brown Sahib decided he should.

Chapter 8

Raj sat next to Jenkins at the wheel while Baruah sat in the back. 'How long has Rajah *Sahib* been catching elephants in these forests?' Raj asked.

'Well,' Jenkins said, 'I think since the last fifteen years or so Rajah *Sahib* holds the forest department contract to catch elephants in the forests. There were quite a few *zamindari* families actively involved in elephant catching, but for the past few years we have found only Parbatipur shows interest in the contract.' Raj listened quietly.

'He has never used any form of force or coercion to dissuade others from competing for the contract, but other parties have retreated from the scene. I'm told they fear some kind of curse, which they believe only the elephant catchers and *mahouts* working in Rajah *Sahib's* elephant camp can dispel,' Jenkins said cautiously.

'But what of this curse? Have you ever wondered about it, given there are now no other contenders for this lucrative elephant catching business?' Raj found himself frowning.

'Many have reported sightings of a young girl leading a hundred-strong herd of elephants. There have been instances of sudden deaths of the *mahouts* and others who have been unfortunate enough to lay eyes on the girl,' Baruah said, joining the conversation from the back. Interested, Raj turned to look at the ranger. 'Really?'

'Every year before the hunt, Rajah *Sahib* organises a tantric ritual to appease the forest goddess and particularly the mysterious maiden who heads the elephants,' Ranger Baruah said in an enigmatic tone. 'Priests from various tantric temples of Assam come to Rajah *Sahib's* place to perform secret rituals in the darkest hour of the night.'

'Have you ever been to any of these rituals?' Raj asked Jenkins, who was concentrating on the road.

'I have heard of them. I assumed they were part of the elephant catching tradition in this part of the world,' Jenkins said, as he looked to Raj, searching for affirmation. Jenkins then pointed up ahead. The massive arched gateway to the elephant camp had come into view. Raj didn't pursue the topic any further. He could perceive Jenkins was thankful, as they passed through the entrance of Rajah *Sahib's* sprawling elephant training camp.

The camp was a huge open compound surrounded by dense sal forests. Raj marvelled at the activity as many men were leading elephants of different sizes around the compound. Jenkins parked inside the gate, which was flanked on either side by a high boundary wall built from large sal logs, blending it into the surrounding sal forest. As Raj got down from the car, he took in the full scale of the place. Elephants were trumpeting, all manner of men were running around, and the trainers were shouting orders at the elephants.

As they walked across the compound, past the pachyderms and their masters, they noticed a line of tents near the boundary of the camp under the shadow of the forest. Ranger Baruah led them to one that looked to be a makeshift office. He asked one of the men the whereabouts of Rajah *Sahib*.

The attendant went and rang the bell hanging outside the largest tent, one with a flag on top of it. The towering Rajah *Sahib* appeared from inside. He was a wearing a long flowing *kurta* and had a pipe in his hand, but he wasn't wearing a turban. His snow-white hair was tied in a long lock and his old eyes were bloodshot yet penetrating. On seeing the party, he managed a friendly smile and said, 'Good afternoon, Your Highness. I am happy that you decided to come.' He offered a cursory hello to Jenkins and ignored Ranger Baruah. He reeked of alcohol and tobacco. 'Why don't you two please come to my tent?' he said after a momentary pause, directly conveying that the ranger was free to loiter around of his own free will.

Jenkins and Raj followed Rajah *Sahib* into his tent while Ranger Baruah walked off towards some acquaintances. Raj noticed that the flag on top of the tent showed a lion taming an elephant, its majestic paw resting on the elephant's head. It looked like the insignia of Rajah *Sahib's* estate. Two attendants pulled apart the curtains of the tent's opening to reveal a different world. They entered an elaborate entryway with comfortable seats and cushions lining both sides. Fans rotated on their axes creating a cool atmosphere about the place, and an adequate number of openings ensured the tent was well lit. Cigar and pipe smoke filled the air. Raj could also smell perfume, undeniably feminine, and he could see closed curtains that no doubt led to other rooms housing other occupants. Rajah *Sahib* gestured for Raj and Jenkins to be seated.

'It is a pleasure to welcome the crown prince of Paschim Behar to my humble training camp,' Rajah *Sahib* said in a formal tone. 'I presume this is your first visit to an elephant camp?' he asked, looking at Jenkins. But he didn't wait for an answer. 'During the April *mela shikar*, we captured two hundred and fifty beasts. Many of them have been transported elsewhere after being trained here. We have still around a hundred and fifty left to be sold locally. Our main hunt will begin in October when we will search the entire division to capture at least three hundred beasts. You can imagine the scale we are talking here.'

'I presume you organise some elaborate rituals before every hunt?' Raj asked, wanting to know as much as he could, as quickly as he could. 'Yes, here in Kachugaon we worship the forest and its powerful custodians so that our hunt can take place without hindrance,' Rajah *Sahib* said in obeisance.

'I have heard of these annual events. If I am here during that time, I would be most interested to attend.' Jenkins said, cautiously adding, 'Are these occasions open to outsiders?'

'Oh yes, of course. The festivity and the feasts are open to all. It is just some of the rituals where only family members are allowed. In the case of Parbatipur, it is only me, as I don't have anyone,' Rajah *Sahib* said, matter-of-factly. Then he burst into laughter saying, 'Yes, I am the last one remaining of our ancestors.'

'What sort of rituals?' Raj asked, ignoring Rajah *Sahib's* segueing into ancestry. He thought it best to clarify things quickly rather than have them linger. 'Do you have any knowledge of a girl who leads a herd of elephants in the forest? Have you ever seen her?'

Rajah *Sahib's* eyes widened at Raj's pointed query. He looked at his visitors then turned around to check the doorway leading to the internal rooms. He cleared his throat. 'Your Highness, she is real. I have not seen her, but my *mahouts*, my elephant catchers have seen her many times. We offer our obeisance to her and she allows us to complete our hunt without mishap. Otherwise, none of my men or elephants would come out alive from Ripu.'

Raj listened to his host, enthralled. He must be nearing seventy, but he looked as strong and powerful as the beasts he handled year after year. His belief in *Pagli Sahan* seemed very real. 'Have there been instances of consequences for people who have not paid the required respect to her?' This time it was Jenkins.

'Ask your Ranger Baruah,' Rajah *Sahib* said with a sneer. 'You must know that he comes from the *zamindari* of Manikpur. Fifteen years ago, they were making most of the catches.' Raj looked at Jenkins. Neither said anything. 'Your Highness,' Rajah *Sahib* stood up, signalling the end of the conversation, 'Perhaps you would like to see some of the camp activities before you retreat for the day? I presume His Highness will be travelling back with you tomorrow morning?' he said, looking at Jenkins.

Raj saw Jenkins give a sheepish nod.

'Well then, let's explore the camp. We will go via our office tent,' Rajah *Sahib* said as he led them outside. They passed a row of what appeared to be residential tents and came across a stockade with an open entrance. A large elephant was steadily making its way toward them, shaking its head.

'Run!' Rajah *Sahib* shouted, shoving Raj then grabbing him by the shoulder. He practically dragged Raj along as the elephant charged straight at them. Just in time, they hid behind the trunk of a massive tree. The elephant stopped and shook its head some more, wondering what to do next.

'Who let Mohan loose?' Rajah *Sahib* shouted, his thunderous voice alerting the elephant to their hiding place. The elephant, with its ears pinned back flat and trunk curled, took several menacing steps toward them but a group of men had quickly gathered and deftly threw ropes over the elephant. The elephant trumpeted in rage as it was restrained by a dozen men, some spearing it with elephant goads.

Rajah *Sahib* stormed toward the group and slapped the face of one of the men. 'Get that rogue down,' shouted Rajah *Sahib*. Raj just stared agape at the scene unfolding before him. Still hiding behind the tree, he slowly realised the gravity of the situation.

A thought struck him.

Did someone in the camp deliberately set a bull in full musth free to attack?

Chapter 9

Raj came out from behind the tree. He was sweating. He ventured over to the elephant and saw the tar-like secretions of *temporin* on both sides of its head, indicative of its heightened state. The elephant refused to be led to its pen. It just sank onto its knees and tried to dig its massive tusks into the ground. In his childhood, he had heard of handlers getting killed in the royal elephant stable by such elephants. He had always wondered how the seemingly gentle giants could turn into such killer beasts.

A red-faced Rajah *Sahib* came over to him. 'I don't know how someone could have been so careless. Particularly, when they all know we have a special visitor such as yourself. I am sorry for what has happened.' By that time Ranger Baruah and Jenkins had joined them.

'I thought,' Ranger Baruah said looking at Rajah *Sahib*, 'you would keep an elephant in *musth* chained to a strong tree and deny it food and water. But this one looks very strong; did it break its chain, or did someone let it loose?'

Rajah *Sahib* began to say something but stopped short. Instead, he turned his attention to Raj and said, 'Let's get on with our tour. We will go to our special training camp.' He led the group to the far end of the compound. A few labourers came running and opened a wooden gate. Raj couldn't believe what he saw; directly in front of them was an enclosed area containing some of the biggest elephants he had ever seen. Raj wondered about the size of the noose and the ability of the elephant catchers to restrain such giants. The elephants were much larger than even the oldest tusker in the royal elephant stable. Rajah *Sahib* explained proudly that the big elephants had been caught by way of a special *mela shikar,* which is used to capture only the biggest tuskers.

He walked with Raj ahead of Jenkins and the ranger, but Raj sensed that the two were deep in conversation, still mulling over the *musth* elephant incident. Rajah *Sahib* looked back at the other two men and said to Raj in a low voice, 'The forest department doesn't mind the arrangement of allotting the elephant catching contract to us year after year. There are many benefits to the department. Revenue aside, our familiarity with the terrain ensures that the number of wild elephants being unavoidably strangled is quite low. New parties would have had higher elephant casualties. We conduct our affairs in a very efficient manner with minimal disturbance to the villagers and other inhabitants of the forests.' Rajah *Sahib* paused and looked back again at Jenkins and the ranger, who had fallen further behind. He continued, 'The only people unhappy with the arrangement are the other *zamindars* and prospective contractors, but they are also afraid of the wrath of the elephant maiden. Let them try if they dare. We respect the forest and the maiden and hence, we get rewarded,' he said, emphasising the transparency and legitimacy of his *zamindari's* dealings with the forest department.

The forest officials quickly caught up. 'It is almost five,' Jenkins said. 'It would be best if we arrive at the IB before nightfall. Shall we get going?'

On their way back, as they passed *Rajah Sahib's* tent, Raj heard the whispering and giggling of girls from inside the tent. He revised his guess of Rajah *Sahib's* age, mentally making him a few years younger. 'Let's leave for Paschim Behar tomorrow,' Raj said to Jenkins when they reached the IB. Tired and overwhelmed, he went off towards his room. A moment after entering his room, Raj flung open the door and rushed out gasping for breath.

'Anybody there?' he shouted, his eyes and nose streaming as smoke trailed out behind him. A short figure came running. Raj asked Gethela to open the windows to let the smoke out. After the smoke dispersed and the windows were closed by Gethela, Raj re-entered his room.

Raj found that Gethela had burned coconut husk to dispel the menacing mosquitoes of Assam's forests but had smoked the room more than was necessary. The short man appeared further shrunken in stature as he offered a reverential bow in recognition of his mistake. 'Can you come and see me in the morning?' Raj asked as Gethela retreated from the room bowing repeatedly. By that time, a few IB caretakers had arrived. One started apologising profusely for the heavy fuming while the other two castigated Gethela in the local language.

The next morning Raj felt like his whole face had puffed up. He looked at himself in the mirror; it was red with mosquito bites. He was irritated as it seemed Gethela had left one of the windows open.

There was a knock on the door. 'Come in, the door is open,' Raj said. Ranger Baruah and Gethela entered cautiously. Raj sat in the armchair and realised that Gethela had brought along Baruah as an interpreter.

'What else have you seen in these forests?' Raj was short with Gethela, who sat on the floor. He was angry with Gethela for his carelessness the night before. He looked at Baruah to translate.

'Your Highness, the list is endless...' as Gethela was getting started, Raj stopped him.

'Have you seen the elephant girl?' Baruah translated for Gethela, asking him about sightings of *Pagli Sahan*. Gethela was taken aback by the query; his small hooded eyes looked up questioningly at Raj. And then he started talking to Baruah, speaking excitedly as if he had to divulge some secret before it was too late. Raj couldn't understand what he was saying. Baruah would query him, and he would explain further until he was interrupted again by Baruah with more queries. Their conversation went for quite some time and the two got so worked up that Raj began to feel as if he didn't exist. Raj could sense that the ranger was trying to get to the heart of whatever Gethela was saying with repeated questioning and no small amount of bewildered admonishment.

After a while, Gethela became restless and started murmuring and sweating profusely. He kept looking towards the door as though checking to see if anyone was there. Baruah looked exasperated with Gethela's rapid narratives and Raj was having trouble understanding any of it, other than a few names. Gethela kept on murmuring and then gave a reverential bow to Raj pointing in the direction of the door seeking permission to go out. Raj gestured that he could go and then directed the ranger to take a seat near the foot of his bed.

'Well tell me — what was all that about? Why did he become so agitated?'

'Your Highness ...,' Baruah started hesitantly. 'He seems to believe that the girl exists. He claims to have seen her on three occasions. He said the maiden is, as of now, near the railway track. She is receiving rations and other essentials before she goes further north to a place called Santhalbari. In fact, he said the old man you saw the other day was carrying provisions for her.'

Raj felt confused and excited at the same time. 'But why was he behaving in that strange way? What was he saying about Brown *Sahib?*'

Raj saw the young ranger hesitate again. 'Gethela said that Brown *Sahib* knows about the white maiden. He has seen her many times.'

Raj was even more confused. 'And what did he say about Rajah *Sahib?*'

'He said there was some connection between Brown *Sahib*, Rajah *Sahib* and the white maiden.'

Now Raj was beginning to understand Gethela's agitated state. He was giving away new and strange facts and secrets. 'What do you think of what Gethela said?'

'Well, I don't know. I am not an old employee like Gethela.

Why don't you check for yourself and clarify all your doubts?' There was a sparkle in the ranger's eyes.

'What do you mean?'

'We can trace the journey of the old man you saw that day. Gethela said the man went to deliver food and other provisions to the maiden who was camping near the track. We could go there and verify it for ourselves. Even if we don't see the girl, it will still be a good walk through the forest.'

'Are you free to accompany me? Can we travel today?' Raj asked, very keen on the idea.

'It would be difficult to go today as it will take a while to ready the men,' the ranger said. 'But I can definitely do it tomorrow. The problem will be finding the spot in the forest where the man got to that day.' Baruah seemed quite enthusiastic about planning another trip and Raj hoped this time the ranger would be able to go with him. 'I hope Brown *Sahib* and Jenkins *Sahib* won't have any problem with yet another train trip,' Baruah said. 'I will inform them of your decision. I will make sure the same driver is there tomorrow and Gethela will accompany us.'

As Baruah flung open the door to leave, Raj saw Brown *Sahib*, scrambling to get away from the doorway, the look on his face revealing he had heard everything that was said.

Chapter 10

Brown *Sahib* waited awhile before returning to knock at Raj's door. 'Your Highness, should I send some attendants to pack your things? Mr. Jenkins is waiting for you in the dining room. He is ready to start for Paschim Behar.'

Raj looked at Brown *Sahib* and said, 'I will join you and Jenkins for breakfast. Give me some time. By the way, how are you feeling today?'

After hearing what was said in your room, how could I feel? Brown *Sahib* felt like saying. Instead, he said, 'The fever comes and goes. Right now, I am feeling very well. We will wait for you in the dining hall.' He went back to join Jenkins who was in conversation with Baruah. His senior suddenly looked very confused and worn out.

'Why on earth does he want to travel again? Is he not going home?' Jenkins almost shouted, as much to himself as anyone else, as Brown *Sahib* entered. He banged his fist on the table. 'I don't know whether I told you this, but he was originally quite reluctant to come here. His wife is not well, and she is expecting a child very soon. I expected him to go back yesterday. I have to go to Dhubri to see my sister as she was expecting me yesterday.'

'I think it is because of the conversation he had with Gethela. He convinced His Highness that he can meet the elephant girl near the rail track,' Baruah said, faltering.

'And he believed that drunkard?' Jenkins asked as he gestured for Brown *Sahib* to sit.

'Well,' Baruah said looking at Brown *Sahib*, 'he wants to take the train ride again to find the elephant girl. He wants to travel tomorrow. He has asked me to accompany him this time.'

Prince Raj Narayan wanted it, or did you encourage him to do so?

'Is he out of his mind? What will he find? And why does he believe what Gethela said? That bastard is full of made up stories.' Brown *Sahib* turned to Jenkins. 'I think you should intervene. You can say the tramway is needed for patrolling tomorrow.'

'Then he might say he wants to join the patrolling party,' Baruah quipped.

'Alright, if he is hell bent on going, I doubt we can stop him. You will have to make the arrangements. I am not feeling well,' Brown *Sahib* said without trying to hide his irritation. His mind raced ahead, thinking of the things he would need to take care of.

'I will make the arrangements. You should rest. Malaria can be quite draining. I hope you have started taking the quinine,' Baruah asked.

Brown *Sahib* stood up. The fictitious malaria was the least of his worries. 'Please have breakfast with the Prince,' he said to Jenkins. 'And do let me know if there is any further change of plan,' he added, his voice heavy with sarcasm.

Jenkins smiled faintly.

On the way to *Lal Bungalow*, Brown *Sahib* knew he had to act fast. He still had a few years of service remaining and he couldn't afford to have an overzealous prince expose all his secrets. He went straight towards the kitchen at the back of the bungalow. Servants and forest guards were loitering around but stood to attention when they saw him approaching. He called to one of the servants and asked him to fetch Ghosh *Babu* and went into his bedroom, banging the door behind him. Shortly after, the head cook ushered Ghosh *Babu* into Brown *Sahib*'s room, and he was asked to close the door on his way out.

'Ghosh *Babu*, I want you to do something for me immediately. You must rush someone to Fakiragram. I need a fire set in the timber depot. If possible, you should go to supervise. But you must do it discreetly.' Brown *Sahib* instructed.

Ghosh *Babu* nervously adjusted his spectacles. 'It is the rainy season.'

'I know the logs are wet,' Brown *Sahib* snapped. 'I don't want you to burn down the entire depot. Just start enough of a fire so I can send Ranger Baruah there.' The clerk nodded.

Brown *Sahib* indicated for him to wait, opened the iron safe on the side of his bed and took out a one-rupee note. He thrust it into Ghosh *Babu's* hand. 'Remember, just a small fire. But the news should be big. Send someone here straight away with the news of the fire.' After Ghosh *Babu* left he thought of his friend *Rajah Sahib* who was blissfully unaware of all the trouble caused by his request for yet another sighting of *Pagli Sahan.*

Greedy old bastard!

There was a frantic knocking at the door. The urgency of it further irritated Brown *Sahib.* He clenched his Beretta and opened the door, all ready to lambast. It was the train driver, Dias, panting and looking utterly crestfallen.

'What's wrong? Didn't they say I was resting?' Brown *Sahib* snarled with rage.

'I had to come. Jenkins *Sahib* and Baruah *Babu* called me to the IB. They asked me why I stopped the train at that place the other day. I had to tell them that you told me to stop there. They were insistent,' Dias said in one breath. A stale smell of alcohol emulated from the driver. Brown *Sahib* had to resist the urge to punch him in the face.

'Did you tell them about the Santali man?' His eyes bore holes into Dias.

'Yes, I had to. Baruah *Babu* threatened me. He said he would throw me out of Kachugaon,' Dias said, panting less now, but still shaken. Brown *Sahib* didn't say anything. He blew on the barrel of the pistol thinking Dias was lucky to still be alive. *How times have changed.*

'What exactly did you tell them about that man?' His enraged voice barely controlled.

'I said I didn't know anything about the Santali man or his brother in the forest. I just stopped because you told me to. That's what I told them.'

'You stopped because I told you to,' Brown *Sahib* repeated with a smirk.

'I will need to take them to that exact spot tomorrow,' Dias said. 'When Prince Raj Narayan travels with you tomorrow, take him to the correct spot and let him out to continue on foot. You follow Das *Babu's* instructions.'

'But *Sahib*, I think the Prince will take Baruah *Babu* with him.'

'You don't worry about that. Ranger Baruah won't be there. He will be needed elsewhere tomorrow. The Prince and his party will go alone. You can wait for him or go back again by noon the next day to the same spot to collect him. If he comes back, well and good. If he doesn't, consider it a royal homage to the forest.' Dias wanted to say something, but was dismissed with a wave of a hand.

Alone with his thoughts now, Brown *Sahib* formulated his plan. He would have to get in touch with the Santali man himself. The old man needed to disappear before the Prince could find him. He would despatch him to Santhalbari, but it would be a race against time. The old man would have to travel for more than twelve hours to get there. He would need to send a party from Santhalbari and they would have to start out that same night to reach the cottage by early morning. If all went according to plan, the Prince would find the cottage empty when he reached. He could not afford the discovery of a white girl deep inside his forest, nor any encounter that could potentially lead to the Prince's death at the hands of those who guarded the girl.

He stuck his head out of his room. 'Fetch Bhola!' he shouted out for someone to get the head cook of *Lal Bungalow*. A servant went running. Bhola arrived at his room not long after. 'Get that bastard Santali old man now,' Brown *Sahib* commanded. 'Make sure when he comes, nobody from the IB sees him.'

As he supposedly had malaria, he had no choice but to confine himself to his room. Lying on his bed, he went over the plan again. Prince Raj Narayan would be accompanied by a few guards and the forest department trackers. They would surely find the cottage as the trackers would easily be able to trace the route from the railway track. The cottage would be empty with all tell-tale signs of inhabitation removed. That would be the best-case scenario.

But what if the Prince and his party reached the cottage before the party from Santhalbari arrived? An encounter would no doubt ensue. The cottage guard would surely attack the intruders. And if he were joined by other archers, that would be the end of Prince Raj Narayan of Paschim Behar. That would be the worst-case scenario, even worse than what happened fifteen years ago.

Brown *Sahib* shuddered at the thought of that wretched

day in 1921. It had been almost fifteen years since then, but he still remembered the logistical nightmare from the outset, with their loads of scientific equipment along with a large number of skilled labourers they brought with them from Bengal: carpenters for making cages, taxidermists for stuffing dead animals, cooks and so on. They literally took over *Lal Bungalow* with their loads of chemicals, tranquilisers, and all manner of other scientific paraphernalia.

To make matters worse, they had already made up their minds where they would be going to look for the elusive rhino.

'No!' Brown *Sahib* shouted, suddenly awake. He had dozed off and was being woken by a persistent knocking on the door. 'Where is the Santali man?' he demanded when he saw only Bhola standing in the doorway with a sullen face. 'Where is that old bastard?'

'*Sahib,* Baruah *Babu* took him to the IB,' Bhola said, his voice quavering. Before Brown *Sahib* could say anything, the train engine's whistle reverberated through *Lal Bungalow*. '*Sahib,* they are all at the station now.'

Brown *Sahib* sank slowly onto his bed. He looked up at the ceiling, gave an open-mouthed sigh and closed his eyes. The thought of what he had done fifteen years ago, and of what could repeat itself in a matter of hours, made him shiver despite the heat.

The whistle blew again.

Chapter 11

'Your Highness, I will be leaving for Dhubri as soon as your train leaves. I will be back tomorrow, by which time you should be back at the IB. We can depart for Paschim Behar tomorrow afternoon,' Jenkins said to Raj who was already seated in the Governor salon.

'I hope you enjoy your visit with your sister. I will be all right with Ranger Baruah,' Raj said. 'Ranger Baruah won't be able to accompany you,' Jenkins said apologetically. 'He has to respond to a crisis. I know it would have been ideal if he accompanied you. But Ranger Das is an experienced man; he has been around for many years.'

A sullen-looking Baruah appeared in the train window, while Jenkins moved away to talk to Ranger Das.

'Why can't some other rangers attend this crisis? Have you checked with others?' Raj asked, gesturing towards Das.

'Your Highness, the timber depot is under my jurisdiction. We just heard about a fire in the depot. I have to go. I do apologize, I really wanted to go with you on this trip,' He then looked around and said, 'The problem is that Brown *Sahib* has really taken the back seat on everything since you arrived, as he is not well.' He lowered his voice. 'Though I do feel he could easily go to check on the depot.' Baruah edged closer and almost whispering added, 'Jenkins *Sahib* doesn't say anything to him.' Baruah looked resigned at the state of the relationship between his seniors.

Raj patted the young man's arm through the train window. 'Don't worry, I will be all right. I would have liked it if you had been able to accompany me, but duty comes first, does it not? I am here as a traveller, but you have a job to do.'

The train was about to depart. He saw Biren getting on, looking tense. Raj knew that Jenkins had asked Biren not to spread the news about what had happened to the Nepali guide, so as not to create panic amongst the forest guards. Raj then watched as all the low-level forest department employees and train workers boarded the train. Leading the party was a very indifferent Ranger Das and with him their prized catch — the Santali man.

Sitting alone in the coach, Raj reminisced on the quick succession of the morning's events. He and Jenkins were reclining in cane chairs, overlooking the IB campus. Jenkins had been somewhat aloof since learning of the amendment to the plans and Raj wasn't sure how he would be spending the day, given Baruah had said the trip would not be possible until the next day. Some servants were bringing fresh produce from the local market, circumventing the bungalow to the kitchen at the back. One deputy ranger had three roosters strung upside down from his bicycle bar. Raj wondered whether the IB attendants knew there wasn't going to be a farewell lunch anytime soon.

Raj was lost in his thoughts as Ranger Baruah approached the bungalow. 'Baruah, I will leave all the arrangement to you for this new trip.' Jenkins said. 'I won't be able to accompany His Highness. You will need to go along with him.'

'The train driver knows the exact spot where that old man got down the other day. Should we also talk to him?' Raj asked.

'Finding the spot won't be a problem ...' Jenkins said to Raj, then turned back to Baruah, '... but how will you know the forest path to take?'

'Sir we will take Bishuram. He is the most experienced tracker. He knows the forest like the back of his hand. He can easily lead us,' Baruah said.

'Hey Dias, come over here,' Baruah shouted out to the train driver, who had appeared at the IB entrance. 'He will know about the Santali man.'

The man came and stood in front of Raj and Jenkins. Others in the IB were gathering, their curiosity sparked. 'You made an unscheduled stop the day before yesterday. You knew full well that His Highness was on board. Who was that man you dropped off?' Jenkins asked.

'Tell the truth or else you will be out of your job and will have to leave Kachugaon in twenty-four hours,' Baruah added.

'Brown *Sahib* asked me to ferry that man. Brown *Sahib* told me that the old man was carrying some provisions for his elder brother,' the driver said, trepidation in his voice.

Jenkins gave a surprised look at hearing Brown *Sahib's* name, but he didn't say anything.

'Who was the man?' he asked again. The driver didn't say anything.

'Who was that man?' Baruah demanded, echoing his senior.

'He is a member of the Bhutan foothill Santali clan. He sometimes comes here to Kachugaon,' the driver said.

'These people are not native to the forests. They don't understand our language and neither we theirs. They look quite different. Lately, they have been spotted around the local markets and other places. Nobody knows where they have come from. When we were young, there was a story about a mythical Santali kingdom in the far north, deep inside the Ripu reserve,' Baruah explained.

'Does the location exist on our divisional map?' Jenkins asked.

'There is no mention of the place on any map. Those who have ventured to that region have never returned,' Baruah said.

'All right, tell us. Where can we find that man?' Raj chipped in.

Dias shook his head. 'I have no idea. I only saw him on the train,' Dias said in a trembling voice.

'You need to stay around. We will be travelling tomorrow to that place,' Ranger Baruah told Dias, who seemed quite shaken by the interrogation and relieved when Jenkins dismissed him.

With a little extra time on his hands, Raj thought of taking a stroll through the small town. As he was about to head off, he heard a strange cry of distress. Jenkins, Baruah and others gathered on the IB veranda and watched a man in khaki dragging along a small, dark-skinned old man behind him. He was agitated and crying out, begging for mercy in a language Raj didn't understand.

'Miri, who is he?' Jenkins asked, surprised at the way Ranger Miri was treating the distraught old man.

'Sir, this man was hiding in one of the old sheds near the station. He could be part of the poaching gang,' Ranger Miri said. 'We also captured his wife. She is being held in the old bungalow.'

Raj immediately recognised the short man with the darting eyes as the Santali man they were looking for. 'He is the one,' Raj said to Baruah who looked unsure.

'Yes, I think it is the man from the train the other day. I couldn't see him properly. Let's get Dias to confirm,' Jenkins said.

Suddenly, the old man gave his captor the slip and took off towards the gate. But Miri's shout alerted the guards standing near the gate and the old man was caught and brought back again. 'This man can do a lot of mischiefs. What should we do with him?' an exasperated Miri asked, as he returned to the veranda.

'Don't worry. Give him to us. We have got a job for him,' Baruah said to his colleague. Then he turned to Raj. 'It will be difficult to hold him for long. I suggest we head off today. Now, if possible.'

'I am ready to start now,' Raj said eagerly. He looked at Jenkins. 'It would be good if you could accompany us, along with Baruah. Now that we have this man we can easily reach the spot and find out if Gethela was telling the truth.'

'Your Highness, actually I have to go to Dhubri to visit my sister,' Jenkins said apologetically. 'Baruah will take care of everything, including escorting you during your trip. I will return tomorrow morning and we will proceed to Paschim Behar.'

Within a few hours of the man's capture, Raj was sitting alone in his compartment as the train pulled away from the platform. He could understand Jenkins not joining him, but Baruah's absence unsettled him a little. He was beginning to like the young man who had a flair for doing things efficiently. It was only ten but Raj felt like it had already been a very long morning as the train chugged through the wet wilderness. Raj wondered whether they would be able to navigate their way through the forest, given the thickness of the undergrowth. He hoped the forest trail was walkable.

The train came to a halt at the designated spot. Raj, the old Santali man, and the two forest guards, one carrying a shotgun and the other a machete to clear the vegetation, got down and prepared for the trek. It was twelve noon. Others who had gotten down from the train to see them off quickly reboarded, and the party set off through a narrow passage of tall elephant grass. Raj looked over his shoulder to see Ranger Das sitting inside the compartment smoking a *beedi*. He had not bothered to check on the departing party.

After walking for around fifteen minutes, the party of four arrived at a point where two forest paths intersected. The old man looked at Raj and attempted to explain something. Raj managed to determine from his utterances and gestures that he thought too many people might startle whatever it was they were looking for. He seemed to want Raj to do something about it.

'Can you two wait here until we come back? The place is nearby and too many people may frighten...' Raj stopped himself before he could mention the maiden to the guards, who had appeared ill at ease from the start. The Santali man pointed to the treetops and enacted the use of bows and arrows, and looking at the guards said something which could have meant, 'Do you wish to get hit with a shower of arrows or you have something better to do?'

'Can we wait on the train with the others?' the guard with the shot gun asked, his voice trembling a little as he spoke. They seemed quite desperate to leave the area, which Raj understood as something to do with the mythical spirit archers who supposedly guard the elephant maiden from the tree tops. They looked at Raj, their eyes pleading. Raj gave his consent and the guards retreated. He saw the old man's mischievous eyes watching the two guards until they disappeared. Then he started walking along the path to the right instead of taking the path straight ahead of them. Raj became worried but realised there was no point arguing with the old man, as now since the guards were gone his fate depended on him. He followed the old man along the path, which was narrower than the previous one, with much thicker undergrowth. The place became darker as they ventured deeper into the wood. Raj heard the unmistakable roar of a big cat. He was unarmed and all alone in the woods with a man he did not trust.

Chapter 12

They travelled for another hour or so through a terrain covered in creepers and thorny bushes.

'How far is the place?' Raj asked in Hindi. The old man didn't reply. Raj felt like blowing his head off with his Winchester. 'I shouldn't have left it behind at the IB,' he murmured.

They reached another intersection where the old man took another right turn. Raj trudged behind him, his boots soggy and pants ripped by thorns. He realized that there was no possibility of the forest guards finding him, if for whatever reason, he needed to be rescued. He was becoming increasingly fatigued whilst the sure-footed old man seemed to be increasing his walking speed. They came across an opening where a sparkling blue stream flowed through the trees. He stopped near the stream to rest but the old man marched on, not bothering to look back. Raj had no choice but to follow him.

After some time, Raj noticed a change in the vegetation. They were in a transition zone — the dense evergreen forest with thick undergrowth was giving way to moist deciduous vegetation. As the open sky became visible, he saw a flock of hornbills taking flight. Raj realised they must have been walking for at least two hours since the guards left them. He now sorely regretted allowing the forest guards to go back. He blamed himself for falling into what was starting to feel like a trap being laid by the old man. He looked at the short, bare-chested man with the squinty eyes - his most hated enemy at that time. But he had no choice but to follow him, like a dog following its master.

The old man signalled for Raj to stop. He cupped his hands around his mouth and let out a shrill ululating sound. Tired and irritated, Raj covered his ears with his hands. The old man waited and made the sound again. Moments later, a similar sound responded, seemingly from dead ahead. The man looked relieved and muttered something to himself. He scowled at Raj, murmuring unintelligibly, and then walked briskly straight ahead through the gradually thinning forest.

They came out of the forest and into an expanse of open grassland. The old man suddenly took off at great speed. Raj could just make out the roof of a cottage ahead. The grass was as tall as he, and the old man being so short was nowhere to be seen. Raj moved carefully through the grass. It ended suddenly, exposing an enclosure surrounded by a trench full of murky water. The enclosure walls were made of sturdy sal logs and were over six feet tall. Through a gap in the log wall, Raj could make out an open courtyard in front of the cottage with a large leafy fig tree growing in the centre. He looked up. High above, on a platform in the tree, was the most grotesque creature Raj had ever seen. He suddenly felt ill.

The creature smiled at him menacingly, its loathsome

face neither that of a man nor a woman. The dark figure had long, shaggy hair and wore nothing but the scantest loincloth. Before Raj could react, the fearsome creature placed an arrow on his bow and pulled back the string. As he was about to release the bowstring, the old man appeared and rushed in front of Raj, shouting something with his hands raised. The archer lowered his bow with a look of defeat, his demeanour completely changed. He descended from the platform with a few athletic moves and commenced an animated conversation with the old man. The old man then made his way along the boundary wall that ended abruptly at the edge of a cliff. Without looking back at Raj, he descended over the steep slope.

Raj crossed the moat over a bamboo bridge and stood near the wall made of logs. To his surprise, a few logs moved like a hidden gate to reveal an opening, and Raj was suddenly face-to-face with the creature, who he could now see was a man, but to his horror, a eunuch. He had left behind his bow, but his quiver of arrows still hung on his back. He was much taller than Raj and had a lean muscular body with long arms reaching almost to his knees. He realised that even with his bare hands, the eunuch would be able to vanquish him in no time.

He suddenly realised where this was leading, and excitement built within him unlike any he had felt before. The eunuch surely wasn't the occupant of the cottage; he would just be a servant or guard to whoever was staying there. In all likelihood he dared hope, the occupant was someone of the fairer sex; someone very beautiful, and dainty enough to need the protection of such a formidable guard. He knew that the harems of the royal houses in India still had eunuch guards.

His thoughts were disrupted by a foul smell coming from

the guard's mouth as he mumbled something incoherent. The guard gestured for him to enter through the gateway into the courtyard. He then directed Raj to a wooden bench in the veranda of the cottage. Raj realised it wasn't a registered forest department property, as no Assam forest department signage was present anywhere. He wondered whether the Kachugaon forest staff even knew about the compound, as he perched himself on the bench. The guard closed the opening in the wall by pulling the log door and latching it tight. Raj took in the unique location of the cottage. It faced the open grasslands but was inaccessible to wild animals due to the presence of the moat and high wall. The compound was at the end of the grassy plateau; one side of which descended steeply to a riverbed below, the path the old man had taken.

The guard sat on the ground in front of Raj and stared at him quizzically.

'What is your name?' Raj asked in Hindi, hoping some amount of conversation would reduce his uneasiness.

The guard didn't respond but instead pointed towards the river bed on the steep side. Raj could hear the river flowing. The guard then took an imaginary something in his hand and acted out, pouring water over his own head. He continued to point at the river with his other hand. Raj thought perhaps he was trying to convey that the old man had gone down to the river to bathe. Raj indicated to the cottage behind him and tried to ask through gesture who lived there. The guard shook his head slowly, his eyes narrowed as if he didn't approve of Raj's curiosity.

Suddenly, from the forest across the river, the sound of gunshots ripped through the air, as loud as thunder. The guard immediately made a sound for Raj to be quiet. He pointed again down to the river and gestured for Raj to listen. All Raj could hear was the sound of rushing water and the dismay of birds on being disturbed by the gun shots as they indulged in their pre-dusk social activities. He could see a flock of green pigeons flying high above, almost in disarray.

Raj looked at the guard, trying to understand. He stood up and tried to see the river bed down below, but the tall grass blocked his view. He could, however, clearly see the forest on the other side of the river, in all its primordial glory. These were the trees of real forests, their bark mottled, not like the uniform *sal* plantations raised by the forest department to extract timber. The guard took a twig and began to draw on the dirt. He drew a long boat with many people in it. He then added wavy lines under the boat to show a turbulent river.

Has the old man gone somewhere in a boat? He gestured again to ask the guard about the old man. He needed the old man in order to get back to the train before dark. He couldn't fathom his disappearance. Surely, he wouldn't go back to the train without him; the forest department people would certainly take him to the task. Raj heard a screeching sound from the sky; flying foxes were out hunting early. He realised with a shudder that he was trapped. Even if the old man returned, it would be impossible to return to the train tonight. He would have to spend the night there. And then he heard it, the unmistakable roar of a tiger. His second tiger in a single day.

Taking a deep breath, he tried to steady his nerves. He weighed his options. If the guard suddenly turned malevolent, he would have no choice but to try and run. He knew that the rivers were the arteries of the forest and if he travelled along the riverbed he might reach a forest village. He might also come face to face with a tiger coming to drink. His ancestors had staged elaborate big game hunts in the Ripu reserve with lavish displays of royalty, machismo, and power — all from the safety of an elephant *howdah*. They had taken down tigers with reckless abandon. His father Bichitra Narayan, in large parties with dozens of elephants, had killed many tigers. *So, if I were to leave this place*, Raj dreaded, *I will surely end up as an offering to the tigers of Ripu from the royal family*. If he stayed, he couldn't possibly spend the night on a bench, facing the obnoxious guard. He had to get into the cottage. He tried his luck again. Pointing to the door he asked, gesticulating, 'Is there anyone inside?'

The guard shook his head as if indicating how impatient he thought Raj was. He again pointed towards the river and gestured with his hands something that seemed to mean, 'Wait some more time.'

A curlew piped up on the river bed as if disturbed by something. Raj felt more nervous and afraid than before. He was now fully regretting the useless trip, taken at the most inappropriate time.

My wife is unwell, expecting our first child. Here I am sitting in the remotest corner of a forest in Assam for no apparent reason with a eunuch who I can't even communicate with, and the worst thing is that I've no clue what he is up to.

As daylight dwindled, Raj had all but forgotten about the alluring maiden on elephant back who had beckoned him to the forest. All he could think of was how to get back to the train. The whistle of that German engine would be the sweetest thing if he could hear it at that moment. Instead, he heard the sound of anklets clinking and the creak of a door opening. It was then he realised there was a second door at the back and someone had just entered the cottage.

Chapter 13

Leaving behind the dirt tracks of Kachugaon, Jenkins pressed hard on the accelerator. He had been feeling dreadful ever since the realisation struck him; he shouldn't have left the Prince. He thought about turning his car around. But he knew the train was now deep in the forest and there would be no way of reaching it. He cursed his ill judgement repeatedly. The Ford A took him to his residence in Dhubri in a record-breaking three hours, despite the pothole-ridden road. He got out of his car and rushed to the door of his quarters. It was locked. A servant appeared from around the back. '*Sahib*,' he greeted. '*Memsahib* has gone to DC *Sahib's* bungalow.'

Jenkins immediately felt thankful for the fact that there was a close-knit group of British officials who would help each other in such times. He was tired after the long drive and wanted to have supper with his sister and then retire for the day. He walked to the bungalow of the Deputy Commissioner (DC), just a stone's throw from his place.

The DC's bungalow was the showpiece of Dhubri. The massive Assam-type house had a front courtyard as big as a football field and the entire compound was bordered by trimmed, enormous hibiscus hedges so that the majestic house was hidden from passers-by. The massive wrought iron gate had a guard room, from which a Nepali guard quickly appeared and saluted. Jenkins walked the long path lined with spotless white bricks. Climbing the steps to the entryway, Jenkins wiped his forest boots on the doormat before knocking on the heavy front door. A servant greeted him and escorted him to the lounge, where the DC was talking with four other officials.

'There you are. Have you heard the news?' It was the Goalpara district DC, raising his head from the deep discussion he'd been having with his deputies and a senior police official. He looked sombre and there was a distinct lack of warmth in his demeanour, despite the fact that they had not seen each other since the Calcutta trip.

'What news? My guard said Janet is here. I thought I would just say a quick hello before taking her home. By the way, thank you for ensuring she has been cared for in my absence.'

'Don't worry about her. She is fine. They are all having a picnic in the backyard. I was referring to Raj Narayan — the Crown prince of Paschim Behar, who you took on a nature trip.' There was irritation in the DC's voice.

'Why? What happened to him?' Jenkins felt a twinge of panic, followed swiftly by confusion. *How did he know about the Prince?*

'Nothing actually, as I'm sure he has been enjoying your hospitality,' his senior colleague said, with a fair degree of sarcasm. 'His father, the *Maharaja* of Paschim Behar, passed away just this morning. A whole contingent of Paschim Behar's armed constabulary and palace officials have amassed and are waiting in the parade grounds. We have to collect the Prince at once from Kachugaon and despatch this contingent to their state,' DC said, all business. 'By the way, there have been enquiries from Shillong, asking what he is doing in Kachugaon. If he is on a hunting trip, why was the conservator not informed or the deputy commissioner's office, for that matter?'

Jenkins tried to make sense of the developments. He looked at the DC, who shook his head and without waiting for him to answer started dispensing instructions to his deputies. 'When can we start for Kachugaon to retrieve your Raj Narayan?' the DC asked again, curtly and loudly. Jenkins knew that his trip home was going to be short, but now he was wondering whether he would even get a chance to say hello to his sister.

The convoy to Kachugaon was impressive. It consisted of the DC in his brand-new Ford A, the superintendent of police in his police truck with his men, and Jenkins. There was a Cadillac from the royal garage to take the bereaved Prince Raj home. There was another car carrying the palace officials. At the end of the convoy was another truck carrying the soldiers of Assam Rifles. On arriving at Kachugaon, Jenkins drove straight to the station. He heaved a sigh of relief when he saw the train standing at the platform.

'When did you return? Is he in the IB?' Jenkins asked the *beedi*-smoking ranger Das.

Tired-looking Das threw his butt away and said, 'We have just returned. Prince Raj Narayan is still in the forest with the

Santali man. He himself sent back the guards I sent with him.'

Jenkins couldn't believe what he was hearing. He wanted to shout at the ranger, instead he asked, 'Where is Baruah? Has he come back?' Thinking fast, he knew he would need Baruah for the rescue mission.

Ranger Das shook his head. 'As I told you, we have just returned.'

'How could you leave him alone in the forest?' Jenkins' voice rose.

'Sir, he is a prince. We are just ordinary people. He asked the guards to go back to the train. They had to obey him.' Jenkins shook his head, left Das at the station and rushed back to the IB. He was relieved to see Baruah there. He had already called all the caretakers and servants. The whole IB compound had sprung to life with people rushing about to take care of the twenty or so unexpected guests. The DC, Police Superintendent, and Jenkins would stay in the IB. The palace officials were to be lodged in Brown *Sahib's Lal Bungalow*. The troops were led to the vacant quarters of the forest guards. With the lodging taken care of, Jenkins asked Baruah to arrange a meeting with all the beat officers, foresters, game wardens and guards who reported to the rangers.

'Should we call Brown *Sahib*?' Baruah asked Jenkins.

'I checked on him after I arrived. He is fast asleep,' Ranger Das said, wandering around. Jenkins felt a flash of irritation at both Brown *Sahib* and Das.

Once all the rangers, deputy rangers and beat officers had

gathered, Jenkins started unveiling the plan for the Prince's rescue. The DC and his colleagues were all confused as they thought Prince Raj Narayan would be in Kachugaon and not some remote location up north. Jenkins outlined that he would need the forest guards and trekkers with the highest level of expertise for the mission. All the department *mahouts* were summoned from their sleep. The *mahouts* and their elephants would march along the track that night, so they would already be waiting at the spot when the train arrived in the morning. The plan was for the train to leave the station at exactly four-thirty in the morning so that by the time it reached the spot there would be enough daylight to venture into the forest.

By the time Jenkins retired to his room, it was well past midnight, with just a few hours left before the rescue mission commenced. He felt worried, very worried, for the first time. He blamed himself for foolishly allowing the Prince to go to the forest in search of the elephant girl. Even if the Prince didn't come across any mysterious creatures, there were enough dangerous beasts out there to kill him. He fell into a fitful sleep only to be woken a few hours later by Ranger Baruah.

The scene at the station was like something from a war zone. Burly Paschim Behar soldiers stood ready on the platform alongside the short tough Gurkhas of the Assam Rifles as Jenkins and the other officials arrived. An orderly was pouring hot tea from a kettle for everyone. Jenkins had never realised his department in Kachugaon had so many employees. There were a number of rangers other than Rangers Baruah and Das, around eight or nine deputy rangers, and many beat officers. All of them dressed in their official khaki uniforms for the rescue operation. The mood in the station was of excitement and trepidation; the large group having no idea of what kind of adversaries they could meet or resistance they might encounter.

As the train pulled away from the station Jenkins could see the relieved faces of those left behind. They were surely hoping for some sleep after all the madness. It was an eerie feeling, sitting in the coach as the train moved into the dark forest. The morning stars faded from the sky as the early dawn created ghostly shadows on the grasslands and the *terai* tracks. There were animal and bird calls, and sounds of all kinds, causing Jenkins to wonder at how the forest could be so alive at such an early hour. He saw numerous pairs of glowing eyes appear and then retreat as the train passed by.

The train jolted to a halt, and he watched the soldiers jump down from the train. Jenkins realised that it wasn't a station. It was a stoppage in the middle of nowhere, the same place where the old man had gotten down three days ago and hopefully the same place where Prince Raj Narayan disembarked the previous day. Jenkins could see some large shadows in the woods — the department elephants waiting for the rescue party. The plan was to take the exact route the old man had taken as soon as day broke.

The two guards who had deserted the Prince the previous day were the reluctant leaders, along with the expert local trekker Bishuram who was known to move with a leopard's grace. They would be on foot, along with a dozen forest employees, while the soldiers and officials followed on elephants. Within two hours the search party had reached the cottage. The soldiers and police officials surrounded the compound, and a few Gurkhas, at the behest of their commander, let off a round of blanks into the air. A few elephants were already at work bringing down a section of the barricade. Once the compound was accessible, the soldiers rushed to the cottage and forced open the door. There they all stopped and gaped.

A stark-naked prince was blissfully asleep in the foetal position on a wooden cot.

Chapter 14

It was the strangest day Brown *Sahib* could remember. So many things unfolded before his very eyes, yet he remained a mute spectator. He was aware of the military-style preparation of the search party, which had started at four in the morning. The night before, when the township had been flooded with troops and police personnel, he realized something big must have happened. The most irritating part was that many loud strangers were brought into his bungalow and escorted to various rooms. In the very early morning, they had departed as noisily as they came in.

After the train left, he couldn't get back to sleep. Sitting on the veranda, he watched the forest in front of him wake up for the day. There were flashes of red as a flock of minivets readied themselves for tree hopping. High up in the sky, he could see an eagle drifting. Sipping sweet, milky Assam tea, he made a few mental calculations. *The Santali man and the Prince must have reached the destination by three or four yesterday afternoon. If the guard had killed the Prince, then it was all over for him. But the old man would hopefully have not let that happen. He knew his wife was being held. The Prince would be spared in all likelihood, but he would have seen it all.*

The distance from the hideout to Santhalbari was about twenty miles. He knew the old man would give the Prince the slip and go ahead to his village to warn the chief. He would need about six hours to get to Santhalbari. If the wild animals didn't attack him, he would have reached Santhalbari before midnight. Thankfully it had been a full moon. By the time the villagers got ready with their elephants, it would have been well past midnight. But elephants move faster than men. Even with the slowest elephants, they would reach the hideout by five in the morning. He looked at his watch as he placed his cup on the table; it was exactly five.

He hoped the old man would remember the stern warning given to him. No matter what happened, he was to rush to Santhalbari to inform the chief that the girl was in danger of being discovered. It was bad enough that he had been captured due to his carelessness. He regretted his decision to house the Santali couple in the abandoned shed. But he was sure the old man was shrewd enough and would manage to send men from his village to collect the girl from the cottage.

It was a mistake on his part to agree to his friend's suggestion. But Rajah *Sahib* was adamant; he wanted to propagate the myth. Their modus operandi, taking unsuspecting visitors to the forest where the large herd could be sighted, always worked. A fleeting glimpse was all that was needed. The viewing was meant to have taken place at the point when the train carrying Jenkins passed over a particular bridge overlooking a vast riverine grassland. The herd was to pass through that stretch at that exact moment.

He closed his eyes and rhythmically shook his head. The

morning forest breeze was still cool. He inhaled the dampness, visualising that, at that very moment, two elephants would be crossing the riverbed through the morning mist. Regardless of where the Prince was at that time, the girl and her eunuch guard would quietly slip away with the villagers and head for Santhalbari. He knew the route by heart.

He tried to count how many times he had been to Santhalbari. Too many to remember. Nobody ever suspected or asked any questions when Brown *Sahib* said he was going on patrol. He missed the longer stays when he was treated like a son-in-law in the village. Due to the increasing number of forest department employees over the years, he could no longer afford to vanish for a week from Kachugaon. But he would never forget the ten days he spent in Santhalbari after accidentally stumbling across the place.

It happened only a few days after joining the Assam forest department in 1905; he was asked to lead an exercise of transect-marking in the forest. The department was systematically trying to create transects in the forest area of Ripu by dividing it into grids. Some of the previously marked rides and parallels needed annual maintenance. The lines helped with patrolling, timber transport and most importantly, in mapping out the forest.

On the Kachugaon forest map pinned to the wall at the divisional head office in Dhubri, the junction of Bhutan, Bengal and Assam remained an unchartered territory. Nobody knew the timber or floristic worth of the area. Previous attempts to venture into that area had resulted in complete disappearances of the parties. This time, an instruction from Shillong had been received, to complete the task of mapping the unknown area of the Goalpara forest division. Leading this task was the new young energetic deputy ranger of Kachugaon.

Brown *Sahib* had armed the guards as the department didn't want to take any chances. It was noon. He had been on an elephant for almost the entire morning. They passed through an area of indescribable forest wealth. He had no idea that such a forest existed. As they were moving through a stretch of elephant grass that dwarfed even the tallest pachyderms, the party was forced to make a sudden stop due to a massive barricade of sal logs that seemed to appear from nowhere. The possibility of forcing the might of elephants against the log wall was negated by the fact that a large moat filled with dark muddy water separated the wall from the party. Attempting to cross the moat would drain the elephants of their strength, leaving them too tired to successfully loosen the wall. Also, the logs were at least a foot in diameter and buried deep. They looked too solid to be dislodged easily.

The party started moving along the moat. They saw watch towers at intervals, and there were skulls mounted on pegs that had been forced into the logs. After rounding the wall, they came to a moat crossing in front of an unmanned gate. Brown *Sahib* marched across with his armed constabulary. What he saw next he could hardly believe. There, in the deepest heart of the wilderness, was a large, well-planned township. It looked bigger than even the biggest forest village under Kachugaon division. They rode along an empty road for some time, before coming across a large building. Thinking they might rest there, they dismounted and went inside.

In the building, they found an ailing old man whom Brown *Sahib* later learned was the father of the village chief. The chief himself was out on a hunting trip with all the able-bodied men. Brown *Sahib*'s party was carrying medical supplies and, as a show of friendship, he attended to the old man's needs.

By the time the male members returned to the village, Brown *Sahib* had befriended the old man along with several Santali beauties. There were some dissenting voices, and so he gave them a demonstration of the power of firearms. The chief had no choice but to extend the hand of friendship to the strong young man and his party — their first contact with an outside civilisation and the Assam forest administration.

And so, Brown *Sahib* found a paradise of love and merry-making amidst the dense forest of Ripu. After ten days, when he took leave of his beauties, he knew exactly what he was going to do.

His thoughts again turned to Prince Raj Narayan. The killing of a prince would be a momentous news. Crown prince of Paschim Behar dies under mysterious circumstances while in search of a mythical maiden in the forest of Assam. Things had changed in Shillong. If an enquiry was held, with so many loose ends, it would be difficult to escape this time. It wouldn't be like last time.

He remembered the Shillong enquiry that happened fifteen years ago.

When he was asked why he, being the representative from the forest department, retreated from the scene, his answer had been simple and very convincing. 'I was at the rear of the expedition. When the elephants from the front turned back after the incident and came running towards me, my elephant panicked and changed direction. My *mahout* tried very hard to make it go to the site, but the beast simply refused.'

'Do you really believe what the surviving *mahouts* are saying about how the naturalists were killed?' One of the members had asked.

'Well, I have been in that region for the last fifteen years. I have seen a great many unexplained things. There are hostile creatures out there that have not yet been discovered by science. Or maybe there are wild tribes, who oppose the intrusion of Europeans on their land.'

'What about the elephant maiden the *mahouts* have claimed to have seen?'

He had been waiting for this question and was ready with his answer. 'The locals are always full of superstitions, but there must be some truth when all of them say the same thing. However, I personally don't believe in any elephant maiden. What I do believe is there are many pockets of the forest inhabited by unnatural beings that have had no contact with civilisation. Hence, the carnage. We have at our disposal hundreds of square miles of good forests for commercial extraction. If there are one or two pockets in the vast forest that some forces wish to keep to themselves, why should we risk our men and reputation for the mere curiosity of zoologists and botanists? There are endless number of areas in our state to study. I strongly believe any future expeditions into Goalpara forests by any party should be closely monitored by the forest department. If those small pockets become accessible due to initial contact established by my local forest guards, we will open them for future scientific expeditions. But until then,' he paused, for dramatic effect, 'we cannot allow these esteemed scientists and investigators from such prestigious institutions to venture into those pockets and endanger their lives.'

Reminiscing about the enquiry, he fell into a fitful half-sleep only to be woken by an excited Ghosh *Babu*. *'Sahib,* they have returned. Prince Raj Narayan is alive.'

Chapter 15

The moment Raj's convoy stopped in the courtyard of the palace, there were ululations from the womenfolk. The future King of Paschim Behar stepped out of the car barefoot, wearing a single piece of cloth. He looked towards the hall. It was full of people. He saw a large number of people out on that sizzling summer day in their heavy ceremonial outfits, waiting for the *Maharaja*'s last rites to be performed by the eldest son.

Raj was accosted by the head priest who presented him with some rings made of grass to wear. Instead of ushering him into the palace, the head priest along with a dozen other priests led him along the path around the palace boundary. He knew where this path would lead. The women of the palace, all clad in white, were looking down from the ornate windows. He was joined by his other brothers, half-brothers, male relatives, palace officials, servants; everyone following the future *Maharaja,* they silently marched along the edge of the long palace building.

The party reached the corner, took a sharp turn and headed towards the back of the palace. As the party neared the huge expanse of the palace courtyard, the crowd's cheers reached a crescendo. Raj saw a sea of people surrounding a raised earthen platform where, on a staked pile of wooden logs was the body of his father — fully covered by fresh white and yellow flowers. With folded hands he passed through the hysterical crowd, men and women almost falling over him, crying inconsolably. Some were trying to touch him, while others were shouting, 'Long live *Maharaja* Bichitra Narayan.'

As Raj approached the raised platform, the head priest asked all others to stay back. He slowly climbed the steps to the base of the wooden pyre. He couldn't see any part of his father. The *Maharaja's* body was covered from head to toe. He asked the priest if he could have a look; he wished to see his father's face one last time. But he didn't get to see the body as the flowers weren't to be removed. Ice blocks had helped keep the body unspoilt until Raj's arrival. He could smell the high-quality ghee, which must have been rubbed all over the body to make it easier to burn. Raj caught a glimpse of a loose strand of his father's hair through a gap in the wooden logs. The head priest came and initiated the ritual.

His father's lifelong wish for a thirteen-gun salute was fulfilled when Raj ceremonially lit the pyre. The cannons boomed thirteen times as a special tribute to the departing king: a concession from the British Government. The hysterical sound of the crowd reached another crescendo as their beloved king was consigned to the flame. And then Raj heard it for the first time. Even in the heat of the mid-afternoon, he felt a shiver run through his entire body at the crowd's cries of 'Glory to *Maharaja* Raj Narayan.' Unconsciously, his hand moved up. He reciprocated by waving to the crowd while his eyes remained on his father's burning body. His mind suddenly shifted to thinking of his own body that had been consumed by a very different kind of fire just a few hours ago.

Raj looked at his brothers, standing at the base of the raised platform. Their white cotton clothes were drenched in sweat and all except one were watching the burning pyre with folded hands. Pran Narayan had his head hung low as if he was searching for something on the ground. All the brothers looked forlorn, but it was as though Pran's gloom was due to something other than their father's demise.

Indra Narayan closed his eyes and began to chant some prayers while his half-brothers poured more ghee onto the pyre. The smell of ghee-embalmed skin dissolved into fat and meat, and the crackling of bones filled the air. The red flames gradually dissipated, bodily signs of the portly *Maharaja* diminished into charred pieces of bones, as the sun started to set. Three hours in the July afternoon sun combined with the heat from his father's pyre and Raj was fully drenched in sweat. After concluding the last-minute rituals somewhat mechanically, Raj was guided back to the palace by the rear entrance. The crowd was still shouting his father's name, and some were hailing Raj as their next ruler.

The six princes were escorted to a large hall in a section of the palace away from their usual quarters. Mattresses lay on both sides along the length of the room with a path down the centre leading to a large mattress. The soon-to-be-crowned *Maharaja* Raj Narayan was to sleep on the floor with his brothers for the next ten days until all the rituals for the departed soul were completed. All the princes would be confined to the hall and were required to curtail their normal routine of gastronomic and other pleasures. Raj wasn't a heavy drinker, but he knew for some of his younger brothers it would be a challenge. They would eat only fruits during the day, and in the evening there would be just one single cooked meal of boiled rice and lentils with some vegetables.

By the time Raj had bathed and changed into a set of white clothes, which he would have to wear for the next ten days, it was time for their only meal of the day. As the six princes sat in a circle to eat, Raj saw his younger brother Pran Narayan's face closely for the first time in many months. He realised his younger brother had aged considerably. He looked older than Raj even though he was two years younger. Alcohol was taking its toll. With the scar on his eyebrow from a childhood fight, he had always emitted a streak of ruthlessness. He was staring at the food, not taking a single morsel, oblivious to the presence of the others.

Next to Pran was Indra Narayan, the suave and stylish youngest brother of the three of them. Technically third in line for the throne, Raj knew very well that if their father had had his way, his favourite son Indra would have been the first choice as his successor. Indra Narayan was about five years younger than Raj. He was well read, well-built and well-mannered. Though Raj held the title of crown prince, the duties of crown prince were mostly performed by Indra as their father had relied on him inherently. The traditional succession system followed by the six hundred year-old Narayan Dynasty of Paschim Behar was that the oldest of the siblings would ascend the throne under all circumstances. It must always be this way to dispel any misplaced notions amongst the brothers that might motivate them to stake a claim.

'Can I have some cut ginger?' Indra shouted.

Raj looked at the three half-brothers who were eating quietly. Indra was chatting to them in a friendly manner while the temperamental Pran sat sullenly silent. After the evening meal, Raj and his brothers readied themselves to retire for the day. Pran was already snoring even though there was a constant buzz of activity all around: servants moving around with juices and fruits, making the princes' beds, clearing away utensils and bringing in various necessities for the princes. Raj saw Indra lying on his bed staring blankly at the ceiling. He had been closest to the *Maharaja* and would feel his father's loss the most. Raj's long stay in London and Pran's aloofness had resulted in a solid bond forming between the *Maharaja* and Indra.

The servants thinned out and all the princes lay on their mattresses — some already asleep and some trying to fall asleep. Somebody dimmed the lights, and for some reason Pran Narayan's snoring stopped. After the hall became quiet, the enormity of the situation dawned on Raj. His father had left them unexpectedly and now he was to become the next ruler of Paschim Behar. Did he want to take it? Did he have a choice? Would Indra be disappointed?

Raj heard a moaning over the sound of lazily spinning ceiling fans. He sat up and walked towards the source of the sound. It was the youngest of the six princes, who was writhing in discomfort. He felt his half-brother's forehead and found it to be hot. He went out of the hall and asked an attendant to fetch a doctor. Raj decided to lie back on his bed to wait for the doctor. He hoped it would be the young Bengali doctor from Calcutta.

The servant returned shortly after. He was followed by the doctor, a distinguished looking older man, with greying hair and a French beard. He appeared to have rushed to attend to the young prince as he was still wearing his pyjamas. As he entered, he saw Raj and acknowledged the future king by giving a slight bow, then turned towards his patient. As the doctor attended to his half-brother, Raj lay on his bed with his hands under his head, thinking back to the days when the same doctor had looked after his mother.

A sudden realisation hit him. In the absence of his father, he became the supreme authority of the palace. He had the right to banish people he didn't like. He would never forgive Dr Delrome for bringing that nurse of his to the palace. That dreadful question lingered. *Had the doctor and his nurse administered something to his mother to get her out of the way?*

As he fell asleep, Raj's thoughts drifted back to the winter of 1910, when the Maharaja's convoy was returning from a royal hunt in the forests of Goalpara. The *Maharani* and her three boys were also part of the group. They had to make an emergency stop at the district headquarters of Dhubri as the *Maharani* was seriously ill. She had a high fever and there was no way the royal convoy would reach the palace before nightfall. She was admitted to Dhubri civil hospital, which sprang into action with the sudden admission of a royal patient. Raj looked on as a young French doctor and pretty Indian nurse did the utmost for his mother. Raj and his brothers were lodged in the district commissioner's bungalow, along with their father. In the morning, the *Maharaja* rushed to the hospital accompanied by Raj. They were relieved to see his mother's condition had improved.

'She stayed with me the whole night,' the *Maharani* said of the young nurse.

'She is ready to go to the palace, Your Highness,' the

111

French doctor told the Maharaja. His father was very impressed with the doctor and offered him a position at the palace. Raj remembered his father's eyes were constantly glued to the beautiful nurse who seemed always to be by the doctor's side, like a shadow.

Within weeks, the French doctor was in residence and became the personal physician to the *Maharaja* of Paschim Behar. The beautiful nurse also came with him to the palace. His mother was constantly falling ill. Dr Delrome and his nurse would nurture her back to health. But a few weeks would pass, and she would fall sick again. The duo took the appropriate care, and his father was always impressed. Over time, however, his mother's condition became progressively worse. His father entrusted the responsibility of looking after his wife to the palace officials and his trusted physician. He would be busy with his card games or trips to Calcutta. He was also spending time planning the royal family's attendance at the forthcoming Delhi *Durbar* to commemorate King George V becoming The Emperor of India. Raj awoke feeling a shiver run down his spine. He had been away, first in Calcutta and then Kachugaon. And like his father, he had entrusted the doctor to look after Divya.

'No,' Raj murmured, 'this doctor must leave the palace.'

Chapter 16

Raj was awoken by Pran's snoring, which reached a crescendo early in the morning. He could make out the silhouette of Indra sitting up on his bed, most likely woken up by the thunderous sounds coming from his brother. The others were all still asleep. As the dawn light gradually brightened the hall, Raj could hear the flurry of activity taking place in the corridor, as the servants prepared themselves to serve the princes. He went to check on the youngest brother, who was just waking up. He touched Jai's forehead. It was no longer warm.

'I am feeling absolutely fine now,' said Jai sleepily. 'Dr Delrome came to check on me.'

'I know; I sent for him.'

'That was last night. He came this morning too, at around four when all of you were sleeping.'

'Oh really? I didn't realise. Anyway, you sleep now. It's still quite early,' Raj said patting his half-brother's shoulder.

As the day passed, Raj found himself surrounded by numerous people: palace officials who updated him on protocol issues, astrologers with a list of dates for the coronation, with the pros and cons of each date, and priests asking him to perform rituals at periodic intervals. Servants were continually moving around with fruit platters and chilled glasses of lemon juice. He would occasionally go out of the hall to greet visitors who arrived in considerable numbers to offer their condolences.

As Raj lay on the mattress in the afternoon, taking advantage of the low turnout of visitors around that time, he realised he had not seen Divya since his return. The women of the palace were mourning in another section. The men and women would remain separated for these ten days leading up to the memorial ceremony. Raj dozed, half-leaning on his pillow. When he awoke, he would consciously try to think about his expecting wife, but as soon as he started drifting off, he was transported to the night he had spent in the forests. Scratches from the bushes and thorns were still fresh on his legs. But his upper body, neck and back had scratches of a different kind. When he was awoken by the loud voice of Pran, who was talking to Indra in a threatening manner, he was thankful he was separated from his wife. Pran swore loudly and rushed out the hall while Indra stood quietly, his face wearing its usual semblance of composure. Raj approached Indra who shrugged. He looked at his younger brother affectionately. *You would make the ideal king for our kingdom.*

He didn't say it out loud, although everyone knew the throne of Paschim Behar did not hold much fascination for Raj. At the same time, Raj knew that the traditional kingdom would never break the usual succession rule even if he did wish to denounce the throne to his younger brother.

But did he wish to abdicate? Probably not, Raj thought. Technically, if he decided to abdicate, the mantle would fall on the second brother: Pran Narayan. Neither Raj nor Indra could ever entertain that possibility.

'How has he been lately?' Raj asked.

'Well, he has realised he has a problem. He has been seeing Dr Delrome. I think if he can stay with us like this for ten days, it would be a great achievement,' Indra said.

'Does he talk to you much?'

'Generally not, except when getting agitated for no apparent reason, like today. Lately, in fact, he has withdrawn even more into himself. The only person I see him interact with normally is your attendant Tapash.'

'Tapash is a helpful aide for everyone in the palace,' Raj said with a smile. 'I think Pran should see a doctor in Calcutta. Dr Delrome is no good. Father died because of his negligence. Maybe mother also died because of him.' Indra didn't say anything. This was another of Indra's traits that made him more suitable for the throne—he listened but didn't always comment.

As he went off to talk to some palace officials, Raj thought again of his mother's death. *Did she die because of the French doctor's negligence... or was his father responsible?* While in attendance of his mother, Raj noticed that his father would often steal glances at the beautiful young nurse. Looking back, Raj thought how very efficient she had seemed, and attentive to all of *Maharaja*'s needs, but at the same time oblivious to his mother's deteriorating condition. It seemed his mother's worsening condition became a boon for the *Maharaja*, as the nurse became a third member of the bedroom. Raj remembered seeing his mother crying in pain while the young nurse attended to the *Maharaja*. One morning when he came to check on his mother, he found the nurse asleep on his parent's bed with his father. As he tiptoed closer, he saw his father was fast asleep, his mouth half open. The nurse didn't have a stitch on and held his father in a tight embrace. She too was asleep. The only person awake was his mother, calling out from the adjoining room.

As Raj went to his mother, she pointed weakly toward the water jug. Little Raj lifted the heavy vessel and poured a glass of water for his mother. Did his mother know that the nurse was sleeping with the *Maharaja* in the next room? Raj still remembered the pain in his mother's eyes. As she sipped the water, tears flowed down her cheeks. She gestured for Raj to come nearer and kissed him on his forehead. A kiss he would never forget as it would be the last show of parental love in his life.

Pran shouting orders at Tapash brought Raj back to the present. An attendant was changing the garlands on his father's portrait. Now that his father was united with his mother in the next world, he wondered what his mother would say to her husband. Would she forgive him after what he did to her? His thoughts turned to Divya. Would she accept him for what he had done?

It was almost five in the evening. There were frantic movements in the corridor. Raj longed for his usual evening cup of tea. He saw the head priest walking towards him carrying a silver cup. The priest briefed him on the rituals to be performed the next day. Still thirsty, Raj was aware that he was undertaking strict penance and was required to observe the rituals the dynasty had followed for generations upon the passing away of a Scion. He looked over at his alcoholic younger brother, still staring out the window, and wondered if he was being disrespectful to the departed soul of their father. He refrained from passing any judgement and was jostled to his senses by the priest sprinkling drops of water from the silver cup by shaking a twig of holy basil.

In the evening, the princes were served a simple vegetarian meal. They ate heartily, all except Pran. After dinner, visitors to the hall dwindled and servants entered to make the beds and clear away dishes and utensils. Once the place was clean and the princes on their beds, the attendants dimmed the lights and fumigated the place with the smoke of burning coconut husk to rid the hall of any night bugs. Pran was now asleep and snoring. Prince Jai no longer had a fever and he too had already fallen asleep.

Raj was exhausted. It had been an agenda-packed day of meetings with special guests and government officials, greeting the ever-steady flow of people offering condolences, and sitting with the priest for the necessary rituals. As sleep drew nearer, he smelled the familiar fragrance of *Jabakusum* hair oil wafting through the smoky air. Raj strained his eye to look at the watch. It was almost nine, time for some of the palace girls to return to their quarters after their shift. He could hear the dim sounds of their anklets as they passed the hall.

Chapter 17

Raj sat as still as stone on the bench as he heard somebody enter the cottage through the back door. He heard a shrill cry coming from the trees beyond the cottage compound. A peacock had just landed and was crying out for its mate. He felt the temperature drop as the sun vanished behind the dense canopy. The booming sound of a bittern added to the eeriness, and Raj experienced a sense of being drawn into this deep forest world, not for the first time that day.

He made up his mind; he was going inside the cottage. He stood up, walked to the front door and knocked. There was no answer. Another knock, with a little more force this time — still no answer. Then he gave it a push and the door swung open.

It was dark inside and he was overwhelmed by the aroma of *Jabakusum* oil. As his eyes adjusted he could make out a delicate young woman sitting on a matted wooden cot, her knees to one side. She was looking straight at Raj, too stunned to say anything or move. For Raj, on the other hand, his arousal was instant. Like a man possessed, he stared at the girl, taking in her white saree, her long black hair, and beautiful face that had a celestial quality; he felt he had seen that face somewhere before.

He took a step closer. 'Is this real?' he murmured as he tried to make sense of the situation. The girl's blue eyes were glued to Raj. He stared at this incredible figure before him. Her body was too white to be Indian, her hair too black to be European. Her unwavering gaze mesmerised him. Raj just stood spellbound, his mind racing and heart pounding.

'Hello,' he said gently, to which the girl said something — her voice sweet and smooth like the most precious wine, drowned out by the increasing chirps of cicadas coming from outside. He loved her voice after the ugly screams of the peacock, but he couldn't understand a word.

As he took another tentative step towards the cot, there was a knock on the door. Startled, Raj retreated to his position near the door. A dark figure entered the room carrying a plate. Bowing continuously to the girl while saying something to her, the eunuch guard fetched a wooden table from the second room and placed it near the cot. He then put the plate on the table, disappeared again and reappeared with another plate, two glasses and an earthen pitcher. He again spoke to the maiden and then retreated from the room, bowing continuously.

It was a simple vegetarian meal. They ate silently. Hungry, Raj cleared his plate in no time. After they finished the meal, the girl took the plates through to the second room at the back of the cottage. Raj heard the sound of splashing water. He followed her, and she indicated for him to wash his hands. As he was pouring water from the earthen pitcher, he heard a noise coming from the river bank below. It was the unmistakable sound of a boat being rowed in choppy water. There was a small window in the room and he strained to see through it. He could just make out a large boat carrying a number of men. They held flaming torches, the light revealing that they were also carrying guns. Another boat joined the first and the men disembarked onto the riverbank and started making their way up towards the cottage.

Raj caught the girl by the hand and they ran out through the front door. He pointed toward the riverbank and she seemed to understand that trouble was brewing. Raj felt very real fear, and then sheer excitement as the girl interlocked her fingers with his. They reached the large wooden wall and stood there; Raj had no idea what to do next. The girl fetched a clamp from behind a bush and fixed it into a gap in the logs. A small opening was revealed, and they slipped through it. Raj pushed the log door closed.

Raj and the girl ran to the bamboo bridge that crossed the moat, separating the cottage compound from the grassland. The moon shone dimly in the sky and they could make out giant shapes in the grassland in front of them. From the muddy smell and grunting sounds, Raj realised that by night the grassland had become the grazing ground for a herd of buffaloes. A bull blew through his nostrils, and even in the darkness Raj could see the grass parting from the beast's snorting gust. The girl clasped his hand tighter, pulling him away. Raj looked back to see the cottage bathed in an orange halo from the approaching torches. A gunshot cracked into the air followed by a hoarse cry.

Is this how I am destined to leave the world? Lost in the forest with an unknown girl?

The girl was shoving him and the next thing he knew he was in the moat. The girl joined him, and immediately both of them were neck deep in the swampy water. She pushed him under the bamboo bridge, her bosom pressing against his chest. He could hear the men as they approached the cottage. If the men reached the bridge and peered through the bamboo poles, they would be spotted. The girl, as if reading his mind, handed him a thin hollow reed. Raj heard the men struggling to find a way through the wooden wall. The girl pushed Raj down by the shoulders and then they were under water, breathing through the reeds.

A thunderous explosion boomed in the sky above. Raj had to surface; he had not been able to take in enough air. He could hear the men from behind the wall. 'The rain is coming. We have to get back to the boat,' one man shouted.

'We will lose all the timber. Let's go, we have to follow the logs,' another voice said. 'Dump the body in the river; the crocodiles will finish it.' The men continued to shout animatedly at each other. Raj realised they must be the dreaded timber smugglers, who were illegally denuding the forests of Goalpara to supply the boat-making industry of Bengal. The river bandits, Jenkins had called them. They had killed the eunuch guard.

The girl surfaced. Thunder rolled overhead. Raj felt a strange tingling sensation under water. He felt down and realised his body was covered with numerous shrimp-like insects. He pulled the girl closer and ran his hands over her body to remove the pests. They remained in a tight embrace as they listened, the shouting was now further away. The forest seemed to fall quiet.

Raj climbed out of the water and helped the girl up onto the bridge. They stood there, facing each other when the clouds burst. The moon was gone, and rain began to fall from the tar-black sky. In seconds, the downpour was immense; the grass bent under the weight of the water and puddles formed all around. They ran together back towards the cottage. A wall of rain moved across the forest and riverbank, and there was no trace of the men or their boats.

The curtain of rain disappeared as suddenly as it had come. An explosion of night birdsong erupted from the dripping trees. The frogs started croaking, the rain invigorating their desires. The screaming of the peacock became louder as the wet bird landed on the tree inside the compound.

Raj led the girl inside; his arms were around her. He removed strands of wet hair from her face and lowered his head to discover her incredible lips; she let out a soft cry. He led her to the bed and lay alongside her — their mouths joined as their limbs tried to discover more of each other's bodies. Their cries joined forces with the cicadas and all other forest animals, as their bodies discovered one another in frenzied passion on the rickety wooden cot.

Afterwards, they lay still, bathed in shadowy moonlight. Raj could hear the river in the valley down below and felt connected to it, as if both of them were trying to outrun each other in the middle of the night.

Raj could smell the girl's wet head buried in his chest while her fingers traced patterns on his body. Soon she became bolder and more expressive. Her luminous teeth flashed in a moment of pure passion as she pawed at his back with her nails. This time the girl did not hold anything back.

At last, Raj fell asleep with the girl completely wrapped around him. Never in his wildest dreams could he imagine that at that very moment they were putting slabs of ice on the lifeless body of his father until the son returned to liberate it from its earthly connections.

Chapter 18

The hall was buzzing with activity as Raj walked to the doorway. The corridor was full of visitors and palace officials. Attendants were ushering people into the central hall where they were offering flowers and paying their respects to the larger-than-life photograph of the late *Maharaja*. They were then quickly ushered away to make room for others.

Standing in the doorway, politely greeting whoever greeted him, Raj saw at a distance the heavy frame of a visitor in a large pink turban. Seeing the limp, it only took him a second to recognise Rajah *Sahib*. He was rather surprised. Paschim Behar was one of the largest buyers of Rajah *Sahib*'s elephants; maybe he had had a relationship with the late *Maharaja*. Raj strode forward to greet his new friend. But Rajah *Sahib* didn't see him and took a sharp turn towards the women's quarters.

Baffled, Raj retreated to his study. He quickly forgot the incident as a string of visitors and state officials came to meet him. The day passed quickly. By mid-afternoon, he was tired and in need of rest. As he opened the door to his study, Rajah

Sahib sprang in front of him. He looked quite different from his earlier demeanour; his turban was gone, his grey hair tied back in a single lock.

'I don't want to take up much of your time. I know you are busy. I also need to go back to Assam. But I have something very important to tell you.' He spoke in a husky voice, doing away with any niceties or commiserations. He looked around to suggest they needed somewhere private.

'Let's go inside,' Raj said leading Rajah *Sahib* into his study. 'I saw you this morning. I thought you were coming to meet me but instead you went elsewhere,' he said as he took up his seat behind the mahogany desk, offering Rajah *Sahib* the seat opposite.

'Well,' Rajah *Sahib* started, clearing his throat, 'It was a bad morning. I went to offer my condolences to the *Maharani*, who happens to be my sister.'

Raj looked at Rajah *Sahib*. Had he heard correctly? 'Sorry, what did you say? Who is your sister?'

'Your stepmother, the late *Maharaja's* second wife is my sister,' he said slowly and loudly as if to reinforce the message. 'Why are you so surprised, Your Highness?' Rajah *Sahib* asked. 'She used to be a nurse.' The disdain in his voice was apparent.

'I know she was a nurse. But I didn't know she was your sister.'

'That's a long story. She has a long history. And surprisingly, she has not changed at all. Some or all of what I will tell you may sound incredulous. There is an attempt going on to annihilate the bloodline of the late *Maharaja* and your late mother,' Rajah *Sahib* said, his tone turning ominous.

Raj looked straight into Rajah *Sahib*'s eyes, hardly expecting to have such a conversation with the man he had met just a few days back. Rajah *Sahib* settled back in the chair and continued matter-of-factly. 'In fact, there were two assassination attempts on your life while you were in Kachugaon. Incidentally, I thwarted both not knowing at the time they were premeditated murder attempts. The first was at *Lal Bungalow*, when I caught a bar attendant mixing something into your drink. He said it was prescribed by your doctor.'

Bewildered, Raj listened silently.

Rajah *Sahib* shook his head. 'I should have made that man drink it. The second attempt was when that rogue elephant was let loose on you. It wasn't an accident. Somebody who was there did both those things. I believe your father was murdered by the same forces. Your wife is expecting. Please send her away. She and the unborn baby are not safe in this palace,' he said with conviction.

Raj tried to guess where all this was leading. 'Who is behind this? Even if I am eliminated, I have two brothers next in line to the throne. So how can they eliminate the whole of my father and mother's bloodline?'

'Everyone knows about Pran Narayan. And your second brother Indra Narayan just survived an assassination attempt in North Bengal while you were in Kachugaon. Even if he becomes the king, he is unmarried. He may have an understanding with my sister that after him one of her children or their children will become the ruler of the state.'

Raj looked at Rajah *Sahib* displaying no emotion.

'I am telling you because I believe someone from my family is orchestrating it. I don't want to mention any names and I don't have any proof. The onus is on you to sit back or act. Just remember that your father's death saved your life even though you were both targeted at the same time. If you had stayed in Kachugaon for a few more days, they might have had the chance to make a third attempt on your life.'

Raj was listening intently. He was trying to put the pieces of the puzzle together.

'You are safe for the time being,' continued Rajah *Sahib*, 'but you have to act fast. First, take care of your unborn baby and wife as an attempt on their lives might be next.'

'I believe you, Rajah *Sahib*,' Raj said. 'How did you know about my father?'

'I don't know. I am just thinking. Based on the happenings in the last few days and over the past few decades. Is it a coincidence that your young mother passed away not long after a new nurse came to the palace to take care of her?'

'How old was your mother?' he continued, 'In her late twenties? How old was your father? He was quite a few years younger than me. He was a fine sportsman, quite an athletic man... and yet he dies, just like that?'

'If I were married, I would have sons about your age, but

I do not, and with my passing away the bloodline of Parbatipur will cease to exist. I don't want the same thing to happen to you.' Rajah *Sahib's* eyes glistened with tears. He took Raj's hand and patted it, then turned around and walked out of the study.

Raj stayed in the study, his head reeling from Rajah *Sahib's* revelations. The head priest had given him an extensive list of do's and don't's for the days leading up to the *Shraddha*. Raj, being the eldest son, was following all the directions given by the priest. The main one, apart from food, was to stay away from the womenfolk. But after what Rajah *Sahib* had told him, he had no choice but to break the rule.

Entering his own bedroom, he felt like a stranger. The room was darkened by long heavily embroidered curtains. In the centre was a giant four-poster bed with tables on either side, each holding a bedside lamp atop an ornate base in the shape of an elephant. On one side of the room was a plush, beautifully coloured sofa, where one could sit and look out at the centre courtyard of the palace.

He was looking for Divya. He could see tell-tale signs of her presence, but he did not see Divya herself until his eyes fell upon what had seemed like a bundled up saree on the sofa.

'Your Highness,' a feeble, trembling voice uttered from the bundle. 'Thank you for coming to see me. I thought I would never get to see you.'

He couldn't believe what he saw; his Divya, emaciated, her beautiful face shrunken and pinched. He crossed over to the sofa and got down on his knees, stopping his wife who was trying to get up.

'What has happened to you?' he almost shouted taking her face in his hands. 'What is going on? You are so sick, and nobody has told me.'

And then he looked down, moving his hand to her tummy that somehow didn't seem as big as when he last saw it. 'Is our child all right? Are you in so much pain because of the baby?'

She started to sob uncontrollably, burying her face in her hands.

'I don't know. I have been very sick since you left. I don't know what it is doing to our baby. What will happen if we lose this child ... like the last time?' Divya asked, reminding Raj of the pain they both bore only a year ago.

'Why was I not informed after I arrived?' he shouted, his voice almost hysterical.

'If the baby doesn't arrive again, will you leave me?' That was enough to break his heart into a thousand pieces. A pang of guilt engulfed him. Divya had needed him by her side in this difficult time and he had failed her.

'I will never leave you,' he said, tears clouding his vision. Then in sudden anger, he shouted, 'Tell me!! Is Dr Delrome the one who has been taking care of you? I am going to kill that bastard! He killed my mother. He is the one who killed my father. And now he is after our baby. Does he think I don't know anything?'

'What are you saying? Why do you think he did all this? He seemed to be taking good care of the late *Maharaja*. He had been very good to me too!' Divya said sounding distraught.

'He just pretends to be good,' Raj said, kissing his wife's forehead. 'But how do we know whether what he prescribes is medicine or poison? I have always disliked that doctor and that nurse of his whom ...' he stopped himself before saying anything more. He stood up, walked over to the door and asked a waiting girl to get Tapash.

'Divya, what do you think of the *Maharani*? Has she treated you well in my absence?' he asked, returning to her side.

'She has enquired after my health every day. She comes once in the morning and once in the evening. She herself makes sure I take all my medicine.' There was a knock on the door. Raj beckoned Tapash to enter.

'I want you to make immediate arrangements for the Princess to be taken to the Calcutta Medical Hospital. Make sure nobody, I repeat nobody, comes to know about this.' Tapash nodded, not asking any questions.

'I will inform your parents so that someone from your family can come to take care of you at the hospital. I don't trust anybody from this palace,' Raj said, as he walked toward the door. Turning again to Tapash he said, 'Ask Gurkha Bahadur to see me at once, he will guard her till she leaves.' Raj again looked at Divya. She looked completely drained. His mind flashed back to three nights ago when the woman in the forest had become a passionate tigress, exhausting him to the point that he had no sense of consciousness until the armed guards broke in. He watched as tears flowed down Divya's cheeks.

'Why did you take so long to come here? Why did you go to Assam so suddenly? What took you so long?' She was on the verge of breaking down. *Should I tell her the truth?*

'I was in search of an elusive animal. I completely lost sense of time. I am so very sorry. I will never forgive myself for this.' He couldn't stop the tears rolling down his own face. Never before had he felt so wretched.

'Did you find what you were looking for?' she asked. Looking into her eyes, Raj felt that she didn't need an answer. He didn't respond. He held her and brought her head to his chest. He felt as if she sensed the truth.

Chapter 19

When Raj returned to the hall, the attendants were about to serve dinner. He sat on the mattress as an attendant placed a stool in front of him, then a large silver plate covered with a banana leaf. It was the same meal as before; a mix of rice, lentils and vegetables all cooked together in ghee served with dollops of butter. Once all the princes were seated, the head priest chanted some hymns and Raj took the first handful, which allowed others to then start their meal. The young princes ate voraciously with the attendants running from one place to another keeping up with demands for salt, butter, water and more food.

Once the meal was over, Raj went to Indra and pulled him aside. 'Tell me, was there an attack on your life recently?'

Indra smiled. 'How did you come to know? I was camping near the border. Someone tried to set fire to my tent. Maybe it was some disgruntled villager from the Bengal side. I really couldn't come up with any other explanation. Anyway, I need to discuss something with you. I will tell you in detail tomorrow,' he said looking around as if to ensure the others weren't listening.

'Good night,' Raj said and went to his mattress. He covered himself with a bedsheet.

'Good night, *dada*.' Indra went to his bed near Pran, who was already asleep but without any snoring this time. The usual routine of attendants removing utensils, fuming the hall with burning coconut husk and dimming of the lights, took place. As the last light dimmed, Raj drifted off to sleep.

Die you bastard, die.

A ghastly cry woke him. He sat up, straining his eyes. He saw two figures in the shadows; one atop the other's chest, plunging a dagger that went up and down. Panic-stricken, he scrambled to the nearest light switch, shouting out to wake up others. As the lights came on, he was met with a horrifying sight. His alcoholic brother Pran was sitting atop the lifeless body of Indra. One of the half-brothers ran out of the hall while the other two surrounded the brothers, but nobody dared to unarm Pran who started laughing maniacally, waving the dagger. Raj felt like passing out.

Pran stood up and dropped the dagger. He folded his hands together and started walking towards the Paschim Behar constabulary soldiers who had just arrived at the door of the hall. As the constable placed Pran in handcuffs, he looked at Raj who gave a weak nod. Pran Narayan, the second heir to the throne of Paschim Behar, was led away from the hall.

Within minutes the hall was full of people. A large procession of the women folk arrived at the scene and started howling, beating their chests. Raj was still shaking from the ordeal and so were his three half-brothers. And then he saw Dr Delrome in his pyjamas near the door, followed by a junior doctor.

'Get away please...', all of you,' Dr Delrome shouted, as he gestured to the attendants who were following him with a stretcher. Indra expelled an 'aahh' sound as his blood-soaked body was bundled onto the stretcher. Dr Delrome, with wild gestures of his hands, shouted at the crowd to make way as he led the attendants out of the hall carrying Indra. Immediately afterwards, palace guards and attendants filled the hall to shift the four remaining princes back to their own bedrooms.

Minutes later, Raj was alone in his room sitting in an armchair. It was impossible to sleep. He was sweating profusely. The bed he shared with Divya was neatly made, with two pillows side by side, his red and Divya's blue. The more he looked at the empty bed, the more he thought of his wife — his loving, caring, beautiful Divya. And then he thought of Rajah *Sahib's* prophecy, Divya's secret departure to Calcutta. She hadn't been prepared to leave so soon. She wanted to stay at the palace. But Raj did not relent. Tapash, with his usual efficiency, had arranged for Divya to be surrounded by attendants and, under the cover of darkness, he had bundled them all into a truck. To any onlookers, it would have seemed like a dozen palace maids were taking a trip to the city.

He thought of his father. He should have visited him before he left for Kachugaon. At least then he would have known if he was sick or if he died due to other machinations. Then he thought of the two attempts on his life and now his favourite brother.

For the first time in his life, he felt vulnerable in the

palace. The sudden realisation hit him that once again, like in the forest, he was on his own. His mother long dead, his father recently departed, Pran Narayan arrested and Indra Narayan - God knows how he was faring, no one had been able to tell him – there was no one else left who he truly trusted.

Suddenly there was a loud banging on his door. He felt irritated and disoriented on being woken as sleep had just come after many hours. Dr Delrome was at the door, still in the same pyjamas only now they were marked with blood. Raj braced himself for the worst.

'Your brother is alive,' the doctor said. 'There is a chance he will recover if we bring in some specialist surgeons from Calcutta.'

He couldn't believe it. How could someone survive such horrific injuries? He knew Indra was the fittest and healthiest of the six brothers. The manly, peppered stubble on his handsome face and wearing the single piece of white cloth, Indra looked like a Greek God during the days of mourning. His dashing smile flashed before Raj. *That's my brother.*

'Do the needful,' said Raj, 'and let the news spread that he is recovering. I don't want this shadowing father's mourning period and the *Shraddha.'*

'I understand and will do what is necessary, Your Highness.'

'Wait,' Raj said. 'Say that there was an accident in the hall. We could say my intoxicated brother thought there was an intruder in the room whom he attacked. But, it wasn't an intruder; it was Indra, and he is recovering now.'

'I will try my best to revive Indra,' Dr Delrome said, as he took his leave.

Raj went back to bed and this time fell asleep immediately. By the time he emerged from his room, it was nine in the morning. The palace had its usual bustle due to the ongoing preparations for the *Shraddha*. As Raj walked past the hall, he saw that it had been cleaned to a spotless shine. The mattresses were gone, and the room had been restored to serve its regular purpose as a visitors' lounge.

'Your Highness, the *Maharani* wants to speak to you. She said it is urgent; it is regarding Prince Indra.' It was Tapash. Raj had not met with the *Maharani* since his return from Kachugaon. While walking to the royal women's quarters on the other side of the palace, he thought about his father's wife. Since the Maharaja's funeral, they had seen each other many times, but they never really spoke. They had always maintained a cordial relationship — respectful yet distant. He always sensed a vulnerability in her despite the powerful position she held in managing palace affairs and to some extent, Paschim Behar. Maybe she was afraid for her role in the palace, now that the *Maharaja* had passed away, but he felt her insecurity was more likely due to the fact there were still people in the palace who knew of her previous identity.

Raj knocked gently. A woman attendant opened the door. *Maharani* Indira Devi, usually so spectacularly bejewelled, looked quite different dressed in white. She stood near the window looking out. As Raj stood before her, she looked more alluring in the simple white saree than he remembered. It seemed the necklaces, earrings, nose rings and the heavy bejewelled sarees hid the beauty of the woman rather than enhanced it. But there was something else he couldn't quite place.

'A lot of disturbing developments have taken place - the *Maharaja* passing away so suddenly. Now this attack on Indra.' Raj was jostled out of his thoughts as she spoke.

'Who do you think is responsible for all this?' Raj asked.

She turned and gave him a surprised look. 'In the case of Indra, we know it was Pran.'

'But why? Why did he do it?'

'I think you know your brother Indra,' the *Maharani* said, looking Raj in the eye, inferring he knew full well of his brother's romantic liaisons in the palace. 'But in this case, Pran was encouraging his wife. I knew it was wrong. But I couldn't do anything about it, as both were consenting and Pran had no issue with it. Even the *Maharaja* knew. Pran never bothered to hide the fact that he had no physical relationship with his wife.'

'Then what could be the motive other than alcoholic madness?' Raj said.

'Everyone knows Indra has little respect for his elder brother, and with his behaviour, Pran doesn't deserve any respect. You were away for many years, and the two of them just drifted apart. I have seen both these men grow up since their childhood. They are so different. But that still doesn't explain Pran's actions. There must be another reason.'

Raj was no longer interested in trying to understand his mad brother's motives. Committing such a dreadful crime just days after their father's passing was a disgrace, and would become a huge source of embarrassment for Paschim Behar in the eyes of the other princely states. They would laugh at the savage ways of Paschim Behar.

'Do you think father was also murdered?' he asked.

'Why do you think that? Has Rajah Paritosh Baruah of Parbatipur said something?' the *Maharani* asked, her expression difficult to read. *She has eyes and ears all over the palace.*

Raj didn't corroborate. 'What do you think?'

'As you know, the *Maharaja* no longer took me in his confidence regarding his health matters. We have not been intimate for years,' the *Maharani* said, matter-of-factly. 'He had a fever a few weeks ago but I thought it was just due to change of season.' She paused, then added, 'I do believe his death was too sudden.'

Attempts on his life in Kachugaon. The Maharaja found dead in his room. An attempt on Indra's life near the Bengal border. Indra attacked by his mad brother. Pran Narayan considered unfit for the throne. The heir apparent becomes Deep Narayan – the twenty-three-year-old firstborn of the Maharani, the nurse.

It felt as if all the pieces of the puzzle suddenly fell into place.

Chapter 20

So, the bloodline of Paschim Behar will run from the womb of this enchanting nurse and not my mother.

The *Maharani* was about to say something when Raj blurted,'What do you have in mind? Why did you want to see me?' The pointless interview with the woman was now causing him great angst.

'Now that the *Maharaja* is no more, you are the heir apparent, with the coronation around the corner. I want to make a few things clear to you,' the *Maharani* said calmly, in contrast to Raj's agitation.

'Go on,' Raj said, trying to regain his composure.

'You should be very careful in these coming days. We believe that bad things happen to the family when the patriarch passes away. It is like a great banyan tree falling in a storm. When the big tree falls, it brings down smaller trees with it. I am not sure whether Indra will survive. Pran is no good, in or out of prison. I really want you to take care of yourself. Be circumspect,' the *Maharani* said.

Raj looked at the *Maharani*. She seemed earnest enough. Suddenly, he felt that the enchanting widow, clad in all white, brought back memories of what had happened in the cottage. It caused a stirring in him. He was aroused and the fact he was wearing just a single piece of cloth around his waist didn't help.

'I understand you have sent Divya away from the palace?' the *Maharani* asked. The question pulled him back to the present.

'Yes, she wasn't looking well. I have sent her away for treatment. With everything going on here, she wasn't receiving the attention she needed.'

'Where is she, by the way?'

'I can't disclose.' Raj wasn't taking any chances with his wife and the baby. 'Thank you for your advice,' he said curtly and left her room. As he walked back to his study he mulled over who to believe: Rajah *Sahib* or the *Maharani*. To add to the dilemma, both had sounded genuine. He missed Divya. She used to tease him that he was the worst judge of character.

Raj was in his study when the *Diwan* walked in. After exchanging pleasantries with the future king, the *Diwan* outlined a list of issues on which his opinion was required. Most of the discussion was on arrangements for the *Shraddha* that included protocol and security issues, and the guest list and seating arrangements. They discussed strategies to ensure that any polarised camps wouldn't be near each other.

In the end, the *Diwan* said, 'I don't know how to broach this, but I think it will benefit from your wise counsel as it relates to the state exchequer.'

'Go on,' Raj said.

The *Diwan* cleared his throat and took a sip of water. 'This is a letter from the late *Maharaja* asking me to release a sum of fifty thousand rupees to an estate in Assam. I wasn't sure of the reason for the transaction.' He placed the letter on the table. Raj saw the letterhead displaying the official insignia of the *Maharaja* of Paschim Behar.

'Did you ask him?'

'No, I didn't get the chance as I only received it the day he passed away. Please advise me, what should I do with the instruction?'

Raj wondered how to respond to the question. It was a large sum of money. 'Under what circumstances would father owe money to an estate in Assam?' he asked.

'I have been *Diwan* for the last eighteen years. Under no circumstances have our state's finances ever been so bad that we had to borrow from small estates. I don't see any reason the late *Maharaja* would need to take out a personal loan either. The only financial dealing we have with an estate in Assam is for elephants.'

'Could it be due to some outstanding amount owing for elephants?' Raj asked.

'The sum would equate to the worth of twenty elephants.

No elephant seller would give twenty elephants on loan,' the *Diwan* said. His stern look indicated to Raj that the matter could be serious.

'In fact, we no longer have any dealings with this particular estate. Our elephant dealings have been with Parbatipur for years now. But the letter asks me to release the money to the Manikpur estate.'

Raj knew he would have to get to the bottom of the matter. 'Don't worry, I will talk to Indra once he is well. He might know something about it.'

He looked at the Diwan. The sixty-something bespectacled Prime minister of Paschim Behar seemed exhausted but Raj knew that his mind was sharp and that he was an intelligent administrator. During the last few days, he had efficiently dealt with various contingencies. However, the letter was troubling him considerably. Raj went out of his study and asked the waiting attendant to bring tea for the Diwan.

'You mentioned Parbatipur estate, our main elephant supplier. Did you know that the *Maharani* is the sister of the Rajah of Parbatipur?' Raj asked, thinking he might take the opportunity to clarify a few things that had been on his mind since his meeting with Rajah *Sahib.*

'Well,' *Diwan* hesitated for some time. 'Everyone knows where the *Maharani* comes from. But nobody discusses this as she disassociated herself from her parental home.'

'Which is Parbatipur?' Raj enquired.

'Your Highness,' the *Diwan* started speaking. 'Parbatipur

is one of the most progressive *zamindaris* in the district of Goalpara. *Zamindar* Paritosh Baruah, whom everyone calls Rajah *Sahib*, and your family, descended from the same ancestry. In the sixteenth century, the kingdom of Behar was divided into Poorav and Paschim Behar. As time passed, with Mughal incursions from the west, Ahom incursions from the east and machinations of the East India Company, Paschim Behar became a princely state under British India and Poorav Behar became fragmented into numerous smaller estates and *zamindaries.*'

Raj nodded. He was aware of this bit of Paschim Behar's history.

'Rajah *Sahib* was one of the three children of his parents. As the oldest child, he was entrusted to look after the estate affairs and the elephant catching operations. The second child was sent abroad to learn film making; he never came back. The youngest child was a daughter who was around twenty years younger than Rajah *Sahib*. She was beautiful and well looked after, a pampered child. Her elder brother, who took charge of the estate at an early age due to their father's debilitating illness, sent his sister to Madras to study medicine.'

An attendant walked in with tea for the Diwan. Raj settled for lemon juice. They waited for the attendant to leave to resume their conversation.

'The sister returned to Assam not as a doctor but as a trained nurse. She was deeply in love with a French doctor who had graduated in medicine in Madras. Rajah *Sahib*, oblivious to his sister's romantic inclinations, started looking for alliances for her. He wanted to find a suitable boy from the *zamindari* families of Bengal. Then came a proposal which completely caught Rajah *Sahib* by surprise. He was unprepared and didn't know how to react.'

'What proposal?' Raj asked.

'Not a proposal actually, it was a straight out declaration that she was going to stay with the French doctor. Rajah *Sahib* didn't like the French doctor,but his sister was head over heels for him. Without asking for her brother's endorsement, she moved out to live with the newly-appointed civil surgeon of the Goalpara district. It served everyone well that no ceremony took place. The doctor didn't have to explain to anyone in his circuit about his native companion and Rajah *Sahib* didn't have to explain giving his sister away to a French doctor.'

'Quite a story,' Raj said.

'Yes, quite a love story. A rebellious one too,' the *Diwan* added. 'Rajah *Sahib* was hurt and humiliated — the daughter of Parbatipur was the mistress of a doctor. But she wasn't bothered, and she severed all links with her brother and her family in Parbatipur. That was in 1909. They were happy there, until...'

'My father saw her when returning from the hunt,' Raj cut in.

The *Diwan* nodded. 'You know what happened after that. After she became the *Maharani*, I once acted as the emissary from her estate, on Rajah *Sahib's* request. Her father died after a prolonged illness. Now that she was the *Maharani*, Rajah *Sahib* expected his sister to return and readied his estate to welcome the royal couple. In fact, the *Maharaja* wanted to go, to offer his condolences to Rajah *Sahib* on the demise of the father-in-law he had never met. But she didn't want to go. The death of her father helped her severe any remaining connection she had with the estate of Parbatipur. As the years passed, *Maharani* Indira Devi became even more detached from her family. She has never entertained any queries on her original home or family lineage. Such queries would always be met with a blank look and stoic silence.'

'Interestingly, her dumped suitor Dr Delrome became quite close with Rajah *Sahib*. And the *Maharani*, once she was initiated into the network of wives and mistresses of other Maharajas, especially as a young bride during the Delhi Durbar, became more resolute that she would never reveal her family background. All the other wives were Princesses from the various princely states. Your mother was from the state of Baroda, but our *Maharani* hailed from an obscure *zamindari* family in Assam. She thought not revealing and remaining an object of speculation was preferable than revealing her identity and suffering from an inferiority complex for life.'

'A heartless woman indeed,' Raj said, unconsciously looking at his watch. It was almost time for his daily evening meal. 'I must go,' Raj said after a terse silence.

Chapter 21

Though the four remaining princes were back sleeping in their own rooms, they were still observing the ritual of eating their only meal in the evening together. During dinner that evening, Raj decided he would use the time to make a conscious effort to bond with his half-brothers. Indra and Pran, of course, would not be present. All he had were his half-brothers who still carried his father's blood. Being the eldest, he thought he needed to reach out to his younger siblings. Despite what Rajah *Sahib* had told him, he found that none of his half-brothers treated him as anything other than the heir apparent of Paschim Behar. All three half-brothers seemed genuinely disturbed with the recent tragic events.

All three of them were fine young men. The eldest of the three, Deep Narayan, had been his father's favourite after Indra. Raj had always perceived Deep to be a proud young man who had scant respect for his elders. However, while talking to him that evening, he felt he had judged him incorrectly. *Maybe I have been biased throughout?* Raj thought.

Later he received a call from Calcutta. Divya was feeling

much better and her sister was with her. Her parents would also visit her before they came to Paschim Behar for the *Shraddha*. It was a huge relief that Divya was now in good care. The plan was that after the *Shraddha*, her parents would return to Calcutta to collect their daughter and go to Bombay. Once she had fully recovered and delivered the baby, the daughter and grandchild would be taken to Gwalior Palace where they would stay for a few weeks. After that, they would return to Paschim Behar before the coronation.

After talking with his half-brothers and getting the call from Divya, Raj felt lighter and he hoped for a good night's rest. As he lay on his bed, mulling over the day's conversations, his eyes fixed on a large photo of his bride, dressed in a bright red and gold saree, but somehow his nostrils still carried some traces of the *Maharani* in her sensuous white. He looked away from the photo and turned onto his side. Divya's image blurred from his vision and he felt the smell of his stepmother wafting ever more strongly in the air.

'Now that Divya is in safe hands, you have to go back and look for her. She needs your help,' said a voice in his head, while he was trying to sleep. *Does she need my help? Or do I just want to be with her again? Either way, I need to find her. Or I will lose my sanity.*

He sighed heavily and got up from his bed. He thought of the only person who could help him out. He went to his bedside desk and wrote a message. Then he shouted out for an attendant to get Tapash, who promptly arrived at his door.

'Tapash, this is an urgent telegram for Bert Jenkins DFO Dhubri Assam,' Raj said, as he handed over the piece of paper. 'Be sure to address it correctly.'

Tapash took the paper from Raj. He looked a bit surprised and was about to leave the room when Raj said, 'I want you also to send someone to Dhubri. He will be hand-delivering a letter of invitation for the ceremony to Jenkins. And make sure nobody knows about this telegram.'

Tapash nodded and left the room. Raj breathed a sigh of relief. It was six days until the main ceremony. The telegram should reach Jenkins by tomorrow afternoon. This would give him three or four days to prepare for the trip. And the hand-delivered invitation would reinforce the urgency. If Jenkins could make it to the ceremony, then they would be able to start for Kachugaon forest the next day. Waiting any longer wouldn't be advisable as the head priest would be declaring a day for the coronation sometime soon. Once coronation day was declared, Raj knew he would be under constant scrutiny and would also have to take part in many rituals leading up to the day. Also, Divya wasn't at the palace. Indra would remain in hospital and Pran would remain in jail. None of his half-brothers would be interested in knowing where he was. It would all be up to the *Diwan*. The old man would have to do some covering up.

'After the hectic nature of the past eleven days, the crown prince is taking a few days off to recover from the recent events. He does not wish to be disturbed,' the *Diwan* saying this would stop anyone from suspecting anything. Raj wasn't bothered by what the *Maharani* would think. He lay down again and his eyelids soon became heavy. His thoughts drifted back to the forest of Ripu. Sleep enveloped him in the halo of that special morning.

Her mouth was open as she slept after their lovemaking. Her white saree, his shirt and trousers were wet bundles on the floor. He was exhausted, but sleep was the last thing on his mind. He watched the rise and fall of her beautiful bosom. She awoke and pulled him towards her. As he curled himself around her, he slowly drifted into a dream world. She would free herself from him and run away. He would be waiting with his hands covering his eyes. She would blow a whistle and hide somewhere, and he would go find her. On finding her, they would kiss, and he would let her go again. There would be another whistle and he would search for her again.

And then he heard a long whistle. It wasn't the sweet sound of the play whistle. It had a sense of urgency and he didn't like the sound. He went out into the forest to look for her. He made up his mind; this would be the last round of the game. Once he found her, he wouldn't let her go. He would hold onto her forever. But he couldn't find her. He looked for her behind every tree, and in every bush, but she wasn't to be found. He went down to the river bank. Was she in the water? He went to the tree where the peacock was sitting. She wasn't there. He looked up at the platform where the eunuch stood. It was empty. He went to the bamboo bridge. The grassland in the front looked green and wet. The water of the moat looked crystal clear. He looked for her in the tall grassland. She wasn't there.

Tired and devastated, he returned to the cottage. He saw a large earthen pot covered with a white saree. He climbed into the pot. He curled up along the contour of the pot and was soon asleep until somebody started shaking the pot. Then someone hit the pot with a hammer, and he came out of the pot in his pristine nakedness like a newborn baby.

Three burly Gurkha soldiers barged into the room. Raj woke up. He felt the bed and looked around. He was completely naked. It took a while for him to realise where he was and what was going on. She wasn't there. He looked for his clothes. They were gone. The white saree was also gone. He looked around the room. It was bare. There was no sign that somebody was staying in the cottage. The door of the cottage had been broken and the soldiers were standing inside the doorway, amused looks on their faces. He heard the sound of many people talking outside.

Tapash appeared in the doorway, carrying some cloth. 'Your Highness, please wear this.' It was a white cotton *dhoti*.

Raj sat up. 'Where are my clothes?' he demanded, but then realised that Tapash wouldn't know. 'Why this *dhoti*? Don't you have any other clothes? Why are you all here? Who sent you?' he asked, covering his groin with his hands.

'Your Highness, we bring very bad news. The *Maharaja* is dead. He passed away yesterday. We have come to collect you. His funeral is waiting, as the eldest son you must light the pyre.' Raj could see Tapash trying hard not to look at the scratches on his body.

Raj sat, dumbfounded. His father had died and the whole of Paschim Behar's state machinery had come to track him down. The soon-to-be *Maharaja* of Paschim Behar. Covering himself with the *dhoti*, he pointed outside, 'Who is with you?'

'*Diwan Sahib*, Uncle Beer Narayan, the forest officer who came to collect you from the palace and many other district officials from Dhubri. And of course, the soldiers of Assam Rifles,' Tapash said. 'All the other princes and the *Maharani* are waiting for you at the palace. Since hearing the news, thousands of people from all over the state have gathered at the palace, as well as many visitors from Calcutta.'

Bare-chested, wearing only the *dhoti*, Raj exited the cottage. All the palace officials bowed. The *Diwan* and Uncle Beer Narayan exchanged glances. He could see a sneer on his uncle's face. There was one face amongst the crowd that he was pleased to see. It was that of Jenkins. But before he could say anything to his host, the palace officials surrounded him and guided him to a waiting elephant. The elephant didn't have a *howdah*, it had only minimal matting. The *mahout* made the elephant sit. Raj mounted the elephant with great difficulty and his head reeled as the elephant stood up. Senior members of the rescue party also mounted elephants. Others were on foot.

'Brahma, you remain here and find out what's going on. Keep a few soldiers with you. I want a thorough report,' Raj heard Jenkins give instructions to a junior as he mounted his elephant. Soon all the elephants were moving through the forest. *Mahouts* prodded the beasts and they moved quickly through the grassland. As soon as the elephants entered the forest, it began to rain, drenching the procession. Raj realised how torturous it was to sit on an elephant without a *howdah*. The rhythmical movement of the elephant back resonated through his entire body. The sweet feeling of his body entwined with the maiden's seemed like a faraway dream, while his testicles were getting crushed by the folds of the elephant's skin.

So, there he was, going to light his father's pyre sitting half-naked on an elephant.

Chapter 22

Brown Sahib was sitting in the veranda of *Lal Bungalow*. He was thinking about Rajah *Sahib*, who was extremely distraught on his return from Paschim Behar. He never imagined that a tough man like Rajah *Sahib* could be so heartbroken. When he was leaving for Paschim Behar, he had been in such a jovial mood. He got the cleaners to shine his old Rolls Royce until it gleamed like polished silver. He was confident of the inevitable rapprochement between him and his sister. He was willing to forget everything and forgive. Before his departure, he had made up his mind that he would provide his sister with all the solace she needed.

Brown *Sahib* wanted to caution him not to be too optimistic. But he didn't end up relaying this thought.

As Rajah *Sahib* departed, his smile never left his face. It was as if he was going to a wedding, not to offer condolences. The previous night, Brown *Sahib* had invited him to stay in *Lal Bungalow*. Rajah *Sahib* had expressed to him how he thought things would change with the death of the *Maharaja*. His sister's three young sons would need a father figure. Who would be better for the job than their maternal uncle? That's what Rajah *Sahib* had said the night before he left while drowning himself in alcohol.

Brown *Sahib* couldn't shake the feeling something bad was about to happen.

'Mark my words,' Rajah *Sahib* had said, 'I am sure this time it will be different. We are both so much older and it is only the two of us left. Surely when she sees her big brother after twenty-five years, her heart will melt. When she left, I was an overprotective brother and she was a young girl madly in love.' Rajah *Sahib* let out a big laugh, reminiscing.

Brown *Sahib* listened to his friend but remained silent. He hoped that Rajah *Sahib* wouldn't be disappointed. Before he left, Rajah *Sahib* had hugged his friend. Brown *Sahib* was a bit surprised, as he had never known such a display of affection from his friend before. But he hugged him back. He thought he saw a tear roll down Rajah *Sahib's* cheek.

After two days, Rajah *Sahib* returned to Kachugaon and came directly to *Lal Bungalow*. Brown *Sahib* was eagerly awaiting him, but not only for the news of his friend's meeting with his sister. He also desperately wanted to know whether the Prince had mentioned anything about his encounter. So far, nobody in the department knew who the Prince had met in the cottage, nor what he had done. Brown *Sahib* was hoping he had kept it a secret. That the Prince was married gave him some solace. When Brown *Sahib* saw his friend after his return from Paschim Behar, he couldn't believe his eyes. Rajah *Sahib* didn't look anything like the man he had seen off two days ago. He seemed to have aged ten years in two days. He was a shattered man.

'I had to beg to get an audience with my own sister. She refused to meet me. All I wanted to do was offer my condolences. She was my little sister whom I have loved unconditionally despite everything,' Rajah *Sahib* told his friend, crying inconsolably.

'You won't believe what she said to me when we finally met. "*Why are you here?*" Those were her exact words to me, as I stood in front of my sister whom I have not seen for so long,' Rajah *Sahib* said, filling his glass with more whisky. His hands were shaking, and his eyes were red.

'Do not let it upset you anymore. You now know that she has not changed. Don't give her any more chances,' Brown *Sahib* said.

'But why this cold shoulder? To her own brother?' Rajah *Sahib* asked. 'I told her that I just came to enquire after her and how she was coping with her husband's death. I didn't want anything from her.'

Brown *Sahib* listened to his friend patiently.

'I was exhausted after the long journey. I had to wait so long. If Dr Delrome had not been there, I would never have met her. She didn't even offer me a seat. Nor did she summon anyone to offer me any refreshment. As soon as I arrived at the palace, I sent a message to her through the officials. I conveyed that Rajah Paritosh Baruah of Parbatipur wanted to meet the *Maharani* to offer his condolences. I did not mention our brother-sister relationship. But my sister didn't relent until I saw our old doctor friend who must have convinced her. Only then did she agree to grant me an audience,' Rajah *Sahib* said, his voice choked with emotion.

'What else did she say?' Brown *Sahib* asked.

'She told something that really troubled me. She said that once the baton of Paschim Behar monarchy passed to her bloodline, she didn't want to see my face anywhere near Paschim Behar. She said I could take solace sitting in Parbatipur that my family has taken over the rein of Paschim Behar. But she would say nothing more. Given that the three children of the *Maharaja* from his first wife are alive, I've no idea how she thinks she is going to become the mother of a king. She is up to serious mischief,' Rajah *Sahib* said, composing himself.

Then he chuckled. 'Do you know what I did at the palace?' Rajah *Sahib* asked his friend.

'No idea,' Brown *Sahib* said. He knew his friend wasn't one to take humiliation easily.

'I told our new friend, Prince Raj Narayan, everything she had said to me. Being the heir apparent, he should know everything, right? That should take care of her,' Rajah *Sahib* said as he gulped down the rest of his drink.

'So, it seems your little sister is aiming very high. From queen to king mother?'

'Don't worry, whatever plan she has will surely fail as I have informed Prince Raj Narayan of her ill intentions. He is a smart, well balanced young man. He will make sure that she is shown her place.' Rajah *Sahib* shook his head as if trying to rid himself of his trip to Paschim Behar. 'I must forget about her. She is not a good woman. I am ashamed to call her my sister. Let's open some champagne to offer a toast to our friend *Maharaja* Raj Narayan,' Rajah *Sahib* said breaking into a thunderous laugh.

It was evening, and Rajah *Sahib* had been drinking since noon. Brown *Sahib* asked his friend to stay at *Lal Bungalow*. Rajah *Sahib*, however, was insistent that he return to his own camp. As he left in his inebriated state, Brown *Sahib* told him he would check on him the next day.

Brown *Sahib* saw the bus of the local contractor passing by. He hailed to stop it. The contractor and the driver got off the bus and ran towards him with folded hands.

'Drop me at the elephant camp. I need to see the old man,' Brown *Sahib* said as he hopped on the bus, which was on its weekly trip through the township. The driver and the contractor scrambled on behind him.

'*Sahib*, it seems you transferred Gethela to Fakiragram,' the contractor said.

'When did you see that bastard? I don't know where he vanished to after spreading those rumours,' Brown *Sahib* thundered. A few passengers on the bus were looking up in awe at Brown *Sahib* as the bus moved off.

'Why, he was in the bus with Baruah *Babu*. They were going to Fakiragram as Baruah *Babu* said there was a fire at the depot. I thought you must have instructed Baruah Babu to take him. I have not seen him since then,' the contractor said.

Baruah never informed me that Gethela went with him. Is he hiding Gethela away from me? This rich son of a zamindar is becoming something of a nuisance.

'Stop!' Brown *Sahib* shouted, as the bus approached the path to Rajah *Sahib's* elephant camp. He got off, threw a coin at the contractor and walked off towards the camp.

Attendants on foot and elephants saluted him as he strode in. Without acknowledging anyone, he went straight to the tent with the flag. It was three in the afternoon, but the tent door was closed. This was unusual, as Rajah *Sahib* usually did his rounds at that time, in discussion with the agents of prospective buyers.

'He has not come out of the tent all morning,' said one of the attendants milling around the tent.

'And you lazy bastards have not bothered to check on him since then?' Brown *Sahib* asked the man. 'Are there any girls inside?'

'I think no...' the attendant said with some uncertainty. 'No, nobody is in there. Champa was there, but she left late last night. Rajah *Sahib* has been alone since then.'

Brown *Sahib* stomped his foot on the ground. 'Bastards, why haven't you bothered to check on the old man? Can someone be inside a tent so long on a hot day like this? Open the flap. Cut it if necessary.'

By then many of the elephant catchers and grass cutters had gathered around the tent. Two men began cutting at the strong canvas with a *dao.*

As the tent door was cut open, the group led by Brown *Sahib* barged in. It felt like they had entered a furnace. The hot draft hit them, and a stench filled their nostrils. At the far end of the tent, the lifeless body of Rajah Sahib was lying on the mattress.

Chapter 23

'Get everyone here. Make sure nobody leaves the camp,' Brown *Sahib* ordered.

Soon he was facing a hundred-strong crowd of elephant catchers, grass cutters, attendants and labourers-- all stunned by the sudden revelation about their master. Some were already crying, some were angry, but the majority were just clueless.

'Did anyone see anything suspicious? This morning or yesterday evening?' Brown *Sahib* shouted, repeating it a few times in different directions.

'No, we didn't see anything suspicious,' came the replies.

'Who saw Rajah *Sahib* last night?' A dozen hands were raised.

'Who saw Rajah *Sahib* today?' No one raised their hand. *This means he died or was killed last night.*

'Were there any visitors to the camp yesterday evening? Anyone who doesn't belong to the camp?' Brown *Sahib* shouted, noticing that the news had travelled, as forest personnel and villagers were joining the ranks of the camp workers. He saw some of his rangers, including Baruah.

One of the camp hands edged over to Brown *Sahib* and muttered, 'Baruah *Babu* was here last night.'

'Why didn't you tell me when I asked?' Brown *Sahib* asked under his breath.

'I thought you said outsiders. Forest department people are always here,' the man whispered back.

Brown *Sahib* gestured him to get away and shouted, 'Were any of our department officers or guards here last night?' Ranger Baruah raised his hand.

'Why were you here? You shouldn't have had any dealings in the elephant camp,' Brown *Sahib* asked with scorn. 'Did you meet with Rajah *Sahib*?'

'No sir, I came to see someone else. I didn't meet with Rajah *Sahib*. I will tell you later. Not in front of all these people.'

'Why later? Tell me now,' Brown *Sahib* wanted to say but stopped himself. 'Alright, first things first. We have to do something with the body, fast.' He gestured for the camp wardens and rangers to follow him to the office tent nearby. He sat on his friend's throne-like chair, its armrests carved from ivory. He asked the rangers to take a seat. Rangers Baruah, Das, Miri and Deputy Ranger Brahma were there.

'Can you get Choudhury?' Brown *Sahib* asked the deputy ranger as he pointed to a middle-aged man who was a senior at the camp.

'So...,' Brown *Sahib* started, addressing the group. 'It is to be business as usual around here. The camp now belongs to the Assam forest department. We will take care of you all. I will go to Dhubri to sort everything out,' Brown *Sahib* turned to Choudhury, as he arrived at the tent. 'Tell all your men they need not worry. Nobody will lose their job. But we will have to get rid of all those servants looking after Rajah *Sahib.* They must find jobs elsewhere. This is now the Assam Government's elephant camp, so only people dealing with elephants will be allowed to stay.' Choudhury nodded silently.

'Ranger Das will be in the charge of the camp from now onwards,' Brown *Sahib* said, knowing full well that Das wasn't the best choice, but he didn't want anyone from the camp. Miri wouldn't be suitable as he constantly fell sick. And Ranger Baruah would obviously be a bad choice.

'By the way, you come from Dhubri, don't you? You are to pack your belongings and leave at once. Your dues, if any, will be cleared later,' Brown *Sahib* said looking at Choudhury with scorn. A man who didn't possess the common sense to check on his elderly master on a scorching hot day had no right to be in charge.

'Sir, can I have a moment with you?' It was Baruah. He leaned towards Brown *Sahib* and whispered, 'Don't dispose of him so quickly. He knows the place inside and out. He knows who the troublemakers are here. It will be difficult for us to handle these hundreds of people if he is thrown out.'

'OK, I understand,' Brown *Sahib* said, moving away from Baruah. 'You will stay and help us,' he shouted at Choudhury who looked startled and relieved.

Brown *Sahib* stood up, clapped his hands together and said, 'All right, can someone get the priest for initiating the ceremony? We will make Rajah *Sahib's* pyre here in the camp, in the presence of his elephants and his men.'

The rangers and some of the camp officials were surprised at the announcement.

'This looks like a suspicious death. Should we not send the body for an autopsy?' Baruah asked. Rangers Das and Miri and a few camp officials nodded and murmured in agreement.

'Are you people mad or blind?' Brown *Sahib* shouted. 'Can't you see the condition of the body? By the time it reaches Dhubri on a hot day like this, the body will have rotted.'

Brown *Sahib* gathered himself up. 'He is my friend and I want to send him off with dignity. I don't want his body to be bundled in a jute sack and handled by those filthy bastards in that dirty morgue in Dhubri,' he said, with all the weight of his authority. He peered out of the tent and pointed to a large fig tree. 'He will be laid to rest under that tree.'

The rangers and camp officials dispersed to prepare for the funeral. Brown *Sahib* went back to Rajah *Sahib's* tent to have one last look at his friend. Soon after, he lit the pyre and did the rituals guided by the priest. He remained next to the pyre while the flames were engulfing Rajah *Sahib*. He kept wiping away the ash and sweat from his hairy chest, as Rajah *Sahib's* pyre burned on.

The Elephant Girl

By the time the large body of Rajah *Sahib* had turned to ashes, it was well past midnight. Brown *Sahib* returned to *Lal Bungalow* and sat in a chair outside. He remembered their one special trip together to Calcutta. The towering personality of Rajah *Sahib* in a white starched *dhoti* and long *kurta* with gold buttons, carrying a walking stick with an exquisite ivory handle carved in the shape of a swan, had many heads turn in the streets of Calcutta. Passers-by would stop momentarily to guess the origin of the aristocratic man. And today the last of his bodily remains were being pushed with sticks by the *mahouts* to ensure everything turned into ash. The same *mahouts* who wouldn't dare come near him or speak to him without bowing.

Sitting alone in the darkness, surrounded by forest creatures that colonised the township at night, he reminisced on his friend and business partner. What a business it was! Yes, they resorted to falsehood; but it saved lives, protected families and helped shroud a royal secret.

He remembered the sparkle in his friend's eye when he told him of the special elephant catchers. He saw them for the first time in Santhalbari when they were taming the largest elephants he had ever seen. They had acquired a certain skill that made them the most effective elephant catchers in the foothill forests. What's more, their stealth and skin tone helped them approach and capture the biggest of the wild tuskers without detection.

The story he heard in Santhalbari was of the elephant catchers and *mahouts* who belonged to one of the *zamindars* of Goalpara, on their annual *mela shikar*. One of the elephant catchers became possessed by an evil forest spirit. He let all the elephants loose and destroyed all of the provisions.

Then, armed with a machete, he killed a number of his team members. Seeing no way to control the man, who seemed to have acquired superhuman strength, the remaining elephant catchers and *mahouts* retreated deep into the forest.

This tired and lost group was discovered by Santali hunters and taken to their village. The punishment for trespassing in Santhalbari was beheading and would have been the fate of the elephant catchers. However, Raghu, the village chief, realised they could be an asset. Their lives were spared, and they became the elephant catchers and trainers for the village. The runaway elephant catchers became part of the Santali society and produced the next generation of stealth elephant catchers who were of mixed race and surpassed their predecessors in skill and agility.

The big elephants caught by the stealth catchers fetched a fortune. The royal houses of India paid the same amount for a large, well-trained tusker as they would for five juvenile elephants. The stealth catcher would sit stark naked on a female elephant that would be on a special diet in order to emit an odour that would drive even the most nonchalant tusker of the herd insane. The love-struck tusker would follow the female for days. Once the tusker became exhausted, it would be captured by the stealth catchers. Santhalbari became the hub for catching the biggest tuskers of the region, very unlike the juveniles captured by the *zamindars* in the southern parts of the forests.

Brown *Sahib* shook his head remembering how eventually he became the conduit for smuggling the giants to the wealthy *zamindar* of Goalpara. That was how he started a symbiotic relationship with Rajah *Sahib* of Parbatipur, which later blossomed into an unconditional friendship. He remembered seeing Rajah *Sahib* so happy with the giants he received from Santhalbari that year. He started a rigorous training regime to ready the giants for the ceremonies of the rich princely states of British India.

But it seemed God had other plans for the trainer.

'What the hell?' Brown *Sahib* was jostled into consciousness by the loud sound of a bamboo stick being whacked hard on the ground.

'Hey! Hoosh!' It was the night watchman who was repeatedly thwacking his stick on the ground, sending something scuttling into the bushes. 'It came all the way to the veranda, *Sahib*,' he said to Brown *Sahib* who had spent the remainder of the night in his chair. It was almost daybreak. Flying foxes were returning to their roosting trees while a horned owl hooted it's last hoot of the night.

'Don't worry about the leopard. It's gone. Go ask them to get me a cup of tea and tell someone to fetch Ranger Baruah.'

Baruah's sighting with Gethela on the bus and his appearance in Rajah Sahib's elephant camp were still troubling Rajah *Sahib*.

With a steaming cup of tea, Brown *Sahib* waited for Ranger Baruah. Baruah had said he had come to the camp to meet someone but not Rajah *Sahib*. He had to get to the bottom of it. Had he made a huge mistake appointing the descendent of Manikpur *zamindari* as a ranger in his department?

Chapter 24

Raj suddenly sat up in bed shuddering.

'Tapash!' he shouted, and his trusted attendant was promptly standing by the bed. Raj wondered fleetingly how Tapash could be at his side so quickly whenever he called. 'We need to save Indra. This old doctor is no good. He couldn't save mother. He couldn't or didn't save father. And you saw what happened to the Princess. She could hardly walk. How can we know he will try to save Indra?' Raj looked questioningly at Tapash. Tapash, as usual, didn't respond.

'Can you arrange to send Indra to Bengal Medical College?' Raj asked.

'But Sir, he is under Dr Delrome's treatment. How can I take him anywhere when I don't know where he is? Nobody in the palace knows. There are many rumours.'

Raj remembered that he had asked Dr Delrome and *Diwan Sahib* to keep Indra away from the public eye. He had no idea they were doing such an excellent job. He then thought of Dr

Roy, the young Bengali doctor who had joined as Dr Delrome's deputy. He would surely know about Indra's condition and his location. He had already made up his mind to appoint him Chief Medical Officer of the Royal Hospital once he took the reins of the state.

'Can you get Dr Roy?' Raj asked Tapash. 'Tell him no one is sick, I just want to talk to him about an important matter.'

Tapash returned after some time, not with Dr Roy but with Dr Delrome.

'How is Indra doing?' Raj asked, hiding his irritation.

'His wounds were too deep. The best I could do was to keep him alive for one more day,' Delrome said.

'What do you mean?' Raj asked, thoroughly confused.

'Prince Indra is dead, Your Highness. He has died. I cremated him yesterday,' Delrome said calmly.

'What the hell is going on? Why was I not informed?' Raj's shouts echoed down the corridor.

'What would you have done if I told you?' Delrome asked, raising his voice. 'If you had cremated your brother during the mourning period of your father, the entire world would have known what a murderous state Paschim Behar has become. Its siblings are killing each other. Do they deserve to rule? Perhaps the state should be incorporated into Bengal as a district.'

The unexpected outburst from the doctor surprised him.

'But you should have at least told me. I am his older brother.'

'Your Highness,' Delrome said, firmly holding Raj's gaze. 'I have been in the palace for twenty-five years. I am morally obliged to uphold the dignity of this state. At this stage, the only thing that matters to me after the *Maharaja's* legacy is your wellbeing. I am not referring to how you are feeling or eating. What I mean is how well these thousands of visitors to the palace are receiving you as the future regent of Paschim Behar. This is a transition period. People are observing you. They are observing your behaviour. If I had shared the news with you, it would have surely cast a shadow of further gloom on your behaviour. It would have affected your dealings with the people and your decisions. You were biased towards your youngest brother and Pran is an outcast to you.'

'But at least I could have helped,' Raj said, his tone milder.

'No, you could not have helped. Nobody survives that kind of a brutal stabbing. Perhaps you should have tried to intervene when the attack was going on. If you had acted swiftly, there would have been fewer stab wounds and your brother might have lived. Maybe you would have been hurt but you would have survived, and Indra might have survived,' Dr Delrome said, his voice bordering agitation. 'Yes, you could have helped, Your Highness, by not avoiding Pran for months and even years. Maybe you would have known what was going on in his mind. Who knows, if Pran knew that his elder brother understood him, maybe he wouldn't have committed such a desperate act. I know you avoided talking to him during breakfast when all the royal family members sat together. Pran would go to breakfast every morning, hoping he would find a sympathetic ear from his father, or at least from his elder brother. But no, nobody paid him any attention. And you

167

see the result.'

'Did... did Indra say anything?' Raj's head was spinning.

'Yes, I tried to ask him why Pran had attacked him; had he ever hurt Pran. When someone is on their deathbed you would think he would tell everything. But no! Prince Indra didn't say anything. He died with many secrets.'

'So, we will never know what happened between them?' Raj said, his throat felt like it was closing up.

'Of course, we will get to the bottom of it. The perpetrator is still alive. We must talk to him, gently. Let's go to meet him now,' Dr Delrome said. Raj looked at his watch. It was eleven at night.

Soon after, Dr Delrome and Raj were walking down the dark corridor that led to the secret incarceration centre. Pran was being held in a building adjacent to the palace that, for all these years Raj thought was part of the royal elephant stable.

They were greeted mildly by some guards whom Raj had never seen. The palace guards were friendly and courteous by comparison. When they reached the end of a long corridor they met a police guard seated at a desk. The large man had a well-oiled moustache and displayed no sign of servitude when he stood up to forward a register for Raj to sign before meeting the royal detainee.

'Beware of the stink. He has been dirtying the whole place, does not use the commode,' the Jailor said, as a strong smell of human excreta hit their nostrils.

Both Raj and Dr Delrome covered their faces and proceeded towards a dimly lit cell where a figure was crouched in the floor. Raj hesitated. 'Is it worth the effort to see this person whose behaviour is worse than an animal?'

'Shh...' Dr Delrome brought a finger to his lips and said in a hushed tone. 'He will behave and reveal everything, as he has been off alcohol for days. First, we should try to cheer him up with some good news.'

The guard opened a metal gate and they had to bend to pass through. The stench was so bad that their handkerchiefs couldn't block it. Raj tried to move to a corner as he felt like vomiting. But he couldn't walk properly, the floor was slippery from vomit and excreta.

'How are you doing?' Dr Delrome managed to say.

'Are you blind?' Came the growling reply from the floor. Once their eyes grew accustomed to the dim lighting, Raj could make out the filthy mass of Pran sitting on the floor. The bearded face was looking intently at him.

'Get me out of here, *dada*,' Pran said when their eyes met. With great difficulty, he stood up and started shuffling towards Raj, who in turn retreated fearing a brotherly hug.

Pran stopped, his dull eyes pleading. 'Is this what I get for protecting you and our kingdom?' Raj could not think clearly from the stench of faeces and urine.

'We will certainly get you out,' Dr Delrome took over. 'Now that Indra is dead, you will be released. He has died of malaria; that's what we have told people.'

Pran was listening with dazed eyes.

'Why did you do it?' Raj suddenly found his voice. 'He is dead. I am in charge. You tell me everything and you will be back in the palace by tomorrow morning.'

'You might think I killed him because he was sleeping with my wife, but he was relieving me of my duty. My wife was happy...,' he paused. 'Is he really dead? Why is everyone so quiet? Nobody can survive that sort of stabbing. I must have stabbed him eight or nine times.'

'He is dead. Believe me,' Raj said.

'But how come no one is talking about it? A prince's murder is big news. Especially when that prince is the famous Indra Narayan,' Pran said sarcastically. 'People would talk.' He pointed at the guards. 'These bastards would have surely gossiped.'

Raj approached Pran. 'It is a good thing. A blessing from our late father that no one knows,' he said, withdrawing again when the stench hit him.

'But what prompted you to do such a thing? You will have to tell us, Pran. Only then can we get you out of this place. Otherwise, you will rot in here for the rest of your life.' Raj's bitterness was returning. He couldn't keep up the charade of a patient, caring brother in front of this murderer for much longer.

'My self-respect,' Pran said curtly.

'But you just said you didn't mind his relationship with

your wife,' Raj said.

'Oh no, not because of that. If I had another wife, I would have offered her too. I am serious. I am not interested in being married. Maybe something is wrong with me, but that is not the issue here. I killed him for two reasons. He was treating me like dirt. While you were in Kachugaon, he was asking father to convince Dr Roy to produce a medical certificate which would deem me unfit for the throne. I overheard the conversation. But that wasn't enough of a reason to kill him,' Pran said.

'Then?'

'I saw him coming out of father's room after midnight. In the morning father was dead.'

'But that doesn't prove anything. He might have gone to meet father.'

'I am sure he killed father. He was drunk that night. As he was passing by me, he swore at me, saying he would have me sent to the Ranchi mental asylum,' Pran said shaking with a terrible anger. Raj hesitatingly put his hand on Pran's shoulder.

'That was the last straw. I decided to kill him. Paschim Behar doesn't deserve a king like him. He was behaving as if you were never going to come back from Assam. As if he had made some arrangements for you,' Pran said very slowly, as though he needed Raj to digest each word.

Raj patted his brother and said, 'I am ordering your release brother. But you won't be allowed to enter the palace in this state.' Raj then added with a slight chuckle, 'You will have to be clean: clean of everything — including alcohol.'

Pran blinked, his eyes reflecting the joy of imminent release.

Chapter 25

Waiting for Ranger Baruah, Brown *Sahib* reminisced about the good old days. He never used to need any proof of complicity, his hunches would have been enough. But times were changing; Indian nationalism was growing and cries for freedom from the British rule were becoming louder. Also, Baruah's family had connections with Shillong. He would have to handle the investigation of Baruah's involvement in Rajah *Sahib's* death carefully. But he knew; he would punish Rajah *Sahib's* murderer and he didn't care about the consequences.

'Sit down young man.' He gestured for Ranger Baruah to take a seat. 'You have some explaining to do. Why did you go to the elephant camp that night?'

Baruah looked surprised. 'I had to meet someone.'

'As far as I know, you don't have any official dealings with Rajah *Sahib*.'

'I went to meet a girl; I owed her some money. And she owed me an explanation. She was supposed to be at my quarters, but instead, she was at the camp.'

Brown *Sahib* knew that Kachugaon was a male-dominated township. Forest employees worked away from their families for weeks at a time. Prostitution was rife. Rajah *Sahib* had hardly remained at his palatial residence in Parbatipur. He was mostly in his elephant camp, leading the same hard life as his elephant catchers and *mahouts*. He even ate in the same communal kitchen. But he had one privilege in the camp, he could have female visitors to his tent. Champa, the girl from Calcutta, couldn't be afforded by everyone, especially not the forest department staff. There was one exception though — Ranger Baruah, the scion of the rich and powerful *zamindari* of Manikpur. This had always puzzled Brown *Sahib* — *why was Baruah working as a ranger?* He didn't say anything. He let the matter pass and shifted to Gethela.

'Why did you take Gethela to Fakiragram?'

'I didn't take him. I was going to Fakiragram by bus, as per your instructions, when he got on. In fact, he told me that you had told him to go and work at Fakiragram. I assumed it was because you were upset with him for telling Prince Raj Narayan all his stories and wanted him to stay away.'

'The bastard has not stopped telling lies. I never told him to go to Fakiragram. In fact, I was thinking...' Brown *Sahib* stopped, controlling his anger with difficulty. 'OK, where is he now? Can you get him back?'

'It seems no one has seen him recently at Fakiragram. If he had joined the timber depot there, they would have at least informed me.'

'So... did you see the girl that night? Tell me the sequence of events, starting from when you arrived at the camp.' Brown *Sahib* went back to the girl.

'I arrived at the camp around eight at night. I needed to pay her some money and remind her that she was supposed to come to my place that night.'

'Go on,' Brown *Sahib* said. 'Don't skip anything. Did she come to you that night?' he asked flippantly.

'She came to my quarters at around ten,' Baruah said, somewhat embarrassed.

Brown *Sahib* took a deep breath. 'This means after meeting you at eight, the girl went to Rajah *Sahib's* tent. She took with her the money, or whatever you gave her. And then she came out of the tent two hours later and went to your quarters. It would have been dark, and your quarters are around one mile from the camp. Did she go alone to your place? Did you wait outside?'

'I think she must have asked someone to accompany her. I was waiting outside my place. I saw her arrive with someone. But she let him go once she drew near to my quarters.'

'And then, go on...' Brown *Sahib* urged. 'I am listening.' Baruah didn't reply. 'Yes, what did you two do?' Brown *Sahib* started circling his interviewee.

'She spent the night at my place and left in the morning.'

'Where is she now? I want to meet her right now.'

'She told me she was going back to Calcutta. She said her contract with Rajah *Sahib* was over and she had received all her dues.'

How very convenient.

'Are you sure she is not around? If I could talk to her, it will help you. Too many suspects are floating around. Think again and tell me, did she really leave?' His patience was wearing thin.

'As far as I know, she left. She must have taken the tramway to Fakiragram or maybe the bus. If she were here, I would know,' Ranger Baruah said earnestly.

'How would you know?'Brown *Sahib* asked with a sneer.

Ranger Baruah remained unperturbed. 'She has no reason to stay. Nobody else could afford her, except Rajah *Sahib* and me.' Baruah said.

'How old was Rajah *Sahib*? He must have been nearing seventy. Maybe he had a sickness we didn't know of and he died because of that.'

'I don't think so. I feel he still had a few years in him,' Brown *Sahib* placed his hand on his deputy's shoulder and looked him straight in the eye. 'Maybe the Calcutta girl poisoned him. What do you say to that?'

'But why would she poison Rajah Sahib? She was happy, getting well paid by him.'

'I don't know why she would kill him,' Brown *Sahib* said,

his eyes weighing down the ranger. 'Maybe someone paid her more money to kill Rajah *Sahib* than she could earn by sleeping with him.' He wanted to ask the ranger how much he paid the girl that night, but he let it pass.

'Maybe Rajah *Sahib* was killed by someone in his family. You must know that his sister is the *Maharani* of Paschim Behar. Maybe there's some family dispute,' Baruah said.

Brown *Sahib* looked at him, trying not to give anything away on the topic. 'You mean someone from his own family wanted to eliminate him? Perhaps the *Maharani* of Paschim Behar?' Brown *Sahib* loaded his voice with sarcasm.

'It could have been because of the big estate Rajah *Sahib* held. He was childless. After his death, all of his estates goes to his only living relative – his sister. Parbatipur could become part of Paschim Behar.'

'You seem to know a lot about the stakes at play. I am a simple man. I think he was killed for some immediate gain,' Brown *Sahib* said looking at Baruah for a reaction and continued, 'What would she do with Rajah *Sahib's zamindari?* It can't be annexed to Paschim Behar. It will stay with the Assam government if the *zamindari* comes to an end due to the lack of a successor. But someone could benefit from his business — his mega elephant-catching operation, don't you think?'

Baruah didn't respond.

'Alright, you can go.'

After Baruah left, Brown *Sahib* thought of his ultimate

trouble-shooter.

When Ghosh *Babu* appeared, he was followed by two forest guards dragging a handcuffed man. Brown *Sahib* had never seen the man before. 'Who the hell is he?' He wasn't in the mood for more issues.

'He has been hanging around for some time. He doesn't belong to this area but one of the guards recognised him from the night you threw the big party for the Prince. Rajah *Sahib* slapped him for some reason and he fled. Today we found him loitering in the market,' Ghosh *Babu* said.

Brown *Sahib* remembered the commotion from the evening of the party. He was blurry on the details, but he clearly remembered his friend giving this man a resounding slap. Knowing his friend, it must have been for good reason. Brown *Sahib* stood up and stormed into his room. He opened the *almirah* and retrieved a long black whip.

'Tie him to the pillar,' he roared, returning outside. He stood with legs straddled, the whip in his hand. The guards dragged the man across the yard and roped him to a post.

'Wait, *Sahib!* I will tell you everything,' the man cried out as Brown *Sahib* readied himself for the first whip. 'I have come from Paschim Behar. I was told by my master to come and stay while the Prince was here.'

'Who is your master? Why did he send you?' Brown *Sahib* demanded, cracking the whip at the ground near the man's feet.

'My master from Paschim Behar told me to stay here as

long as the Prince stayed. I had to carry out the instructions provided to me by couriers. They said they would take care of my family if I did as he said,' the man blurted out.

'And what did you do? Who gave you instructions here in Kachugaon?' Brown *Sahib* asked.

'*Sahib*, I stationed myself in the training camp. I know elephant handling. I helped with the elephants. I was given instructions by the girl who used to stay with Rajah *Sahib*. The beautiful one, who came from Calcutta.'

'There you go!' Brown *Sahib* shouted, landing the first lash of his whip. Hearing about the girl, Brown *Sahib* couldn't control himself. 'Bastard! Taking instruction from that girl...' a second and third whipping followed in quick succession.

'*Sahib*.... Why are you whipping me? I am telling you the truth!' the man cried out in pain.

'Tell me... what did she tell you to do?' Brown *Sahib* flogged the ground hard right in front of him.

'Wait! I will tell you everything. She told me to go to your bungalow on the night of the party. I was to be like an attendant, bringing in all the bottles. If anyone asked me who I was, I told them I came with the Prince. So, I was moving freely around the kitchen. She gave me a powder and asked me to mix it in the Prince's drinks.'

'And Rajah *Sahib* caught you, red-handed?' Brown *Sahib* asked.

'Yes,' said the man, now crying. 'He gave me a big slap. It

hurt so much. I ran to the elephant camp.'

'And what mischief did you do there?' Brown *Sahib* growled.

'When the Prince came to visit the elephant camp, I let Mohan loose on him. I did exactly what I was told to do,' the man spluttered out, then added, 'Rajah *Sahib* saved him again.'

'So next time you turned on Rajah *Sahib*. Isn't that right? Brown *Sahib* dropped the whip and crossed over to the man, his eyes burning with rage. With one hand, he held the man up by his neck while he was tied to the post. He held him in that position, strangulating him till his face turned blue. The man let out a cry of agonising pain. Brown *Sahib* let go of the man's throat and he dropped down like a scarecrow.

Chapter 26

It was a busy day in the Dhubri office for Bert Jenkins. Some officials had come from Shillong to discuss working plans for the Kachugaon division. This was his first submission of a working plan for the division under his tenure and it would decide the fate of the forest for the next five years. Brown *Sahib* had arrived to discuss the aftermath of Rajah *Sahib's* sudden death and the forest department's newly acquired elephant camp. The department was now the custodian of hundreds of elephants along with the hundreds of people looking after them.

Jenkins was looking forward to the evening. He had organised a dinner in honour of the visiting officials. He extended the invitation to the district officials too. It would be a good opportunity to make up with them — particularly the DC, he thought. His sister Janet was busy directing various cooks and attendants in preparation for the dinner. Things had returned to normal since the aftermath of the Prince's visit. Due to the incident-free evacuation of the Prince from the forests of Kachugaon, no explanation was being sought by Shillong. His friend, the DC, however, was still cross with him.

Hopefully, the dinner would help smooth things over. He knew shepherd's pie was the DC's favourite dish and had asked Janet to include it in the menu.

'I have this letter from the Commissioner's office. How was the crown prince of Paschim Behar a guest in my district for five days without my knowledge? I hope you can help me with a response,' the DC had said to him the other day. Later he had asked, 'Why did you let the Prince go to the forest alone and come to Dhubri by yourself? You should have been with him the whole time.' Jenkins had no suitable response to either of the allegations for he knew he should not have left the Prince on his own. He could not foresee that Ranger Baruah would have to go to the timber depot, or that Ranger Das would turn out to be so callous and irresponsible. He was hoping time would slowly heal their relationship.

But the sudden demise of Rajah *Sahib* with rumours of murder had changed the atmosphere again. Paritosh Baruah, *the zamindar* of Parbatipur, found dead in his own elephant camp didn't make for good news in the vernacular press. And that he was loved and respected by the government agencies in Shillong didn't help the matter. That morning, after Brown *Sahib* arrived, he had provided a first-hand account of events along with his thoughts on the suspects.

'That man from Paschim Behar is responsible for Rajah *Sahib's* murder. He was also responsible for the two attempts on the Prince's life. He was working with a prostitute from Calcutta,' Brown *Sahib* told Jenkins.

'But why did he do it?' Jenkins asked.

'He said his master worked in the elephant stable of

Paschim Behar, but who is this master from Paschim Behar? This is where I have hit a dead end,' Brown *Sahib* said with frustration writ large on his tired face.

'I understand someone from the palace might want to settle a score with Prince Raj Narayan. I have heard of all those dynasty politics amongst the royal families in India. But why would someone from Paschim Behar kill Rajah *Sahib*?' Jenkins asked.

'Exactly!' Brown *Sahib* said, clasping his hands together, his eyes shining brighter. 'The same instruments were used by two masterminds. One wanted to get rid of Prince Raj Narayan and the other, Rajah *Sahib*. The common instruments were the girl from Calcutta and the man from Paschim Behar.' Brown *Sahib* spat red betel nut juice and with a contorted face, added, 'You should have seen the man, such an obnoxious character.'

'But I still don't understand why the man from Paschim Behar would kill Rajah *Sahib*?'

'These are professionals. They look very harmless. This man failed to get the Prince. So, our old man was an easy victim. He gets paid. The money won't come from Paschim Behar but from someone in Assam. Someone from Kachugaon.' Brown *Sahib* waited to see Jenkins' reaction.

'Go on, I am listening. Who in Kachugaon would want to kill Rajah *Sahib*?' Jenkins asked.

'The suspect said he got his instructions from the Calcutta girl, and she was sleeping with Rajah *Sahib* and as well as Baruah,' Brown *Sahib* paused. 'Gethela was also last seen with Ranger Baruah. Maybe the girl was passing on instructions from her lovers in Kachugaon and Paschim Behar?'

Jenkins could guess what Brown *Sahib's* insinuations were, and on whom the aspersions were being cast. He didn't comment on Brown *Sahib's* hypothesis. Instead, he said, 'We should talk to the police. We are not in the business of crime-solving.'

Brown *Sahib* didn't look at all happy with the suggestion.

The office of District Superintendent of Police Baker was a stone's throw from Jenkins' office. Brown *Sahib* narrated the whole story to Baker who seemed convinced that it was too complex a case to be handled by either the forest department or the local police.

'This should be handed over to the criminal investigation department in Gauhati,' Baker said looking directly at Jenkins. 'I am serious. It involves a powerful and connected *zamindar* and then there is this *Maharaja* connection. Only the CID can handle this. By the way, what have you done with the suspect?' he asked Brown *Sahib*. 'When can we get him here? We will need to interrogate him and try to get to the bottom of it quickly. I can tell you that he can't lie to my men.'

'He is in Kachugaon,' Brown *Sahib* mumbled. 'After his arrest, he fell sick. I am not sure about his present condition.'

Baker looked at Jenkins questioningly. Jenkins shook his head.

Brown *Sahib* stood up and said, 'We will definitely hand him over to the police once he recovers.'

Jenkins realised that Brown *Sahib* wasn't ready to hand the man over to the police yet. But Baker didn't relent. Perhaps he was aware of Brown *Sahib's* style. As they walked back to his office, Jenkins asked, 'What have you done with the man? How hard did you hit him? Are his injuries serious?'

'Don't worry. He is all right,' Brown *Sahib* said with a laugh. 'These people are useless,' Brown *Sahib* said pointing back at the police headquarters. 'They couldn't even catch those picketers who blew up the railway track right under their nose.'

Jenkins only hoped that Brown *Sahib* would turn the man in to the police in one piece.

On the forestry front, most of the discussions were continuing smoothly. Only one contentious issue had cropped up. There was a proposal from Shillong to make Kachugaon a game reserve, a move that would restrict forestry extraction. The officials were divided on the issue. Brown *Sahib* was totally against this change in status. The officials from Shillong wanted to enact the change. Jenkins wasn't sure either way.

'One thing will lead to another. After a few years, Shillong will want it converted into a sanctuary. And then what happens? The extraction of fine timber from the forest will come to a complete halt. Sal trees from previous working plans have now reached maturity. That's a big profit waiting there to be collected. I recommend focussing extraction on Kachugaon reserve, and Ripu reserve should be put into regenerative mode. Let's keep our Goalpara forest out of this game reserve and sanctuary classification. Our animals are well protected. They don't need any more protection,' Brown *Sahib* said.

'How can we reduce extraction in Ripu? We have invested heavily in the tramway infrastructure,' one of the Shillong officials countered.

'I am not worried if the tramway ceases operating in Ripu. If we are making a profit from the other reserves within the division, why should we worry whether or not the tramway is hauling timber? Let's look at the big picture,' Brown *Sahib* said.

Jenkins realised that what Brown *Sahib* was saying made sense. The tramway was just a mode of extraction. If the profitable areas lay outside the tramway hinterland, it could remain inoperative. But the Shillong officials didn't agree with this.

'We have not utilised the full potential of the forty-mile-long tramway for extracting timber,' the Shillong official said.

'It is only twenty miles. The rest of the line runs through a non-forestry section,' Brown *Sahib* countered.

The heated discussion continued for some time. Jenkins remained neutral. They decided to break for tea.

It was a sunny day outside. A slight breeze from the river reached his office. Sipping his tea, Jenkins thought about Brown *Sahib's* arguments. Brown *Sahib* was dead against turning Kachugaon into a game reserve, but he had proposed upgrading the north-west corner of Ripu into a wildlife sanctuary. It did not make any sense. According to official records, that part of the reserve was a swampy savannah. But Jenkins felt that for some reason, Brown *Sahib* wanted all forestry operations confined to the southern part of the division.

Jenkins thought it would be good to arrive at a consensus while Brown *Sahib* and the Shillong officials were present. Just as he was about to go back to his office to continue the meeting, he saw a khaki-clad postman heading towards the office. An attendant quickly accosted the postman and took from him a folded piece of paper and then came running over to Jenkins. It was a telegram. As Jenkins read it, he wondered what he had done to deserve such friends.

It read:

Need to visit Kachugaon urgently with you. Same spot. Please be my guest this Sunday when we are solemnising the Shraddha of our father and the departed Maharaja.

Your friend Raj Narayan

Jenkins mulled over the telegram for quite some time. Prince Raj Narayan, who was now soon to be *Maharaja* Raj Narayan of Paschim Behar, wanted him at the palace in three days. As the Prince had cleverly made it an invitation letter for the religious ceremony and feast in the honour of his father, Jenkins realised he had to go.

There was another reason he wanted to go to the palace. That day when the Prince was rescued, he had made a curious sight. His departure was so sudden that he didn't get to ask him what had happened in the cottage. Most importantly, did he meet the girl? Why was he asleep without any clothes on? These questions had been disturbing him since that day.

Finding the Prince naked that morning became something

of a joke amongst the forest guards. He had heard the guards making comments like 'did you go to the forest to find Prince Raj Narayan's clothes?' Raj riding the elephant wearing a white loin cloth had been a funny sight indeed, inciting comments such as 'the white *dhoti* – the perfect choice for elephant-riding?'

On that day, after the Prince and his convoy left for Paschim Behar, Jenkins returned home to see his sister. Brother and sister talked for hours. She was curious and wanted to know everything about the Prince's adventure and the rescue mission. Jenkins told her about the Prince's trip and his search for the white girl on the elephant.

'Forget about the Prince. You will be working in these forests for years to come. What if the girl is real and you come across her? What will you do then?' his sister asked. 'And what if she is breathtakingly beautiful?' she added teasingly.

Chapter 27

Top government officials, heads of states, the families of dozens of princely states, the Governor of Bengal and the Chief Commissioner of Assam had already confirmed their participation in the *Shraddha* ceremony. The Viceroy would send his representative from Delhi. A meeting was scheduled between Raj and political agent James Maxell to discuss all the protocol issues.

Raj had heard a great deal about the political agent, who wielded the clout of the British Government on Paschim Behar through his office. The Englishman was only twenty-nine years old. He was arrogant but close to the *Maharani*. Raj arranged a briefing session with Dr Delrome, who had become his new confidant, to learn more about the man.

'Your father gave many liberties to the young man. When you were in England, he was a constant companion of the royal family on all outings. Since your return, however, his engagement with the palace has been mostly official. Or he has met discreetly with Indra or the *Maharani*.' Dr Delrome said.

'With the *Maharani?*' Raj repeated.

'The *Maharaja's* increasing desire for the thirteen-gun salute status and decreasing desire for his wife of twenty years made it easy for him.

Raj was aware that his father lamented the fact that Paschim Behar was an eleven-gun-salute state. The late *Maharaja* always felt that the protocolary privilege for the state was beneath what it deserved. 'What happened then?' Raj asked.

"It all started in the state guesthouse in Darjeeling. The *Maharaja* and the *Maharani* were holidaying there. I was there too. The *Maharaja* extended an invitation to the new political agent Maxwell, which he gladly accepted. It was winter in the hills. Things happened quickly.'

'What things?' Raj asked, fully knowing what Dr Delrome was alluding to.

'It was a cold Darjeeling night. The lounge room was warm due to the log fire. The air was full of tobacco smoke. There were laughter and the clinking of glasses. When the *Maharaja* was engrossed in a game of bridge with his European planter friends from the hills, the *Maharani* excused herself from the group, feigning tiredness. As she was leaving, she cast a momentary glance at Maxwell who didn't fail to notice the invitation, even with his eyes on the cards he was holding. And as you know, being her old lover, I knew that look she gave him. After some time, the young Englishman excused himself from the group saying he wanted to go for a walk before bed. It was indeed a short walk for Maxwell, who went around to the back of the guesthouse and entered the *Maharani's* room. She had locked herself in but kept a window ajar. Do you know what I did?' Raj shook his head as he had no idea. 'I followed Maxwell,' Dr Delrome said with a chuckle. 'I stopped by the room and placed my ear to the door. I heard familiar sounds that transported me back to the days of Dhubri civil hospital when I used to take her on the doctor's table itself.'

Raj didn't expect the old doctor to be that candid.

'I felt sorry for the *Maharaja*. My loyalties lay with the man who believed in me through thick and thin.'

'Did you say anything to the *Maharani*? I mean your ex-lover?' Raj asked.

'I don't have any rights to my ex-lover since she became the *Maharani*.'

Raj shook his head. What a tangled web it all was. His thoughts shifted to what Pran had said about the *Maharaja*'s death.

'Did you check on father that morning? Who actually found him dead?'

'I was sent for by the *Maharani* at around nine in the morning. She said an attendant had found him unresponsive when he went to the *Maharaja's* room for his morning duties. I had a good look at the body. It had cyanosis,' Dr Delrome said.

'What is that?'

'Blue colouring of the skin due to lack of oxygen. My first reaction on seeing him was that the *Maharaja* had been smothered to death.'

'Pran said he saw Indra coming from the *Maharaja's*

room,' Raj said. 'What about the *Maharani*? Could she not have gone to father's room at night and smothered him to death with a pillow?'

'Yes, it's possible, but what does she gain from that? You become king. Or if you were eliminated, Indra would have become king...' Dr Delrome said, his voice trailing at the end.

Raj mulled it over.

The *Maharani* openly liaising with a political agent? Maybe she hadn't seduced Maxwell for her physical gratification. Maybe the *Maharaja* encouraged it. If the *Maharani* did it for the *Maharaja*, she wouldn't harm him. But if she had engaged in the relationship without the *Maharaja's* knowledge and he came to know of it, then silencing him would buy breathing space to his stepmother.

The Maharani courting Maxwell. The Maharaja encouraging the Maharani. Indra supposedly strangling their father. Indra murdered by Pran. There was one missing link — the relationship between Indra and the Maharani.

'Let me walk with you to the hospital. I want to see the place,' Raj said to Dr Delrome.

As he entered the building, he was hit by a strong smell of disinfectant mixed with the rust-like scent of blood. He went past the administrative office and the doctor's rooms to the main hall where there were rows of metal-framed beds, some occupied by patients and others empty. Most of the patients were palace officials or servants or their family members.

The doctor stopped in front of a door and Raj peered through the glass panel into a room that held only a single bed.

He imagined his handsome brother lying there, writhing in pain. He thought of Indra looking around for his elder brother and trying to say something but not being able to speak. He imagined Dr Delrome administering him a dose of morphine to alleviate the pain. Given his chest and abdomen had been punctured in so many places, without the morphine, he would have an agonising death.

'This is the room where he took his last breath,' Dr Delrome said. Raj felt wretched.

'Tell me, what was Indra's relationship with the *Maharani*?' Raj asked. He sounded desperate.

Dr Delrome put his arm around Raj. This was the first time he had done anything like that. Raj felt strangely comforted. 'Let's go outside and talk in the open air.'

Once they were out in the hospital grounds, Dr Delrome lit his pipe and said to Raj, 'Tell me, what is troubling you?'

'There are so many intrigues going on. Liaisons, insinuations and then two deaths in the same week. I feel scared to stay in my room. I don't know if someone is coming for me with a dagger,' Raj said what he had in his heart.

'Your fear is not unfounded,' Dr Delrome said. 'But I think it's all over. You should now concentrate on taking the rein and consolidating your hold.'

'But, Pran is out there. I let him go. He could become a maniac again and turn on me next,' Raj said.

'Pran never wanted to be king when you were around. If you hadn't returned from London or if you decided to abdicate, he knew Indra was the *Maharaja's* favourite and he would surely have made Indra the king in place of Pran. That is what hurt him the most. But he never uttered a word to his father. However, his younger brother crossed the line. He was overconfident and dismissive of Pran's capability. You remember what Pran said in the prison?'

'Yes, about self-respect?'

'Yes, precisely. One time, Indra and the *Maharaja* were discussing the succession criteria. *Diwan Sahib* and the head priest explained that as per tradition, a man with physical or mental inability couldn't ascend the throne of Paschim Behar. On Indra's instigation, your father made a strange request of me. He said I must declare Pran to be medically unfit. I should declare him mad. I refused. I think somehow Pran came to know of this, which fuelled his hatred towards Indra.'

'So much hatred to kill him?' Raj asked.

'No, this happened a long way back. If you were here to take over the rein, Pran wasn't bothered by what Indra thought of him. But your sudden Kachugaon trip and the *Maharaja's* death changed everything. Pran felt Indra was moving towards his goal of becoming the king. And he felt Indra was after your life. So, he acted, thinking he saved you and his self-respect. You really don't have anything to fear from Pran. He loves and respects you a great deal. In fact, he loves you enough to kill,' Dr Delrome said thoughtfully.

Raj was nodding, trying to digest what Dr Delrome was saying. 'I think I should be going.' was all he could think of to say.

'I will walk you back to the palace,' Dr Delrome said as

they started walking. 'You were asking about Indra and the *Maharani*. I guess Indra had been adopting a carrot and stick policy with the *Maharani*. The carrot could be that after him the rein of the state would pass to her children as he had promised not to marry. The stick was that he was fully aware of the liaisons she had with the political agent.'

'You mean Maxwell?' Raj asked.

'Yes, Maxwell,' Dr Delrome said giving a sad smile. 'They are still going strong. But she is also quite naïve. Indra must have told her — mind you, I am just guessing here — that as he is unmarried, any of the *Maharani's* sons could become the king after him. So, although she has not done anything to foil your succession, Indra has the poor lady convinced that you may not be interested and hence, the mantle for ruling Paschim Behar would fall to him.'

'But her relationship with Maxwell; do you think father was aware of it?' Raj enquired.

'Yes, the *Maharaja* might have been aware of it. He was a clever man. But he didn't create a scene. Indra would threaten the *Maharani* that if word of her relationship with Maxwell got out, the people of Paschim Behar would turn against her. So, he was playing a game with her — tormenting and fooling her at the same time. What is the guarantee that he wouldn't have married after becoming the king? The *Maharaja* of Sambalpur married at the age of eighty-six and produced an heir.'

'So, Indra really wanted to succeed our father?' Raj gave a sigh.

'He was a confident young man. His ambitions were understandable given he was the *Maharaja's* right-hand man for over ten years. Your long stay in London followed by your indifference to the state's affairs upon your return; your subsequent preoccupations with married life, coupled with the pursuit of your own interests, Indra seriously thought that you weren't interested in ruling the state. Maybe he was projecting his own desires, as you haven't made any such utterances that you would abdicate. But Indra was sure of one thing, if his older brother wasn't in the race, the mantle would fall on him, as the middle brother was considered unfit for the throne by all palace officials. The British political agent Maxwell wouldn't make any distinction between him and you if the transition was smooth and trouble-free. So, to ensure facilitation from Maxwell, Indra approached the *Maharani*.'

'If it was you who found out about Maxwell, how did Indra come to know of it?' Raj asked.

'It's true I was the one who heard them that first night in Darjeeling, but as you know, Indra had ears and eyes everywhere. After that episode, they might have met up many times. I have not seen them, but that doesn't mean others have not.' They had reached the palace. The doctor turned to face Raj. 'Good night, Your Highness,' Dr Delrome said, not without affection. He turned back to return to the hospital.

'Good night doctor. Are you not going home?' Raj asked.

'Your Highness, I was looking after some patients before I came to see you. I need to check on them,' Dr Delrome said.

Raj checked his watch; it was ten at night.

Chapter 28

It was the tenth day after the *Maharaja's* death. The palace was busier than usual. People were milling around attending to a variety of tasks. Raj had been busy with the priest since early morning, conducting the required rituals. All five princes were tonsured in readiness. Raj saw many surprised looks at seeing a clean-shaven Pran moving around, pleasantly greeting visitors. A few made enquiries after Indra. The official line was that Indra's condition had worsened due to malaria, which he had contracted in the hospital, and he had been transferred to Calcutta.

Raj's legs ached from sitting cross-legged on the floor for such a long time. He was relieved when the priest said he could take a break. 'I need some time to prepare for our next ritual. In that one, we will be offering obeisance to the nine generations of our late *Maharaja's* lineage,' the priest said as he rushed to catch up with his assistants.

Raj saw Dr Delrome carrying a small bottle in his hand. 'Should I let the *Maharani* and Deep Narayan know about Indra?'

'Shhh....' Dr Delrome said bringing a finger to his mouth. 'Don't even think of divulging it to anyone before the *Maharaja's* ceremony. But, Your Highness, I have got this cream with antiseptic properties, which you may like to apply on your head,' Delrome said, pointing to his shiny bald head.

'Thank you very much, Doctor. Why don't you take a seat? I wanted to ask you something.'

'Something about Indra again?' The doctor had a knowing smile.

'I can't stop thinking about it,' Raj admitted. 'Do you know if Indra had any dealings with an estate in Assam known as Manikpur?'

A frown appeared on Dr Delrome's face. 'Manikpur, it does ring a bell. It is a small estate near the larger estate of Parbatipur. Oh! Yes, I once treated the landlord of that estate in Dhubri.'

'Do you think Indra had anything to do with that palace?' Raj repeated his line of questioning.

'Many years ago, I remember he visited that place. He said he had to meet his good friend from Kurseong.'

'Good friend from Kurseong? In Manikpur?' Raj asked, somewhat exasperated.

'In fact, that friend of his has been to the palace a few times. Fun-loving young man, quite good looking. It seems Indra and the young man were quite close.'

'So, Indra had a good friend in Manikpur, is that right? But… I'm confused, if he was from Manikpur, then how was he also from Kurseong?'

'They studied together in Kurseong at the Forest Rangers College. The young man returned to Assam to become a ranger and our Indra came back to the palace.'

Raj remembered when he was in England doing mechanical engineering, Indra had not yet made up his mind about his future. The *Maharaja* wanted to send his favourite son to the Presidency College in Calcutta to study arts. But his brother wasn't academically inclined. Like other princes, Indra wanted to join the Indian Military Academy. But the *Maharaja* selfishly wanted him to remain closer to home; Calcutta was the furthest he was inclined to let him go. His eldest son was in England and he felt he could not rely on his temperamental middle one. So, they struck a compromise. Indra would be sent to the Forest Rangers College in Kurseong — to instil discipline and impart physical training. The *Maharaja* didn't want his son to become a forest ranger, but a British World War I veteran, who was a good friend of the *Maharaja's*, had taken over as principal of the college and encouraged the *Maharaja* to send Indra to Kurseong.

Raj had all but forgotten about this part of Indra's life.

'By any chance was Indra's friend's name Baruah?' Raj asked.

'Both the estates Parbatipur and Manikpur are ruled by the Baruahs; they all come from the same stock. But they were at loggerheads for many years,' Dr Delrome said.

'Why is that?' Raj asked.

'Elephant catching, Your Highness! It is the most lucrative industry in Assam. The two estates competed for the yearly contract for catching elephants in the forests of Assam for almost fifty years. The Assam forest department kept the competition going and benefitted from the royalties. But in the last ten, maybe fifteen years, the contract has been given only to Parbatipur and that is bleeding Manikpur dry. They don't generate as much farming income as Parbatipur.'

Maybe Indra wanted to help his friend's estate? Maybe the letter wasn't from the Maharaja. He could have forged the Maharaja's signature.

'But how can a department be partial? Does it not have to follow the tendering procedure?' Raj asked.

'The Assam department is above board,' Dr Delrome said quizzically. 'But apart from Parbatipur, no other parties have shown interest in bidding.'

'Because of the elephant girl curse?' Raj said.

'Ah! You must have picked that up on your Kachugaon trip. A strange belief has spread throughout the superstitious elephant catcher community that if they work for any operator other than Rajah *Sahib* of Parbatipur, they and their families would be doomed. They believe only Rajah *Sahib* knows how to appease the forest goddess, so no harm will befall his elephant catchers.'

'Meanwhile, Manikpur is losing its share of elephant catching revenue. Its scion is working as a ranger in the

Kachugaon division,' Raj said, thinking things might be finally falling in place.

'Yes, that could be the same man who was Indra Narayan's good friend in the college days,' Dr Delrome said. 'But what has suddenly prompted you to ask about this connection?'

Raj pondered this for a while. Dr Delrome seemed to know so much. He decided it was better to confide in him fully.

'Well, *Diwan Sahib* said there was a letter from the *Maharaja* asking the Treasury to transfer fifty thousand to the Manikpur estate. He feels there was no valid reason for the *Maharaja* to ask for such a transfer. So now I'm thinking, the letter could be forged. I was told about the letter the day before Indra was stabbed. I didn't get a chance to ask him about it,' Raj said.

'Hmmm… one thing is for sure though, this can't be just for the sake of an old friendship,' Dr Delrome said with certainty.

'I asked *Diwan Sahib* to verify the *Maharaja's* signature. He said it was a copy but not an exact copy. Somebody has forged father's signature. Yes, the timing of the request seemed a bit bizarre to me that with everything happening here, Indra should be thinking of helping his friend's estate. Surely that could have waited. This is, of course, assuming it was Indra,' Raj said.

Dr Delrome looked directly into Raj's eyes as if conveying he still had a lot to learn. 'Based on what I know of the relationship between Indra and the late *Maharaja*, if Indra wanted to help the Manikpur estate, he would have done it long ago. The *Maharaja* wouldn't have batted an eyelid at such a request. To me, it seems he needed to pay someone for an immediate favour.' Raj didn't say anything. 'What did you think of Baruah? Did you notice anything suspicious about him?' Dr Delrome asked unexpectedly.

'Well, Baruah was one of the most efficient and diligent officers I've met. He was much friendlier and more helpful than his superior — that Robert Brown,' Raj said, disdain appearing on his face.

'Did anything unexpected or suspicious happen when Ranger Baruah was around?' Dr Delrome pried.

Raj thought for a moment. 'I am not sure about it, but Rajah *Sahib* said there were two attempts on my life when I was in Kachugaon. Somebody tried to mix something into my drink, and Rajah *Sahib* caught him red-handed. The second attempt, I wasn't even aware of it. Someone let a rogue elephant loose when I was in Rajah *Sahib's* camp. Ranger Baruah was around on both the occasions.'

'Hmm... both incidents happened while you were in Kachugaon,' Dr Delrome frowned, his face pensive. 'Nobody would have suspected anything. The crown prince of Paschim Behar dies of excessive alcohol consumption at a wild party in the forest of Kachugaon, or crown prince of Paschim Behar trampled to death by a rogue elephant in Assam. Big news but not suspicious. You are very lucky indeed,' Dr Delrome said. His tone was serious.

'But who could be behind it?' Raj implored the doctor.

'Let's not jump to conclusions. You have your theories

and I have mine. Let's work through it. We must meet our old friend Rajah *Sahib* again. But for now, let's concentrate on tomorrow's ceremony. It will be a long day for you; we want everything to go smoothly.'

Outside, on the steps of the palace, Raj watched the workers erecting a large ceremonial tent. It would be used to serve lunch to the guests. All of Paschim Behar's townspeople were expected to attend. The *Maharaja's* well-wishers from other parts of the state had already started arriving in the capital. Raj caught up with the *Diwan*.

'Provisions have been made for around forty thousand people. No one should go without having eaten,' the *Diwan* said.

'Have all the cooks arrived?' Raj knew hundreds of cooks were due to arrive from Calcutta to prepare a feast comprising both vegetarian and non-vegetarian dishes.

'They have all arrived and preparations are well underway,' *Diwan* Sahib said.

Raj was also looking forward to the next day for another reason; the five princes would be having their first proper meal on that day.

'Our subjects will be led to the central hall to pay respects to the departed *Maharaja*. They will be served lemon juice and water and then led out of the palace to tent number one where they will await their turn to dine,' the *Diwan* explained.

'What is the dining tent capacity?'

'It can seat around three thousand and we estimate we will have to serve about ten rounds. If we start the first batch at twelve, we can feed the last visitor by evening.'

Raj nodded. He had never seen such grand preparations in Paschim Behar. His wedding had been a series of functions on a smaller scale. An attendant came to summon Raj as the head priest was ready for the next ceremony.

'What is the arrangement for our European guests?' Raj asked as he headed inside to the function hall.

'Government officials from Bengal, Assam and Delhi, European guests, members of the royal family and other royal families will be received and entertained within the palace. We have converted five rooms in the palace into dining rooms. We are expecting around two thousand special guests,' *Diwan* said, following at Raj's heel. Raj had no interest in the two thousand special guests. He was expecting one special guest from Dhubri and was hoping he wouldn't be disappointed. He sat on the straw mat with his hands folded as the priest sprinkled holy basil water on him.

Chapter 29

The eleventh day was the auspicious ceremony of the *Shraddha* - celebrating the life of the late *Maharaja* Bichitra Narayan and of paying obeisance to the gods to ensure the *Maharaja's* soul was at peace in the other world.

Since early morning, Raj had been performing a series of religious ceremonies under the guidance of the head priest. The chanting of hymns in praise of the lord and the departed soul could be heard throughout the whole palace. The head priest was directing a number of ceremonies simultaneously and the five princes were busy with different priests worshipping different gods. Pran was earnestly following a priest's instructions while sitting at the base of an altar.

Raj smiled wryly. The irony didn't escape him; the murderer of the *Maharaja's* favourite son was praying for the eternal peace of the *Maharaja*.

By noon all the religious ceremonies had concluded, and the five princes were ushered to bathe and change into normal clothing. They then proceeded to the communal dining hall in the palace grounds. They walked with folded hands, paying obeisance to the subjects of the state, Raj leading the procession of brothers. Raj sat to eat his first proper meal in ten days. The feast laid before him made him salivate — he felt like never getting up and simply eating to his heart's content — but he finished quickly as he was keen to open the dining area to the many visitors. As per the ritual, the community feast could begin only after the deceased's eldest son had taken his first proper meal after the days of mourning.

As the day moved into early evening, Raj looked down at the large *pandal;* it was still feeding thousands of people. A crease appeared on his forehead.

'The estimate is that thirty-five thousand have been fed so far,' *Diwan Sahib* said. Raj looked at his watch; it was almost five in the evening. 'Don't worry Your Highness, we have arrangements in place to feed the remaining thousands. The final tally is expected to be forty-five thousand.'

Raj's thought turned to his father: *hope you are happy, wherever you are*. His thoughts quickly rested on Indra. Was it his destiny that his life be cut short by one brother for orchestrating attempts on another brother's life? His exit from this world remained unmourned and uncelebrated.

Raj walked towards his study, dragging his feet. Since the ceremonial meal, he had been constantly on the move: meeting and greeting as many visitors as he could. He spent an equal amount of time in the various halls; talking to the invited guests, as in the outside tents greeting the subjects of his state. He saw the delight in their eyes when he made himself approachable. Fortunately for him, with so many people to talk to, he could spend the shortest amount of time possible with anyone.

As he sunk into his cushioned chair in his study, he thought of the two special guests he didn't find amongst the crowd.

Fear of further humiliation from his sister might have kept Rajah *Sahib* away. But he wondered why he had not seen Jenkins; he would surely have received the telegram three or four days ago. It was almost nightfall, a strange feeling of hopelessness descended upon him.

There was a knock on the door. 'Your Highness, a *Sahib* from the Assam forest department wants to meet with you. He said you sent for him,' an attendant said.

'Get him in, quick.' Raj had no doubt who it was.

Moments later, the beaming face of Jenkins appeared in the doorway. However, he quickly became sombre as he said, 'I am very sorry for your loss, Your Highness. My heartfelt condolences.'

'Good to see you, my friend,' Raj said as he got up and greeted his friend with a warm hug. 'You surely took a while to arrive. When did you start?

'I started out this morning. But on reaching your state, I had to slow down considerably as the roads were filled with people coming to the palace to pay homage. And on arriving, I was a bit lost as there were so many people. In fact, I arrived over two hours ago.'

'Alright, you are not going anywhere anytime soon,' Raj said as he gestured the attendant to call Tapash.

'By the way, how is Rajah *Sahib* doing? I had hoped he would come although I wasn't expecting,' Raj said.

'Rajah *Sahib* unfortunately passed away. It is almost a week now.'

'What? How did that happen?' Raj was stunned. Before Jenkins could reply, Tapash arrived.

'Arrange for Jenkins *Sahib* to stay in state guest house number one,' he said to Tapash. 'I wish you could have stayed here. But the palace rooms are already full of guests from other states,' Raj said looking at Jenkins.

Once Tapash left the study, Raj said, 'Tell me, how did it happen? I can't believe that Rajah *Sahib* is gone.'

'We are really not sure. Brown *Sahib* has some theories. He was quite close to Rajah *Sahib.*'

'Brown *Sahib*?'

'Yes, they were quite close. In fact, I didn't realise just how close they were. He is a broken man. He doesn't think it was a natural death. He suspects foul play and is hell bent on finding the perpetrator.'

Raj raised his hand to stop Jenkins. 'We will talk about all this tomorrow. Now you should go for your long overdue lunch. You look exhausted. It has been a long day for you.' He went over to the doorway and gestured to Tapash to come in.

'Take Jenkins *Sahib* to the dining hall.' Raj turned to Jenkins. 'I need to get going as I have more guests to meet. I will see you again before you retire for the night. Please feel free to ask Tapash for anything you need.'

After Tapash led Jenkins away, Raj came out of his study and was once again lost in the sea of people. *Diwan Sahib* came rushing to tell him the Bengal Governor wished to have a few departing words with him. Raj knew he was in for a long night. He had already seen off the Chief Commissioner of Assam, Secretary to Governor General of India and a number of prominent leaders of the Congress party. Thankfully most of the heads of the royal states were staying back and Deep Narayan and the other relatives were looking after the overnight guests. His stepmother, the former Maharani, dressed in white silk carried herself with poise and dignity, was also looking after the royal families.

It was around nine. Some semblance of quietness returned to the palace. Tired members of the royal families had retreated to their private chambers. Raj was back in his study while an attendant was massaging his bald head with oil. Tapash brought Jenkins to the study.

'I wanted to ask you something,' Raj said with a business-like attitude.

'Is it regarding Rajah *Sahib's* death?' Jenkins asked.

'No, no... Rajah *Sahib's* death is very unfortunate. But I have something else to discuss with you,' Raj said. 'Tapash, close the door and wait for *Sahib* outside.' He turned to Jenkins and said, 'Actually, I want to go to the Kachugaon forest with you again.'

'Your Highness, we didn't get an opportunity to talk that day. What happened that night?'

'What do you mean?' Raj asked, knowing full well what he meant. He knew Jenkins deserved to know what had happened.

'Did you see the elephant girl?'

'She is real. I met her. But she ran away before we could talk,' Raj said, trying to sound casual.

'Why do you want to meet her again? Where will you look for her? She is surely not at the cottage.'

'This time I plan to go to the place she is from,' Raj said calmly. 'I want you to come with me.'

'But how will you find her place? How do you know where she's from? It will be impossible to trace her to her village or any place inside Ripu. Your Highness, the forest in that part of Assam goes for hundreds of miles,' Jenkins said trying hard to remain calm himself.

'I know where she's from. We will go to Santhalbari,' Raj said, watching Jenkins for his reaction to the revelation.

'I am not sure about the existence of the place. Some of the forest guards and local people of Kachugaon are convinced that a kingdom of Santalis exists in the far north-west corner of the Ripu reserved forest. But according to our department's map, the area is marked only as a swampy savannah. The area was surveyed decades back by Brown *Sahib* himself,' Jenkins said, somewhat despairingly. 'I am not really sure how a trip to that area can be arranged. No one from the forest department has gone to that area. Even if it exists, is it worth taking the risk?' Jenkins asked earnestly.

'What risk are you talking about?' Raj asked.

'Your Highness, you are no longer the crown prince,' Jenkins stated as politely as he could. 'You are the ruler of Paschim Behar. Last time there was the incident at Rajah *Sahib's* elephant camp. Your life was in danger. It will be very difficult to provide you sufficient support and protection if you just go through me,' Jenkins said. 'You are better off making a request through the department headquarters at Shillong.'

'My life is no more or less valuable than anyone else in this palace. My father was a ruler, today he is a handful of ashes, but life still goes on,' Raj philosophised.

'Assam Government protocol won't allow me to host the *Maharaja* of Paschim Behar. I hope you can understand my limitations,' Jenkins said with a considerable amount of anxiety.

'Who said I will go there as the *Maharaja*? It won't be an official visit. It will be a discreet visit. A friend visiting his friend's forest. Believe me, I don't want to inconvenience you or put you under any undue stress.'

'When do you want to go?' Jenkins said, with trepidation.

'Tomorrow,' Raj said. Jenkins looked as if Raj had given him an electric shock.

'How can you leave the palace tomorrow for the long trip to Santhalbari?'

'Yes, I want to go tomorrow. My coronation is in a week's time. After that, all my movements will become ceremonious, with all the fanfare. I just want to vanish for a few days. I will be back before anyone realises. I have a very capable *Diwan*,' Raj said.

'You really want to go that badly?'

'Yes, I really want to go. I hope you understand. Do you know why I want to go there again? And go sooner rather than later?' Jenkins looked on, his eyes blank. 'I met the girl. I think she may be trapped. It simply doesn't feel right. She is different and doesn't belong to them at all,' Raj said as if he was talking to himself.

'Different from whom, Your Highness?' Jenkins asked cautiously.

'Different from those around her. Different from the people who guard her. Leave aside Santali, she doesn't even look like an Indian. She is a European girl,' Raj said, nearly shouting.

'A European girl? In Ripu?'

'Yes, she is white. Just like you, and very beautiful,' Raj said while walking towards the door. He cracked it open and gestured to Tapash to enter.

'Tapash, I am going to Kachugaon tomorrow morning with Mr. Jenkins. I leave it with you to make all the necessary preparations. And listen, no one is to know about it.'

Astonished, Tapash didn't say anything but nodded.

Chapter 30

Suddenly, the two deaths, endless hosting and rituals, and the previous ten days, all began to fade from Raj's mind. He was thinking about the trip the following day. Jenkins was turning the pages of a memorial souvenir that had been published that day to commemorate the *Maharaja's* life and times. He looked tired.

'Should I get Tapash to escort you to the guest house?' Raj asked. Before Jenkins could respond, there was a knock on the door. It was Tapash. 'Your Highness, Dr Delrome wants to see you.'

Raj wasn't sure whether or not to inform the doctor of his intended trip. Given that Dr Delrome had shown he was privy to many important matters, Raj thought he would have to confide in him. But that could wait until after he told of the news concerning Rajah *Sahib*.

Raj broke the news. 'Rajah *Sahib* had passed away under suspicious circumstances.'

Dr Delrome looked shocked. He was about to say something, then stopped when he saw there was someone else in the room.

'Dr Delrome, meet Mr Bert Jenkins, DFO Assam forest department. He is from Dhubri and was my gracious host during my stay in Kachugaon.'

After the usual pleasantries, Dr Delrome asked, 'Tell me about Rajah *Sahib*'s death. When did it happen? Are there any suspects? What is our friend Brown *Sahib* saying?'

'You know Robert Brown?' Jenkins asked surprised.

'Oh yes..., I know him very well. We go a long way back,' Dr Delrome said. He looked like he was reminiscing for a moment. 'Do we have any leads or suspects?'

'The incident occurred not long after he returned from his visit to this palace. He was very upset when he returned. Brown *Sahib* did all he could to take care of Rajah *Sahib*, given his distressed mental state. But that night, it seems he couldn't convince Rajah *Sahib* to stay back at his place. When he returned to his camp, he was in a bad shape. And then things get murkier. There was this girl in his camp. Brown *Sahib* suspects the girl. But he said that she might have been just the instrument. The girl left Rajah *Sahib* and went to a ranger working in our department and spent the night with him,' Jenkins said, exasperated as he narrated the sequence of events.

Dr Delrome was deep in thought. 'Did anybody examine the body?'

'Brown *Sahib* decided against it. He didn't send the body

for an autopsy. He didn't even bother to take the mortal remains to Rajah *Sahib*'s Parbatipur house. I hear many of the distant relatives and many employees as well are aggrieved at this. He cremated the body at the elephant camp,' Jenkins said.

'Impatient old bastard,' Dr Delrome muttered under his breath. 'How can we investigate foul play when we can't have a post mortem done?' Dr Delrome said shaking his head. 'What about his tent? Is it still intact?'

'My department has taken charge of the camp. We have stationed a ranger there permanently. Rajah *Sahib*'s tent is off limits to everyone. We have barricaded it and it has remained untouched since Rajah *Sahib*'s body was discovered. Dhubri police officials are not very happy with the way the forest department, and by that I mean Brown *Sahib*, cremated the body so hastily. But then Brown *Sahib* had his reasons. He said due to the summer heat the body would rapidly decompose. The stench was already unbearable. He did what he thought was best at the time.'

'A legendary elephant catcher and fun-loving bachelor killed in his camp. Somebody must have had a motive. Nobody would dare to take such a risk with Rajah *Sahib* unless they were desperate. I knew the man. Nobody messed with him. To be killed like that, a lot had to be at stake,' Dr Delrome said thoughtfully, as the piercing gaze of his blue eyes looked to the others for an answer.

Raj could see Dr Delrome was overwhelmed with the news of the passing away of Rajah *Sahib*. He had come to realise that the French doctor, who had spent three decades in the region, knew and had seen much more than he ever imagined.

'What was that ranger's name, the one who was seen with Rajah *Sahib*'s girl?' Dr Delrome asked.

'His name is Amaresh Baruah. One of our most efficient officers,' Jenkins said.

'Baruah!' Dr Delrome repeated. 'Does he belong to any *zamindari* family?' He turned to Raj. 'Is he the same man who took good care of you and who you said was from Manikpur?'

Raj nodded. 'Yes, it's the same man. I noticed that there was no love lost between Rajah *Sahib* and Ranger Baruah.'

'Ranger Baruah belongs to Manikpur. Rajah *Sahib* belongs to Parbatipur. And our Brown *Sahib* is happy with this ranger? I doubt it,' Dr Delrome looked quizzically at Jenkins. Jenkins didn't respond.

Dr Delrome turned toward Raj. 'This ranger is Indra's friend from Kurseong. He was the intended recipient of the fund.' Then he stood up, walked over to Raj and whispered, 'Somebody from the palace wanted to eliminate both you and Rajah *Sahib*.'

Raj just shook his head, he was no longer surprised.

'Your Highness, I heard you are planning a trip to Assam tomorrow,' Dr Delrome asked casually, speaking louder now.

'How did you come to know?' Raj muttered, looking at Jenkins who shook his head to suggest it wasn't him. Raj knew there was no point hiding anything from the doctor.

'Yes, I am planning a trip to Kachugaon tomorrow with Mr Jenkins.'

'Kachugaon? With him?' He said pointing to Jenkins. 'But why?'

'Nothing is planned. I was just thinking of getting away from the palace for a few days to recover from all this,' Raj said trying to keep his voice even.

'Of all places, you have chosen the forests of Kachugaon again. Why not Calcutta or the hills?'

'The last trip had to be cut short due to father's sudden demise,' Raj said, not sounding very convincing.

'Can I accompany you to Kachugaon?' Dr Delrome asked.

'Why doctor? Is there something in the forest of interest to you?' Raj asked. He couldn't help feeling disdain despite his new fondness for the doctor.

'Have you found something in the forest that is calling you back right now? Right when your father has just passed away, and you are expecting your first child in a week's time? Your coronation just around the corner?' the doctor countered.

Jenkins coughed nervously, given the way the conversation was heading.

Dr Delrome continued, 'Tell me, did you see the elephant girl?'

Raj gave up; he was neither angry nor surprised. He was convinced there was no point hiding anything from the omniscient doctor.

'I would like to meet her,' Raj said, omitting 'again' at the last moment.

'There are suggestions that you were rescued from her hideout,' Dr Delrome persisted.

'Well, I need to go there again,' Raj said.

'This means you saw her?' Dr Delrome asked uneasily.

'Yes, I met her, but she ran away before I could talk to her,' Raj lied.

The French doctor's face flushed red. Raj's first trip after the *Maharaja's Shraddha* ceremony should have been to Calcutta to see Divya. Instead, he was planning a trip to Santhalbari. The doctor had every right to be surprised and angry.

'So, Your Highness, you met the girl, and you want to go and meet her again?' Dr Delrome spoke slowly, breathing heavily. Raj wasn't sure what was troubling the old doctor so much.

'Yes, I met her. And I want to meet her again. And I request you keep this trip a secret,' Raj said. 'By the way, how did you come to know that I was planning a trip to Kachugaon?'

'Tapash came to me asking for medicine, quinine and first aid for a forest trip. And then I saw you were holed up with our friend from the Assam forest department while guests were still enquiring about you. So, I guessed you must have decided to take another trip.'

Raj didn't say anything. He understood Dr Delrome wasn't the late *Maharaja's* most trusted advisor for nothing.

'So, Your Highness wants to meet her again?' Dr Delrome probed further.

Up until now, nobody had asked Raj what had happened in the heart of the forest, or who he had met. The urgency to return to Paschim Behar for his father's funeral overshadowed all curiosity anyone might have had. Once he was out of the grip of the Assam forest officials, nobody in the palace knew what he'd been up to in the forest. Having these pointed questions directed at him by Dr Delrome was unnerving.

'Well, I am curious; what is a white girl doing in the deep forest of Assam? And then there are the reports of her leading a hundred-strong herd of elephants. That's why I want to go to Kachugaon first. From there, we will hopefully be able to get to this place Santhalbari where she might be taking shelter,' Raj was surprised at how rational it sounded.

'But why do you want to go to Kachugaon to get to Santhalbari? Your Highness, can I have a map of the Assam and Bengal region?' Dr Delrome asked.

Raj took a map from his collection and unrolled it on the table. Dr Delrome began tracing his finger along the Sankosh River from the point it joined the Brahmaputra up north towards Bhutan at the foothills of the Himalayas.

'So, on the right is Assam and on the left is Bengal. Paschim Behar is a landlocked state surrounded by Bengal. And as I go up, on the right side is the reserved forest of the Kachugaon division and to the left is the mixed land holding of Bengal province. As we keep going north along the river we hit the Bhutan hills. This is the tri-junction of Assam, Bhutan, and Bengal. And now look at this.' He kept his finger on the northwesternmost point of Assam. 'Now to reach this point from the Assam side, you must start from Kachugaon and then walk or take an elephant for miles. But...' Dr Delrome paused and smiled at Raj and Jenkins, who were both bent double over the map, 'to get to the same place from the Bengal side, you only have to cross the river and you are in Santhalbari.'

'So, there is no need to go to Kachugaon?' Raj asked to confirm. He was surprised and relieved. 'This means we can just drive north up to the Bhutan border and cross the river to the Assam side to reach Santhalbari?'

'It's not that simple. But it's much easier than taking the route through the forest of Assam with the Assam forest department personnel,' Dr Delrome said. 'Especially with those who don't have any idea that a place called Santhalbari exists in their forest.

Raj knew that the jibe was for his friend Jenkins.

Chapter 31

It was six in the morning. Dr Delrome and Jenkins were already in the study with Raj sorting out the final details. Jenkins was studying the same map they had used the previous night.

'That area in our departmental map is definitely marked as swampy savannah. This area doesn't have any timber. Also, there have been many incidents of attacks by archers in that region; generally, we avoid that area from the Assam side. If that is where Santhalbari is, then we must be careful even if we approach from the Bengal side. It could be very dangerous.' Jenkins sounded apprehensive, his face clearly sleep deprived.

'How dangerous do you think? Have there been incidents of attack or harming of forest department people other than what happened to Daju?' Raj was determined.

'Gethela has told us of many such attacks in the past. I didn't believe him until our guide Daju was shot dead by an arrow,' Jenkins said.

'Yes, Gethela the storyteller,' Raj said, looking up from some paperwork he was completing for the *Diwan*.

'Your Highness, you were very lucky. Nobody escapes those archers if you go near their place uninvited. Maybe at that point, they didn't see you as a threat,' Dr Delrome said re-joining the conversation. 'But not everyone is that lucky. Your guide was not lucky. And your father was definitely not lucky on one particular day fifteen years ago.' Dr Delrome said, looking at Jenkins.

'How do you know about my father?' Jenkins asked in surprise.

'Paul Jenkins was a world-famous naturalist. It was big news all over India. I met him when they were camping in Kachugaon. I used to go there regularly to meet my friend Brown *Sahib*. And now I've met you, I see a strong resemblance,' Dr Delrome said.

'You mean to say he was killed by the Santali spirit archers?' Jenkins' voice wobbled.

Jenkins went to say something more when there was a knock on the door. It was *Diwan Sahib*, accompanied by Tapash. The bespectacled old man was thoroughly confused to be summoned to the study at six thirty in the morning. It seemed he was never able to get any sleep. Raj handed him the paperwork and told him about the planned trip, and the requirement to keep it a secret.

'Your Highness, a lot of people will be looking for you. What will I tell them?' the *Diwan* asked, looking quite distraught.

'That's your problem *Diwan Sahib*,' Dr Delrome said before Raj could reply and gave Raj a wink. 'This is an opportunity for you to show your crisis management capability.'

'Alright, let me think,' *Diwan Sahib* said, scratching his bald head. Peering through his spectacles, he looked around the room. 'Great, I know what I will say!' he shouted, his face suddenly joyful.

'What will you tell people, *Diwan Sahib*?' Dr Delrome asked playfully.

'The *Maharaja* had one last wish,' *Diwan Sahib* said looking at Raj. 'He wanted his ashes to be immersed in the rivers flowing through his state from Bhutan. Your Highness, today, wherever you are going, you are going to take an urn of the *Maharaja's* ashes, and you will dispense the ashes in the river up north.'

Raj and Dr Delrome looked at each other, both immensely pleased and relieved.

'What a great idea *Diwan Sahib*!' Raj said and shook the old man's hand in thanks.

'And I can openly tell anyone who asks that you have gone to the Bhutan border to disperse the ashes of our late *Maharaja*. Nobody will question your absence.' Turning to Tapash, *Diwan Sahib* ordered, 'Get the urn of *Maharaja's* ashes and load it into the car.'

The old man looked at Raj and, folding his hands modestly said, 'Your Highness, I have a humble request. Please don't lengthen your stay like the last time. The stated purpose of your visit ideally shouldn't take more than a day or two. I hope you understand.'

Jenkins couldn't contain a smile. He looked at Raj who was trying to hold back his own. Soon Raj and Dr Delrome were seated in the comfortable Daimler Double Six followed by two other vehicles carrying the trip's provisions. Jenkins was driving his own Ford. The destination was Kumargram to the north of Paschim Behar at the Bhutan foothills, a relatively short journey of three hours.

'Santhalbari is just across the Sankosh River, which flows between Bengal and Assam. You should thank me for saving you from that long perilous journey through the forests of Assam,' Dr Delrome said breezily as the convoy took a sharp left at the intersection to take the road to North Bengal, leaving behind the straight road that led to the Assam border.

'If the place is so accessible, how do people not know about it?' Raj asked.

'Who said people don't know about the place? Ask the fishermen. Ask the local villagers of Kumargram. Everyone knows about the place. However, outsiders including the Assam district and forest administration, are unaware of it. For them, it is a stretch of inaccessible swampy savannah that is best avoided. And that's how Santhalbari has existed as an almost independent state, right under the nose of the Assam administration,' Dr Delrome said.

'I still find it hard to believe that it has managed to remain undetected for so many decades.'

'They won't be detected as long as Assam and Bengal

district officials don't talk to each other. Even if they do, there is hardly any reason for the Bengal officials to raise the topic of an obscure hamlet to their Assam counterpart,' Dr Delrome said.

'Whoever founded the place must have been a genius.'

'There was a visionary by the name of Raghu who established the settlement. After the discovery of tea by Robert Bruce in the eastern frontier of Assam, there was a widespread conversion of forest land into tea plantations by the European tea planters. The population in Assam was small and farm labour wasn't readily available. A large-scale import of plantation labourers from other parts of India occurred. It was a forced migration. They had to leave everything, and there was no going back,' Dr Delrome explained.

'Did Raghu come as an Assam tea garden labourer?'

'No — our hero Raghu Murmu was the chief of a Santali village in the Chota Nagpur region around a hundred years ago. The villagers heard about Assam from those who were forcibly removed to work on the tea estates. But this group of villagers decided to journey to Assam of their own free will, to lead an independent life in the cradle of the deepest forests. Raghu had heard that the forests were plentiful, there was no shortage of wild animals to hunt, and there was no competition, as the region didn't have a local population.'

'Raghu led a group of about one thousand young men and women with a few children on a long journey to a dream destination called Assam. As the contingent started progressing towards the east, their numbers began to deplete. Some defected, while others simply perished. By the time the group reached the Assam border, they numbered only around seven hundred. But they were determined in their mission, to establish the nucleus of a Santali state in the heart of the Assam wilderness.'

'This man had real courage,' Raj remarked.

'He was both courageous and clever. The region he chose for his kingdom was near the border where the Sankosh separated Assam and Bengal. Both sides of the river were covered by dense forest. The group crossed the river to find a suitable plot to settle in the forests of the Goalpara district. They didn't plan to move further into Assam territory for fear of discovery. They were afraid they might end up in the tea estates, like the thousands of others, if they migrated any further east.'

'So, after crossing into Assam, the group began to move northward through the dense forest. In the process, they discovered the unique forest and wildlife, quite different from the dry deciduous forest of the Chota Nagpur plateau. Their industrious leader decided to settle on a plot bordered by the turbulent waters of the Sankosh in the west, a steep gorge of the Bhutan hill in the north and the vast expanse of an oxbow lake in the south. The only direction from which there was the possibility of discovery by Assam administration or depredation by wild animals was the sal forests on the eastern side. Raghu and his men concentrated on erecting barricades to the eastern side, and eventually, over the years an impenetrable wall was built. It was made from sal timbers and had watch towers built at intervals where sharp shooters would be positioned as sentinels.'

'Has anyone in the Assam forest department seen that

wall?'

'Any explorer, forest official or hunter from the Assam side who stumbled upon the wall, never made it to the village. They were always shot dead by the Santali guards, and their heads were displayed as a warning to possible intruders. The heads of the dead were always positioned facing east, to warn outsiders from the Assam side.'

'And that's how Jenkins' father got killed?' Raj asked, slightly off balance.

'I think that's how he and the others were killed. After that incident, the region became an absolute no-go zone for the Assam forest department,' Dr Delrome said.

Raj, shaking his head asked, 'How do you know so much about Santhalbari?'

'I go there regularly...' Dr Delrome began but was cut short by Raj, who looked totally bewildered by now.

'You visit Santhalbari regularly?' Raj almost shouted.

'Yes, Your Highness, I go often. Someone lives there who is very close to my heart,' Dr Delrome said. Raj could see tears forming in the doctor's eyes.

'I don't understand...'

'Do you remember the royal hunt after the Delhi Durbar?'

Chapter 32

It was the most tumultuous phase of Raj's life. Young Raj had lost his mother, and his father remarried soon after. He had been hearing about the durbar from his father and palace officials for months leading up to the event. The royal family, with a large contingent of palace officials and servants, finally set off for Delhi by train. It was a journey that would take four days.

Raj wanted to travel in his father's carriage. But his father locked himself away inside with his beautiful bride, and he only saw his father when they arrived in Delhi.

The days in Delhi were frantic for his father, networking with other royal families and preparing for the presentation of tribute to the Emperor and Empress of India. For Raj and the other children, it was a sightseeing bonanza by a horse-drawn buggy. The broad avenues of Delhi unfolded many delights for Raj. There were evening outings to the lanes of Old Delhi where the children would savour street foods and buy trinkets. The month passed quickly. During the return journey to Paschim Behar via Calcutta, he overheard conversations about planning for the biggest royal hunt of the decade.

As the day of the royal hunt drew close, there was a debate at the palace around whether or not to take *Maharani* Indira Devi along. He heard his father saying that there was absolutely no way they could change the date for the royal hunt as it had been decided months in advance. Later, Raj realised that there were important reasons for organising the hunt just after the Delhi Durbar. It meant they could rope in several high-profile British officials from Delhi, the new capital of British India. The *Maharaja* wanted to impress the officials and support a recommendation to the new Emperor through the Viceroy, to upgrade the status of Paschim Behar to a thirteen-gun salute state. The *Maharaja* had persuaded the *Maharaja* of Kota and the *Nawab* of Junagarh to join him for the hunt so that they could also put in a good word for Paschim Behar.

Raj remembered passing through the non-descript township of Kachugaon on their way to the hunting camp. Before the gory chapter of the hunt began, the camp in the middle of the forest had a carnival-like atmosphere. The site chosen was an open patch bordered by woodlands on three sides and a steep gorge on the fourth that overlooked a vast expanse of river valley. Temporary fencing that ran hundreds of metres was erected along the border of the gorge to prevent children and drunk adults from tumbling into it.

There were parallel rows of tents, each row housing different categories of guests. One row of tents was for the *Maharaja* and his invited guests — heads of princely states and European officials. The second row was for the womenfolk of the palace and the third for the children and high-ranking palace officials. The last row was reserved for local facilitators and forest officials. Bordering the woodland in a circular fashion was the basic accommodation for the numerous servants, cooks and caretakers. There were also long storage tents to store provisions to feed the city for a week or so. Raj recalled the red letter boxes that were set up at various locations.

A typical day began with a banquet breakfast. Long tables were laid between the rows of tents. The *Maharaja* and his guests would be treated to a sumptuous feast consisting of European and Indian delicacies. Bread and cakes were brought in from Calcutta. Pooris fried in an open fire in the busy makeshift kitchen would be served piping hot with bhajis and potato curry. Afterwards, the menfolk would discuss the details of the day's hunt with the local facilitators and the professional hunters who had been hired to ensure the biggest of the trophies went to the special guests and the *Maharaja*. Womenfolk busied themselves with knitting or playing board games, enjoying the late winter sun of the foothill regions. There would also be games of badminton, musical chairs, pass the parcel and others. Lunch would be a short affair, given an elaborate dinner commenced at five sharp each evening and lasted till past midnight. The children of the camp would be regaled with movies and bioscopes. There was a special tent that housed toys of all kinds while another tent acted as a makeshift library.

The camp was a busy place for young Raj. He explored every corner of the tent city and he would venture out with a trusted servant to trace the source of incessant pecking. He would see the golden back of the woodpecker taking flight as he approached. He would crane his neck to see the capped langurs sitting at the tops of tall trees overlooking the camp township. There would be roars of the Bengal tiger from the immediate vicinity. They would invariably fall prey to the shots of the hunters who sat mounted on the howdah of elephants as hundreds of beaters would corner the prey. Hearing the roar would bring smiles to the faces of the hunters and guests who would congratulate each other for the excellent choice of site.

Raj's favourite pastime would be to sit on the edge of the steep gorge, his face pressed between two bamboo sticks of the fence and his back to the hullabaloo of the camp. He would look out at the vast valley down below with its unfolding vista of rocky riverbed and expanses of grassland, buffered by light woodlands of the riverine forest that eventually merged with deep, dark green forest. He would see herds of buffalo, deer, bison and elephants on the track below, all oblivious to the men and machines congregated above to annihilate them.

As the sun set on the western horizon, vanishing in the heart of the dark green wilderness, Raj and some of his companions would sit and watch as darkness engulfed the whole valley, while festivities awoke in the township behind them. Hundreds of torches and lamps would be lit along the rows of tents making the whole place resemble an illuminated city. Long tables covered with starched white cloths would be laid. There was a table for the special guests, one for government officials, one for the forest officials and one for the prominent aristocratic but nationalist citizens from Bengal and Assam. It was a vast networking session and an intense balancing act for the *Maharaja*. There were rulers from neighbouring states who were staunch supporters of British rule; there was aristrocratic gentry from Assam and Bengal who were ambivalent and there were die-hard nationalists who were prominent members of the Congress party. But during those days in the camp, differences in ideology didn't matter and most just enjoyed the hospitality offered by the *Maharaja*, reciprocating by keeping him in good humour.

Every dinner would start with an appetiser like quail or small game and there would be spirits of all kinds to drink. The children's tables would be served with various bhajis and pakoras, quickly followed by mains as the children would need to be taken to their tents soon after as the atmosphere drifted toward more of an adult nature. The menfolk would retire depending on their state of intoxication and opportunities for illicit liaisons.

Maids would be moving from one tent to another to organise bedding for the guests. They would be in a hurry to finish their chores, so they could have their share of fun with the other servants, cooks and orderlies, while the guests were partying.

Once the young children were herded back to their sleeping tents, young Raj would ask for a storyteller to come to the tent he shared with his two brothers. The brothers would be fast asleep, and Raj would plead with the storyteller to tell him about the nearby body of water during dusk. The man would vividly describe the animal or rather spirit that lived near the water, with legs so long and strong that people mistook them for tree trunks. Then he would tell the true story of how the creature killed one unwary forest guard who had committed the mistake of going near the water. There were stories of monsters that flew from the hills of Bhutan and swooped down at the hunters who had entered the forests without paying due respects. There were stories of strange animals like panthers; darker than the darkest nights, and tigers white as cotton. And then the stories would gradually shift from animals to spirits — some good but mostly bad. Raj would feel strangely comforted by the story of a benevolent spirit called the Respected Old Man who would roam the streets of the Kachugaon township at night, wearing a starched white *dhoti kurta* and an impressive turban. Then there was the time when he first heard stories of the dark ghosts who would glide from one tree to another with their bows and arrows. Anyone encountering them never returned. The spirit archers — that's what people used to call them.

Ultimately, an attendant would come in and urge the storyteller to leave so young Raj could get some sleep. The storyteller would leave with a promise to return, and Raj would have a hard time falling asleep thinking of the spirits roaming all around. He would take solace from the fact that the tent opposite his was occupied. It was referred to as the *Maharani* tent and it was where his stepmother stayed. She was the nurse whom his father had married a few months back. With a big swollen tummy, she stayed inside the tent with a few maids and a young French doctor, who was in continual attendance.

Chapter 33

'I do remember the 1911 royal hunt,' Raj said. 'I also remember hating you.' He added with a chuckle.

'I can understand; you were just a child,' Dr Delrome said in a way that seemed as though he still considered Raj a child. 'In that camp, I was looking after everyone's health, including the *Maharaja's* new wife's.'

'What has that royal hunt got to do with your frequent visits to Santhalbari now?'

Dr Delrome looked fondly at Raj, understanding his impatience. The car slowed down as it was passing through a small hamlet. Half-naked village children ran after the car shouting joyously. The driver turned around and asked Raj if he wanted him to stop. Raj gestured him to keep driving.

'Answer me, what is the connection?' he said, turning to Dr Delrome.

'I think it was the sixth day. It was late in the evening. As usual, the men were discussing the day's hunt over dinner. The womenfolk had finished their dinner and had gone off to their tents — playing board games or gossiping. Your father was drinking with some of his close friends and invited dignitaries. I was with him for some time, before retiring to my tent. The *Maharani*, your new mother, was in her tent with a maid waiting on her. It was around eight on a cool March night, when her water broke. The maid, as per prior instructions, ran straight to fetch me. I was sitting in front of my tent,' Dr Delrome said. He smiled, 'I was enjoying my pipe.'

'I didn't realise that Deep Narayan was born in that camp,' Raj said.

'It was a normal delivery. We had to cover the tent with an extra cloth to muffle the deafening labour cries of the *Maharani*, lest your father and his guests were disturbed. I had the shock of my life when I took into my hands this cute baby girl with a bald head, blue eyes and pink wrinkly skin that dispelled any chance that the *Maharaja* could be the father,' Dr Delrome said. 'It was not Deep Narayan.'

'It was a baby girl? And the baby wasn't the *Maharaja's*? But how was it possible?' Raj asked. He looked at the driver and hoped he wasn't listening to the conversation.

'As you know before she became the *Maharani*, she was my nurse, and we were in love. Your father started courting her when she was still in love with me. When he married her, she was still seeing me secretly. I was hoping that the baby would be the *Maharaja's* as I believed she had slept with her new husband more than with me, but no...' Dr Delrome gave Raj a sheepish look. Raj remembered how the new *Maharani* was always cosying up with the young handsome French doctor whenever her portly middle-aged husband wasn't around.

'I was at my wit's end when I held that baby in my hands. And when I looked at her mother, I forgot she was the *Maharani*. I saw my lover, lying exhausted with her legs still spread, emotions ranging from complete shock to elation. She was trying hard to keep her eyes from closing, to see the baby she had delivered. I was trying to muffle the baby's cries by wrapping her in a bundle of clothes. The *Maharani* succumbed to exhaustion and passed out, and I began to think of the consequences,' Dr Delrome said. Pearls of sweat had appeared on his forehead.

'What consequences? I don't understand,' Raj said.

'Well, Your Highness, think of your late father's reaction, if he came to know that his wife had delivered a white girl, or if the news got out amongst all his friends, other royal families, government official, notable public figures from Assam and Bengal. Then there were people from the palace — relatives, priests, astrologers, and others, whose job it was to ensure the continuity of the Behar dynasty through a pure bloodline. Even if the *Maharaja* would have accepted the child, others obsessed with the purity of Paschim Behar lineage would have had that child eliminated. I had no choice. In the camp, I had befriended a very efficient young forest officer. His name was Robert Brown. I ran to the camp of the Assam forest officials, carrying the baby through the darkness. I told him that I had to hide the baby. I told him everything. Thankfully, the young officer understood my predicament.'

'You mean Brown *Sahib*, the ACF of Kachugaon? He was there? I've met him. I found him to be an obnoxious old man. He was very efficient though; I have to admit I was impressed with his planning and organisational capability,' Raj said.

'Yes, he was there at that time. He wasn't only my saviour, but also the *Maharani's* and the little baby's. The biggest thing that he saved was the royal family, from a huge embarrassment. I told him I would give him whatever he wanted. He said he didn't want anything and told me that he himself would take the baby to a place nobody would find.'

'And that place is Santhalbari,' Raj said, his eyes opening wide.

Dr Delrome nodded. 'And that tough man just vanished into the dark forest carrying the baby. He knew the risks and so he didn't even wait until the morning.' Stroking his white beard and shaking his head, Dr Delrome continued, 'I will never forget that sight. It was around eleven at night. That young officer had the baby in one hand and a rifle in the other. He carried a few bottles of milk in a bag for the little one.'

'What did you tell everyone? What did you say to my father?'

'Well, the *Maharani* was told that the baby was stillborn and had been quickly buried in the forest. She was hysterical of course. Some of the attendants were suspicious, and I had to win them over with gifts,' Dr Delrome said. 'And most of the guests in the camp were unaware as none of them had seen the *Maharani*. She was always inside her tent.'

'And father?'

'He was playing cards. I went to him and quietly broke the news in his ear. He nodded and continued playing. Don't judge your father. He was a good man. But maybe he knew what was coming and wanted to give his new wife another chance. Or maybe he believed what I told him. I never had any relations with the *Maharani* again.'

'Does the *Maharani* know her daughter is still alive?'

'She doesn't know. While the *Maharaja* was alive, I had to keep it a secret. Now that he is gone, I am not sure. I don't know what her reaction will be, learning that she has a daughter,' Dr Delrome said uncertainly. 'I think I will keep it this way, at least for the time being.'

'Did Rajah *Sahib* know that his sister's daughter, his niece, was growing up in Santhalbari?' Raj queried.

'Rajah *Sahib* didn't know as he wasn't in the hunting camp at that time. Your father asked the *Maharani* if she would like to invite him, but she strongly declined. It would have been interesting if Rajah *Sahib* had been in the camp that night. Anyway, he later came to know of a white girl growing up in Santhalbari from Brown *Sahib*. So, he thought of a way to use her. I am sure he wasn't aware of any link between the girl and his sister. If he knew, it would have been different.'

'What would have been different?'

'Rajah *Sahib* was very rich. He had no heir in Parbatipur as he never married. His brother never returned from Germany and his sister deserted him. If he knew that the girl growing up in Santhalbari was his niece, he would surely have brought her to Parbatipur and raised her. He was a kind-hearted man,' Dr Delrome said.

'That would have been ideal, wouldn't it?'

'Yes and no. Yes, for the girl; she would have had a far more comfortable life. But on the downside, it would have become known that the *Maharani's* illicit daughter was being raised by her brother. She maintains no relationship with her brother but that doesn't stop everyone from knowing that she is Rajah *Sahib's* younger sister. I feared for my daughter's life far more outside the forest than inside.' The doctor sighed heavily.

'The young *Maharani* was trying to gain a foothold in the royal establishment. If I revealed the truth to her, I wasn't sure what she would have done — torn between the revelation of her daughter and her predicament of what this discovery might do. I had doubts about her, but I could have been wrong. And there were others obsessed with the purity of the lineage that might have harmed the child. I became determined that under no circumstances would I tell the secret of the girl child growing up in Santhalbari. I didn't even tell Rajah *Sahib* and forbade Brown *Sahib* from telling him.'

'Was she not curious about her firstborn? How could she believe you without question?'

'She did question me continuously about her delivery in the forest camp. I stuck to the story; it was a stillborn baby. I told her the baby was white though. I think that did the trick; she stopped asking me after that. And soon she was pregnant with her first child with the *Maharaja*. Baby Deep Narayan was born, and the girl was forgotten.'

Chapter 34

The road to Kumargram wound through tea gardens interspersed with shady trees and green patches of deciduous forest. It was midday by the time Raj's convoy reached Kumargram, the northernmost hamlet of Bengal, located at the Bhutan foothills.

'I will go to see the village chief. We will have to leave our cars and men behind. Just the three of us will go on: you, me and that forest officer from Assam,' Dr Delrome said.

'Can we take Tapash along?' The last few days had made Raj realise the worth of his personal assistant.

'I think not. We will be constrained by our mode of transportation. Don't worry, he will accompany us to the mid-point,' Dr Delrome said and excused himself to talk to the diminutive old Nepali man who was the village chief.

Raj got out of the car and approached Jenkins to enquire about his trip. The attendants got busy setting up a temporary tent for lunch. Kumargram was a village of mixed population;

Nepalis, Rajbangshis and Bodos. Bengali seemed to be the common language.

Dr Delrome returned from his chat with the chief. 'From here, we will walk to the river. It is a short walk, maybe a mile. It is not accessible by car. The chief will arrange for a boat to transfer us to the other side of the river.'

'And then we reach Santhalbari?' Raj asked apprehensively.

'No, not that easily, Your Highness. We cross the first part of the river, walk over the island in the middle and then cross the river again. It is very difficult to get a boat without prior notice. No boatman wants to go from Kumargram to Assam. They generally just go upstream or downstream but not across.'

A small party comprising of Raj, Dr Delrome, Jenkins, Tapash and two villagers headed off   towards the river. They walked through a patch of freshly stripped and burnt forest where the soil was an ashy brown. It was a slow walk on the soft earth, the ground dotted with tree stumps and burned trees. After some time, the rich brown soil gave way to silvery sand with tall riverine grasses. Raj heard a thunderous roar.

'What is that sound?'

'That's the Sankosh, Your Highness,' Dr Delrome explained. 'The river, as it descends from the Bhutan hills, unleashes all its fury onto the rocky bed of the plains. We have to cross that river to reach the middle island that, at its widest section, is about five miles. The river island, a part of Assam, acts as a buffer for Santhalbari from the fishermen of the Bengal side. Then we have to cross the second part of the river to reach Santhalbari.'

'Will we have to walk five miles after crossing the first stream?' asked a worried Jenkins.

'Not really. We can't cross the stream at this point as the water is too rough. We will have to go downstream and then attempt to cross it. The land mass there is maybe two miles as the island becomes narrower downstream,' Dr Delrome said.

And then Raj saw it. The mighty Sankosh dividing Assam and Bengal flowing over the rocky river bed. It looked like an undulating sea of froth covered with a mist rising high up as if its strength knew no bounds.

As Raj approached the river, a chill ran through his entire body. He went over to the water's edge and bent down, gliding a hand through the water. It was ice cold. Tapash approached, carrying the urn. Raj cupped some water, lifted his hands and then released the water back to the river, uttering a prayer. He took the urn from Tapash, held it with the utmost care, and then poured the contents into the fast-moving water. The ashes of the *Maharaja* of Paschim Behar, who may have crossed the Sankosh many times to hunt, were carried away in the immense current of the river. All of them prayed silently for the eternal peace of the *Maharaja's* soul and then readied themselves for the next part of the journey.

'Your Highness, this way,' Dr Delrome directed Raj further downstream where he saw the shadow of a boatman emerge from the mist with a boat. One of the village guides gave Dr Delrome a long bamboo pole with a patterned square cloth tied onto one end. The cloth was black, red, and yellow and looked like a flag.

'What is that for?' Raj asked as he boarded the boat.

'This is the flag of Santhalbari. Anyone trying to cross the river and entering into Santhalbari without the flag will be killed by the archers. I am the only one who has this protection flag,' Dr Delrome explained as the boat was drawn downstream by the swift current.

Raj saw the vast expanse of the river island. It was a silvery sea of grass interspersed with tall green *sissoo* trees. As they were drifting downstream, Dr Delrome pointed out a *sissoo* tree where a few black dots could be seen in the green canopy that appeared to be larger than cormorants.

'Can you see them, the spirit archers? I think we are within the range of their arrows,' Dr Delrome said. 'But this is protecting us,' he said, waving the bamboo pole with its flag of Santhalbari flying.

'I can't see them,' Raj said, craning his neck to look up at the trees that were quickly disappearing from view.

'Don't worry, they are everywhere. There will be many more of them,' Dr Delrome said.

After a rough ride, the boat slowed. The fury of the water receded, and the boatman uttered some prayers as he angled the boat directly towards the river island and started rowing across the river.

Dr Delrome cupped his hands into a funnel and let out a shrill whistle. Raj realized it was the same sound the old Santali man had made. Bows were lowered, and one archer replied with the same call that was repeated from tree to tree eastward and relayed all the way to Santhalbari that some visitors were expected.

Dr Delrome instructed Tapash and the boatman to return to the same location the next day. 'From here on, we will be in the company of these people,' Dr Delrome said. When everyone had alighted, they made their way gingerly across the rocky shallows to dry land. Dr Delrome was still carrying the pole with the flag, and the boatman took off at speed with Tapash.

As Raj walked onto the sandy beach, he was spellbound by the expanse of scenery before him. There were miles of glistening sand covered with green and silver of river grasses and tall *sissoo* trees. Herds of spotted deer came into view and enormous butterflies fluttered everywhere. Raj and Jenkins realised they were in an undiscovered paradise.

Raj and Jenkins marvelled at the lean-built young men, their dark complexion, long heads, flat noses and curly hair. They did not appear happy to see the visitors, but they respected Dr Delrome who was still carrying the flag.

On reaching the other side of the island, the archers ran to the river bank and pushed three dinghies into the water. Three men stood boarded each dinghy and gestured to each of the visitors to get in. Within moments the archers were pushing their long poles into the river bed, steering the dinghies to the other side.

The ride across the stream with the Santali warriors only took a few minutes. The warriors secured the dinghies' anchors into the rocks of the shoreline and Dr Delrome led the way toward the path that would lead to their destination. As they approached the settlement, half a dozen semi-naked children came running to greet them, two of them totally white. The children shouted at the approaching party but disappeared as soon as the Santali guards hurled some harsh words at them.

Raj looked at Dr Delrome who shook his head. 'No, not my children. One is enough.'

Chapter 35

Brown *Sahib* was sitting in the front courtyard of *Lal Bungalow*. He wasn't able to concentrate on the papers Ghosh *Babu* had left for him to sign. 'Stupid man,' he muttered under his breath. The Superintendent of Police was right; he shouldn't have hastily cremated Rajah *Sahib*. If only he had sent the body to Dhubri, they could have found the cause of death. It may have been malaria, or kala-azar, even plain old-age ailments. Or, it could have been poisoning.

Given the heat, the body would definitely have begun to decompose but the hospital staff would have dealt with it. But at least he would have been able to find out the cause of his friend's death. He shook his head. He was irritated with his useless deputies; they could have given him some advice if they had any brains at all. He was still in shock at learning his good friend had died. He remembered Baruah advising him not to go ahead with the hasty cremation. If only there had been more voices that day to dissuade him. He felt miserable; his friend was dead, and the cause of death was a mystery.

A pair of red jungle fowl came out of the bushes to

forage on the unkempt lawn. The male looked proud with his glistening golden plumage and erect red comb, as it twitched its head to attract the drab hen's attention. Brown *Sahib* was amused seeing their courtship over food. Normally, he would have just picked up his gun and the birds would have been lunch. But there was a rumbling noise and the birds vanished into the bush as Brown *Sahib* heard the rolling sound of heavy wheels coming down the street.

'Hey, you bastards! Where are you taking that?' he shouted at the three forest guards who were pushing an empty cage on wheels. The men left the cage midway and came running to him.

'*Sahib*, Das *Babu* told us to take it to the station. We need to take it to the Raimona range. Apparently, a leopard has been sighted in number sixteen and it appears at night,' one of the guards said.

Brown *Sahib* was recently made aware of the problem faced by forest village number sixteen. The village was in a meadow with a deep evergreen forest on either side of it. Running through the centre of the village was a sparkling stream. An abundance of wild foods growing in the nearby forest had made the villagers lazy. They had stopped cultivation and became gatherers, which was when the problem started. The area around number sixteen had the highest population of big cats in the entire Ripu reserve - tigers, leopards, and the tree-dwelling ones which he never bothered to learn to differentiate from the leopard. As per reports, the problem animal was a black panther that had become a blood-thirsty hunter of poultry and had graduated to village dogs and then to children. Within months, the animal had acquired malevolent spirit-like notoriety. Villagers had reported to the department that it had been creeping through the nearby brush seeking out its next victim. The village had some expert hunters. But they were also clueless as they said its paws barely made a sound as it moved around. A seventh unsuspecting child who had gone to play in the stream had been taken.

Brown *Sahib* looked at the guards. He didn't say anything, as they waited. He wondered whether it was the right cage for the animal. He had captured many trouble-making leopards by luring them into cages with a bleating goat tied inside. It was an easy and effective way of capturing leopards and sometimes tigers for selling to zoos and circuses. Kachugaon forest had supplied tigers and leopards to zoos all over the world. But the animals had become wary of the cages, refusing to get inside. They needed greater enticement. Around fifteen years ago, he made one of the most dangerous innovations in the field of big cat capture.

Brown *Sahib* remembered the killer of Kachugaon and how it had struck terror into the township. It was an old leopard that had started preying on unsuspecting inhabitants of Kachugaon. Brown *Sahib* came up with a plan to ensure he would capture the animal. An extra-large cage was placed in a strategic location near the village. For prey, there was no bleating goat or buffalo calf; Brown *Sahib* positioned himself inside the cage. He didn't have to wait long. As night descended, Brown *Sahib* saw a bright pair of eyes in the darkness rushing towards the cage. A split second before those mighty paws could tear into him, a trap door fell from the top separating the cage into two sections. As the metal barrier appeared before the predator, it unsuccessfully tried to claw at its victim, but realised it was a trap and turned to get out of the cage. That was when a second trap door at the mouth of the cage descended. It was the first successful use of the innovation that became known as Brown *Sahib's* Big Cage. Since then there had been quite a few discreet uses of the Big Cage. Capturing big cats for selling to zoos and circuses became another feather in the cap of ACF Robert Brown.

Brown *Sahib* thought about the captured man from Paschim Behar. A special modification, so that the middle trap door didn't close, would be needed. He wasn't very keen on saving the life of the 'bait' on this account. It would be a quick and easy disposal method for the captured murderer as well as trapping of the nuisance animal.

'Go and take this back where you brought it from and get the Big Cage,' Brown *Sahib* instructed the guards. The guards looked at each other. 'Don't waste time. Fetch that arrested man from Paschim Behar. Set up the Big Cage as soon as you reach the village. And you know which door shouldn't close.' The guards left hurriedly. Brown *Sahib* remained seated on the reclining chair. He shook his head, relishing the thought of the rascal and his master together in the cage. That criminal was just an instrument, a pawn. He must have had a mastermind. Brown *Sahib* wished he could put both of them together in the cage. That man-eater would have a double treat. The bastards would never know when the ghostly-silent cat would pick up their scent and then keep an eye on the cage from the bush. Then, in the pitch-black of the night when the moon was hidden behind clouds, the beast would sit back on its haunches and whisk its tail before springing with all its terrifying might into the cage where they would be sitting huddled, tied to the bars.

Brown *Sahib* was jostled to reality when he heard a bicycle. The rider was Ranger Das who was panting and looking distraught. Brown *Sahib* realised that he'd been half-asleep under the morning sunlight for quite some time.

'Gethela's decomposed body has been found in a remote corner of the timber depot in Fakiragram.'

Brown *Sahib* was startled, but this time he knew what was to be done. 'Get the body to Dhubri civil hospital as quickly as you can. Take the train.' Ranger Das gave him a surprised look. 'We have to know how Gethela was killed. There is a murderer prowling amongst us. The autopsy will tell us how he was killed.' Brown *Sahib* was trying to be as patient as he could.

'Sir, why do you need an autopsy for that? He was shot in the head. I found these bullets in his half-eaten maggot-infested brain,' Das said, taking the bullets from his trouser pocket.

Brown *Sahib* took one of the bullets in his hand and immediately recognised it. 'A 91-grain bullet from a Colt 1908. He was killed by one of our department people,' he announced, knowing full well the firearms distribution amongst his staff. Das had a shot gun, the other rangers had old Winchesters and he himself had a beretta. Ranger Miri, the senior-most ranger, had a colt. And there was one colt in the *almirah* in the safe room. Only one ranger was without any official firearm. Looking after the tramway wasn't considered as patrolling and hence, he didn't sanction any firearms for Baruah. He knew well that being the scion of the Manikpur *zamindari,* Baruah could afford his own firearms. But a Colt 1908 was a rare pistol and nobody except he and Ranger Miri had one in the region.

'Where is Miri?'

'Sir, he is in his quarters. He has been unwell for some time,' Das replied.

Brown *Sahib* was aware of the ongoing health issues of his old ranger. *But why would he kill Gethela?* He went inside and opened his *almirah* where they kept the department ammunition. He took out the bullet case. Three bullets were missing.

It couldn't have been Miri. I have not fired a shot for months. This means Gethela has been murdered using my weapon by someone who didn't have a gun of his own.

'Das!' Brown *Sahib* yelled at the ranger. 'Get to the station at once and check if they were able to take the Big Cage and the man.'

'I saw them loading the Big Cage. They said you wanted it sent to number sixteen,' Das said. Then he looked around and came closer to Brown *Sahib*. 'They also took the man.'

'I want him back. Send someone to the station to get that wretched man back. But leave the Big Cage there. Very soon I'll be sending the man back... with his master,' Brown *Sahib* said, rising from his chair.

'Who is his master?' the ranger insisted.

'None of your business. Now get lost; I don't have time for your stupid questions.'

As Ranger Das hurried over to his bicycle, Brown *Sahib* called after him, 'When you come back with that killer, keep him hidden behind the cook's quarters. Keep an eye on Ranger Baruah. As soon as he is not home, search his place thoroughly and if you find anything suspicious, bring it to me. Take Ghosh *Babu* along.' Ranger Das stood still, not knowing whether to move.

'Don't touch any of his personal belongings or valuables. And be ready to arrest him when I tell you. I want no mistakes. And you have permission to shoot. Now get the hell out of here,' Brown Sahib shouted. The ranger took off on his bicycle toward the station like a man possessed. Once Das was out of sight, Brown *Sahib* went inside. Sitting in the sun for so long made him feel dizzy. He quickly grabbed a chair handle for support and then slumped down into it. He realised he wasn't young any more. Age was catching up, but he wasn't going to let his friend's murderer go unpunished.

I owe it to you, my friend.

Chapter 36

Santhalbari revealed itself as a well-planned settlement. There were rows of thatched roof houses with mud walls. Each had a small courtyard fenced by bamboo. The households had vegetable patches of potato, runner beans, carrots, turnips, herbs and corn, guarded by numerous scarecrows of different size and shapes. There was a central thoroughfare with bigger cottages, and parallel to it ran a few smaller roads. The whole township was laid out on a grid pattern. There were a school and a hall for public functions. Raj and Jenkins were surprised at seeing such a well-planned township in the middle of nowhere.

When the party reached what looked like the main street, the guard said something to Dr Delrome and left. As Raj, Dr Delrome and a thoroughly bewildered Jenkins, walked along the main street, curious onlookers stared at them from both sides. There were old men with sunken eyes, grandmothers with timeworn skin, giggling young girls and naked kids.

Raj saw a structure bigger than all other houses at the end of the road. 'What is that building?' he asked, pointing to the massive wooden tower-like structure billowing smoke. Before Dr Delrome could answer, an old Santali appeared from one of the side alleys and exchanged greetings with the doctor. All four of them started walking towards the structure which had the appearance of a temple. By this time the thoroughfare was lined with almost the whole of Santhalbari, all of them watching the visitors and murmuring excitedly among themselves.

As they climbed the steps of the wooden temple, the scent of burning incense wafted through the air. The whole structure began to reverberate with the beating of drums. And then there were eerie ululations that sent shivers through Raj's body. The old man now took the lead and opened the heavy wooden door.

It was dark inside and at first, Raj could not see through the smoke of burning incense and coconut husk. As his eyes adjusted, he saw her, sitting on a pedestal. Her upper body was gyrating, her eyes closed in a trance while the men and women sitting around her chanted and clapped. They were holding pigeons in their hands; some alive and others headless, squirting blood out of their severed necks. There was a fire burning in front of where she sat.

'Who is she?' was all that escaped from Raj's mouth. He watched stupefied, as the maiden he had made love to, grabbed a pigeon from one of the men, bit off its head and drank blood from its body.

'She is my daughter,' Dr Delrome said as his eyes welled up.

'Your daughter?' Raj asked.

'She is your stepsister if you care to consider her that.' Raj watched, intrigued and revolted in equal measure, as she danced a ghastly ritual around the fire, ululating to the beat of the rumbling drums. The men and women surrounding her were stretching their hands to touch her. Some were throwing flowers at her as if she were a living goddess. He couldn't take it any longer. His head started spinning and he turned and ran down the stairs as the drum beats reached their crescendo. He rushed to a small pond near the steps, bent down and threw water onto his face. He collapsed onto a bench overlooking the pond.

'What is your daughter doing inside that temple?' a bewildered Raj shouted as he saw Dr Delrome climbing down the steps, quickly followed by Jenkins.

Dr Delrome gave a long sigh. 'When she was a toddler, she was everyone's favourite. All the women wanted to be her mother. But she was growing up fast, along with the village boys who were turning into men. Soon the men started seeing the adolescent girl as a prospective bride. And this is when I had an idea. I was in Nepal with your family. We went to the Pashupati Temple to pay annual homage to the mother goddess. In that temple young pre-pubescent virgin girls were worshipped as incarnations of the mother goddess. After I came back from Nepal, I headed to Kachugaon to meet up with Robert Brown. He was a fun-loving bachelor, but he was also equally worried about my daughter. In fact, he was worried that his own children may cause her harm.'

'Brown *Sahib's* children?' Jenkins asked, his eyes widening.

'Those white kids you saw this morning are Brown *Sahib's*

children, but he also has grown-up kids. We met with the chief, the grandson of the founding chief Raghu. It took some effort, but we managed to convince him to agree to the plan. We also took the priest into our confidence. He was the old man who escorted us here. After that, the temple of Santhalbari became the guardian of my daughter. We introduced a hybrid ritual of virgin worship and *devadasi* in Santhalbari to create a safety barrier for the girl,' Dr Delrome said.

And it had kept her safe until she met a married middle-aged man one night. 'Did it make her safe? Many of those girls in the temples of South India have become victims of rich people's desires,' Raj asked, alluding to the fact that most *devadasis* ended up as prostitutes.

'We had thought about it,' Dr Delrome said. 'That's why we created the hybrid. We brought in elements of an oracle to *devadasi*. The only way I could protect my daughter was by making her untouchable. We befriended a witch doctor, a healer and diviner in the village. The Santalis believe in magic and witchcraft. My little girl is a 'witchfinder' amongst the community. It was the only way a white girl could survive.'

Raj was shaking his head in disbelief. 'You could have just taken her home with you. That would have saved the girl from all this.'

'And likely get her killed,' Dr Delrome said matter-of-factly.

'What do you mean? Who would kill her? Surely they wouldn't have come out of the forest to go after her.'

'Your father would have come to learn she was the

Maharani's daughter. Even if your father didn't act on it, the palace officials or the family would surely have done so. How could the *Maharani* of Paschim Behar while married to the *Maharaja* produce a European child? There was no way they could accept a disgrace like that. But now that the *Maharaja* is gone, you will rule Paschim Behar. Can I trust she will be safe outside?' Dr Delrome looked imploringly at Raj.

'Yes, we have to get her out of here.' It was Jenkins who spoke for the first time. Raj couldn't help noticing the sense of eagerness in Jenkins' voice.

'Mr. Jenkins, you have no idea what an important role you will have to play in this whole affair,' Dr Delrome said. 'In return for my daughter, we will have to give them something. It will be my daughter's freedom for their freedom.'

'Of course, I am ready to do anything I can to get your daughter out of here,' Jenkins said. 'So, Brown *Sahib* has known about this place all along?'

'Yes, he was the one who brought her here.' Then he told Jenkins how Brown *Sahib* had brought the baby girl to Santalbari two decades ago. When he was done, Jenkins was silent. 'There is not a single day I have not thought of her. Every night when I sleep on my comfortable bed, I think of my daughter sleeping on a bare wooden cot. I had to stay at Paschim Behar so that I could at least see her occasionally.'

'Does she have a name?' Raj asked.

'Yes, her name is Teesta,' Dr Delrome said with a smile.

'Teesta? After the river?'

'Yes, she was conceived near the bank of the river Teesta. I was with your father and stepmother on a hunting trip in the Jaldhapara region. One starry night, when the *Maharaja* was busy with his card games, I snuck into her tent and we could not restrain ourselves.' He just shook his head trying to blink back more tears, but they escaped and slid down his cheek. Raj looked at him; so many secrets, hidden for so long, were finally free.

Chapter 37

Raj, Dr Delrome and Jenkins were seated on a wooden bench around a circular table under a gazebo with a thatched roof. They were outside the chief's house. Winds from the Sankosh blew across the hamlet, creating wavy ripples over the leafy sal forest to the east. They were eating cool cucumbers and sweet jackfruits while they waited for the chief. A Santali girl came and gave them an earthen pot filled with water. Raj felt he had never tasted such cool sweet water.

The chief, a bright young man of around thirty came out of the house. Raj assumed he would be the great-grandson of their founding chief Raghu Murmu. He was followed by a few advisers and counsels who were much older. All of them appeared despondent.

Raj looked at Jenkins as Jenkins would have to lead the discussion. The area was part of the Ripu forest that belonged to the Assam forest department. He hoped his friend had a plan of some kind.

As the chief sat across them and muttered something to

one of his advisers, Raj realised that Dr Delrome's knowledge of the Santali language was too basic for him to act as interpreter for Jenkins. An anxious crowd had gathered around the meeting place. Dr Delrome shouted for someone. A man who didn't look like a Santali came forward.

'He will be the interpreter as he knows Santali and Bengali, and a bit of English,' Dr Delrome looked at Raj and said. 'He was a fisherman from Bengal whose father used to help these people using his boats near the Bengal border. He fell in love with a Santali girl. Luckily for him, the local people accepted him. There are very few outsiders like him here.'

The chief looked at Dr Delrome, Raj and Jenkins, unsure of whom to address. He said something quite long-winded, pointing to his people. Raj tried to guess if there were any threats in his speech. They were just three unarmed outsiders. The chief could easily have their heads displayed as trophies. He remembered the guards carrying bows and arrows. He also remembered the eunuch guard he met in the forest. Looking back later, he realized it was a miracle that he hadn't been killed that day. The three of them turned to the translator.

'He is asking what will happen to his people,' the interpreter said, looking at Dr Delrome.

'Is that all he said?' Jenkins asked.

'In summary, yes,' the interpreter said.

Jenkins gestured to Dr Delrome that he would take it from here. He looked at the man and started explaining his plan. Dr Delrome joined in, in Bengali, to help the interpreter who seemed to be a smart young man. The chief listened intently.

As he listened, his demeanour began to change. Slowly a smile spread across his face, easing the frowns and the troubled look, which he reflected onto the anxiously waiting people. Once Jenkins finished, the chief shouted excitedly toward the crowd. Chattering amongst the crowd increased and soon turned to jubilation. They raised their hands and cheered. By the time the meeting concluded, a celebratory mood prevailed in the entire area.

The chief stood up and addressed his people. A wide smile appeared on his taut, dark face.

'Tonight, there will be a celebration dinner in your honour,' the interpreter proclaimed happily, while the chief excused himself from them to mingle with his people. Raj could see Jenkins was happy with the outcome. He felt relieved for his friend.

'Congratulations,' he muttered. Jenkins gave him an amused look. 'You have become the proud owner of an advanced township of more than two thousand people occupying a prime portion of your reserve. You should thank Brown *Sahib* for this,' Raj said with a chuckle.

Jenkins shook his head and smiled.

Raj went to say something but stopped when he saw her coming through the crowd. Her hair flowed to her waist and she wore a slight smile on her face as she strode confidently towards them. She was wearing a knee-length white saree, baring her shapely white legs. As she came nearer, she rushed to embrace her father, who stood with his arms wide. She buried her face in Dr Delrome's chest, breaking into sobs.

Dr Delrome consoled her. She lifted her head. Dr Delrome said something to her and pointed toward Raj and Jenkins. Her eyes revealed a glimmer of curiosity and interest.

Raj noticed that she displayed no emotion on seeing him. He didn't know whether to be sad or relieved. They had never seen each other in broad daylight. She looked happy to be with her father, but her pain was clear in the crease of her lovely brow. She peered through sweeping eyelashes and burst into laughter as she whispered something to her father, those same white teeth gleaming.

'She says that the monkeys will come and play drums on your bald head,' Dr Delrome said, laughing. Raj laughed at the girl's spontaneous joke, feeling thankful that she might not have recognised him due to his shaven head.

Raj watched her through the corner of his eyes. His heart skipped a beat. What if her father asked her if she remembered meeting the bald man? He looked at Jenkins; he seemed transfixed. He saw their eyes meet. She looked at her father and his friends and with a complete lack of self-consciousness ran off.

At a distance, a group of small children under a berry tree were trying to bend a branch with a hooked pole. They shouted excitedly when their elder sister joined them. She reached up and bent the berry-loaded branch down for them.

'That's my poor girl, leading the life of a possessed woman in a temple and a carefree girl in love with nature. It is time for her to move on,' Dr Delrome said, looking over at her fondly. 'She has grown up in these great forests. She has many friends. But these days I rarely see her doing what she is doing now.'

They could hear laughter and light banter as the children threw berries at one another.

'Over the years, she has been slowly made to withdraw, to spend more time in the temple in the company of the priest. It's affecting her.'

'What do you mean?'

'You saw today what she has become. As people began to worship her, the priest started moulding her for his own benefit. He encourages her to get lost in her prayers to the deities and she has started behaving like someone who possesses divine powers. Lately, she has been offered animal sacrifices and asked for healing. She goes into trances. It is taking a toll on her,' Dr Delrome said with leaden voice. 'If we don't save her now, I fear she will be lost forever.'

'Did you know why she was in Ripu recently?'

'I know Brown *Sahib* and Rajah *Sahib* occasionally take her to the forest. She loves riding the elephants. She rides the tame elephants and approaches the wild herds. It is like a playful outing for her. But she has no idea that whenever she is seen, she is propagating a myth. But I didn't know about the recent trip as this is my first visit in three months. That's why she was so upset with me.'

'How did it all start?' Raj asked.

'It all started when Jenkins' father came to Ripu in search of the two-horned rhinos,' Dr Delrome said.

'Two-horned rhinos in India?' Jenkins was suddenly back on earth. Dr Delrome took a deep breath and gestured for them all to take a seat. He began.

Chapter 38

'Brown *Sahib* had scant respect and little patience for those he called the intruders. Botanists, who spend days in his forests discussing some leaves or the ornithologists mist netting some small drab bird. The biggest trouble-makers were those who were after live mammal capture. He understood elephant capture; but he could never get why anyone would go to the trouble of capturing a pig, bison or rhino when you could just shoot them instead.

When Paul Jenkins and the four other naturalists reached Kachugaon, instructions from the conservator were to provide all logistical support to the expedition. They were reputed scientists from the London Zoological Society. They were there to study the habitat and ecology of the rhino in the eastern part of India. They would be capturing two young adults, to be exported to the London and Bronx zoos. They had already made up their minds about where they would be going to look for the rhino.'

'What did Brown *Sahib* do?' Raj asked.

'Brown *Sahib* was definitely not happy about receiving them at Kachugaon. The stretch of forest under his jurisdiction runs for sixty miles along the Bhutan foothills. It is a huge expanse measuring eighteen hundred square miles with quite a few rhino-bearing areas. The forests to the East of this stretch had already been gazetted as the North Kamrup Sanctuary by the government, for protection of the Indian rhino. Brown *Sahib* tried to persuade the team to go to the already identified rhino habitats, but the scientists were fixated on this triangular border junction of Assam, Bengal, and Bhutan. They reasoned that it could be the only area in the entire world that could harbour both Indian one-horn rhinos and Chittagong two-horn rhinos. Brown *Sahib* had to give in.

The expedition troubled him greatly. If the survey party were to come across Santhalbari instead of a swampy savannah, he would be seriously taken to task. The forest fell under his jurisdiction and the original survey was done under his leadership. Even if he could reason the township was a subsequent encroachment, he should have detected it during regular patrolling and reported it those higher up. Another issue would be explaining the appearance of a half-dozen Anglo-Santali children he had fathered over the years. But his biggest worry was the ten-year-old white girl. If the residents opened their mouths about their protector in the department, he would be doomed. The Assam Government would prosecute him for smuggling a child.

So, Brown *Sahib* hatched a plan to prevent the naturalists from reaching the spot. It was a huge risk but if it worked he'd be able to keep Santhalbari away from outsiders for years to come.'

'But what is the connection between the girl and the

naturalists?' Jenkins asked, a frown forming on his face.

'The forest was rife with stories of a mysterious white maiden riding a tusker leading a herd of elephants. The *mahouts* developed a belief that they were the worst enemy of the maiden as she wanted to protect her herd from the catchers. Brown *Sahib* took advantage of the belief.

My little girl naturally took to elephants. She took a long apprenticeship under the elephant catchers of Santhalbari. When Brown *Sahib* saw how capable she was, he approached the chief. The chief liked the idea as he thought it would keep his kingdom hidden from the prying eyes of the scientific and commercial worlds.

On approaching Santhalbari from the Kachugaon side, the sal woodlands give way to a clear patch of grassland ahead of a large expanse of moist deciduous forest. This area marked the start of the official no-go zone. All these years, Brown *Sahib* has managed to keep his men out of this stretch by ensuring the felling zones and the working circle areas were nowhere near it. Ripu is a very large reserve with plenty of good timber zones. With the advent of the train line, preferred timber extractions zones were conveniently selected near the track. Santhalbari is miles away from the train track. The rail tracks made Santhalbari safer and the possibility of discovery by anyone from the Assam side became more remote, till those adamant naturalists turned up.

The stage set for the sighting would be the grassland. The archers would be in the trees overlooking the grassland, but they were just a contingency. Brown *Sahib* was sure that nobody would get past the grassy track. The girl, dressed in a white saree, would be mounted on a giant tusker and would move laterally along the wood on the other side of the grassland, ahead of the wild herd. The party would certainly turn back on seeing the eerie sight. He was relying on the superstitious *mahouts.*

It was around nine in the morning. The party had been on elephant for more than two hours. The guide elephant was leading the party to the designated spot. The instructions were to take a route through the woodland avoiding any clearing or grasslands. These were foraging areas and any wildlife spotting by the naturalists would delay progress. The timing was crucial.

As the party approached the grassy track, Brown *Sahib* instructed his *mahout* to stop while he pretended to inspect the timber quality of some felled logs.

As the five elephants came out into the open patch, a sense of anticipation built amongst the naturalists at the prospect of viewing some wild animals. They were glad to be out of the dark wood and into the grassland that could very well be the habitat of the horned pachyderms. Then one of the naturalists pointed to a herd of elephants. But it wasn't the herd that attracted everyone's attention, but a girl on a giant tusker a few metres ahead of the herd. The *mahouts* reacted with immense fear and immediately prodded their elephants to turn back. One of the naturalists instructed his *mahout* to follow the girl and elephants. The *mahout* protested, but the man took out a pistol and threatened him. The other naturalists did the same. The party started moving rapidly in the direction of the wild herd and the girl, but the moment the elephants reached the middle of the grassy patch, the naturalists fell from the elephants one by one. The archers lost no time. The panic-stricken *mahouts* then turned the elephants back to the woodland. Some of them had seen these spirit-like archers in the treetops, their bow string stretched.'

'What happened was a very unfortunate accident. Brown *Sahib* didn't plan it that way,' Dr Delrome explained. Jenkins was shaking his head, his eyes narrow and gaze fixed down.

'I am not trying to defend my friend. He has killed many people trying to protect the forests of Kachugaon, but he didn't plan the killing of your father. It was an accident. He has regretted it for a long time. And my little girl played a role without even knowing it,' Dr Delrome said.

Raj didn't say anything. He looked at Jenkins. There was sorrow and maybe rising anger. He wasn't sure whether this would lead to closure or retribution.

Chapter 39

Lying on his bed listening to the night birds, Brown *Sahib* mulled over the recent events: who has killed Rajah *Sahib?* Is there a link between Rajah *Sahib* and Gethela's murders? Is Ranger Baruah the the missing link? The thrashing meted out to the captive hadn't revealed any relationship with Baruah. He had insisted that someone from the Paschim Behar palace was directing him and that he had never met or talked to Baruah. He opened his eyes. The room was dark despite the kerosene lamp. He closed his eyes again and took a deep breath hoping to fall asleep. Do I have any personal vendetta against Baruah? But the fact that Manikpur estate was the catcher of the largest number of elephants in the Goalpara forest before its monopoly was seized by Parbatipur estate, made it difficult for Brown *Sahib* to convince himself that Manikpur wouldn't like to regain its lost business. Baruah was the only person set to gain from the situation with his competitor dead.

He could always see Rajah *Sahib's* deep aversion to Baruah.

'You are biased, just because he comes from Manikpur,'

Brown *Sahib* used to tell Rajah *Sahib*.

Eyes heavy with sleep, he felt the Prince's visit was jinxed. Since then, so many things had changed in Kachugaon. Rajah *Sahib* was dead, and Gethela too.

There was a frantic knocking on the main door of *Lal Bungalow*. 'Who is it?' shouted Brown *Sahib* from his room. He wondered where the night watchman was. It seemed that the bastard was always falling asleep.

The flame of the lamp on his bedside table flickered. He looked at his watch. It was one o' clock.

'Who the hell is it?' Brown *Sahib* yelled, as he got up from the bed and collected his beretta from the safe. And then he heard a voice shouting in Santali.

As he opened the door, a tall dark shadow stood in front of him. 'The Prince and *Sahib* from Dhubri have reached Santhalbari along with Doctor *Sahib*,' the shadow blurted out before Brown *Sahib* could say anything.

It was a eunuch guard. He knew Santhalbari had a dozen eunuch guards who were responsible for guarding key vantage points and the chief's female quarters. They were a ruthless lot. He realised that he couldn't show any signs of weakness.

'You don't worry. Nothing will happen to Santhalbari,' he managed to say.

The eunuch guard didn't look convinced. 'And *Baba*... has not come back to the village,' he growled.

Baba, the eunuch guard in the charge of the girl in the cottage was missing. Brown *Sahib* raised the lamp and looked at the eunuch's sweaty face. He didn't like the look in his visitor's eyes.

The eunuch retreated a few paces. Brown *Sahib* knew that the eunuch had enough deftness to send an arrow from his bow straight to his heart in under a second. Brown *Sahib* realised there wasn't anything he could do about Santhalbari. Its discovery was inevitable. Perhaps getting rid of some hot-blooded elements from the settlement might help it assimilate with the outside world.

'I have to do this,' Brown *Sahib* muttered as he quickly raised his hand. One pop and the eunuch slumped to the ground as the bullet hit his forehead.

He looked around and felt thankful that the watchman wasn't there to see. This was the first time in three decades that someone from Santhalbari had contacted him directly at *Lal Bungalow*. And this was the first time someone from Santhalbari had dared to threaten him.

He rushed inside the bungalow and into the safe house that held the arms and ammunition, and items seized from poachers. He picked up a dusty, web-covered rhino horn. He went outside and wet the horn in a muddy puddle before shoving it in the dead eunuch's hand.

He rushed to the backyard to wake up his sleeping servants and cooks. And then he went to the last room of the quarters where the night watchman was sleeping peacefully. The watchman was woken up by a few kicks to his stomach.

'A poacher has come all the way to my bungalow to kill me and you are asleep!' He lined up the guards and the attendants.

'By morning this body should be taken inside the forest. Recover everything that killer has before you dispose of the body.' He pointed to a forest path behind the quarters. Next to the cook's quarters, there was a bamboo gate. If one walked a few hundred yards past it, the roar of a tiger or the purr of lesser cats was often heard.

'Nobody should know about this attack. You will all lose your jobs,' Brown *Sahib* pointed his finger at the night watchman who was bent over with pain. 'Especially you!'

Brown *Sahib* knew they would have to walk for a mile or so. The path was well trodden at the start but soon it became difficult to navigate as it had been a while since the undergrowth had been cleared. With no forestry activities going on during the rainy season, and the fact no illegal fellers dared to intrude on the forest behind *Lal Bungalow*, he was sure the eunuch's body wouldn't be discovered before it was eaten by the carnivores.

He was keen for them to dispose of the body before the superstitious residents of Kachugaon and other forest guards saw it. And more importantly, Jenkins shouldn't know about this encounter.

Returning to his room, his mind raced; he couldn't fathom why the doctor would take Jenkins and the Prince to Santhalbari. There were two men other than him who knew about the existence of Santhalbari. One was dead, and the other had done the unthinkable.

The room suddenly felt hot and stuffy. He opened the window; he looked out at the dense foliage of the forest circling the backyard of *Lal Bungalow*. An owl hooted for the last time as it flew past the moonlight-splashed trees and the scurrying of rodents ruffled the leaves. When sleep came, the shafts of morning light were coming through the window. A cuckoo singing soothed him.

By the time he awoke, it was late morning. A groggy Brown *Sahib* tottered out to the backyard.

'Why didn't you all wake me up?' he thundered at the idling servants and the guards. He went over to the night guard who still looked scared. 'Has the body been taken care of?'

The guards nodded.

'Good, now get Ranger Miri.'

He went back to his room and pulled out a large suitcase. He wasn't sure how long his stay in Dhubri could be. He would wait there until Jenkins returned and he would surrender all his secrets. He was ready for any consequences.

A short while later, the sickly old Ranger Miri appeared.

'Listen, I am going to Dhubri now. You are in charge. Make sure that killer from Paschim Behar doesn't escape. You and Das continue to keep an eye on Baruah. Make sure he does not leave his place. I will take care of him after I come back from Dhubri,' Brown *Sahib* blurted out his instructions.

Miri looked nervously at Brown *Sahib*. 'Sir, I have to

report an encounter,' Miri said feebly. A pair of treepies was screeching high up in the forest. Brown *Sahib* was getting impatient.

'How many were killed?' he asked flippantly. He knew it was the season of the river bandits. He had given the patrolling forest staff a free rein to shoot dead any poachers or illegal loggers entering his reserved forests by the river routes. They were supposed to report these encounters into the departmental log book.

'One person,' Miri fumbled.

'That's all? You are in charge from now. Write the report. I need to go,' Brown *Sahib* said dismissing the ranger.

Brown *Sahib* knew that unlike Ranger Das and the other ruthless young deputy rangers, Miri didn't have much of a killer instinct. He knew the ranger's tally in his long career would be less than a dozen. He had much bigger problems than some petty timber smuggler shot dead inside Ripu.

As Miri was walking away, Brown *Sahib* shouted after him, 'In which area did the encounter take place? How many of them were there?'

'Sir, it wasn't in the reserve. It was at Fakiragram,' Miri said apologetically.

'Fakiragram? Who did you shoot there?' Brown *Sahib* was astounded. The Fakiragram timber depot, in the middle of the small town, was the last place to shoot a smuggler. 'And what the hell were you doing there?'

'Sir, I was standing in for Baruah. It was dark, and I couldn't see properly. I told him to stop. I was thinking about the arson the other day. I shot, not realising it was Gethela,' Ranger Miri said as he broke down.

'You shot Gethela?' Brown *Sahib* asked seething in anger. 'And what else did you do? Did you take bullets from our storage?'

'My ammunition got wet as my roof has been leaking. I just took three bullets from the store. It was dark. I had no idea it was Gethela. I didn't even know that he had died as he fled after I fired. Or else I would have reported it straight away.'

He went back to the bedroom and took out the letter Ranger Das had brought him after searching Baruah's house. He read it again: both sides. He shook his head throwing the letter to the floor in despair. Nothing made any sense to him.

Chapter 40

Sitting under the gazebo in the courtyard of the chief's house, the trio of visitors watched an enchanting dance performance by the Santali girls. The girls wore red, white and black wooden jewellery and knee-length sarees. They danced rhythmically to the sound of drums being played by the men. In the gleaming moonlight, Raj craned his neck to see if Teesta was amongst the dancers. If she were there, she would have surely stood out.

'Don't you think we should be taking your daughter with us now?' Raj broached the topic, raising his voice to be heard over the loud music. Jenkins nodded in agreement and looked at Dr Delrome. The three of them got up and walked over to the edge of the forest while the festivities carried on behind them. The smell of stewed venison wafted into Raj's nostrils. High up above them, a giant squirrel jumped from one moonlit tree to another.

'I know these people. They know me very well too. But when it comes to Teesta, they don't feel anyone has the right to make decisions about her future apart from one person,' Dr

Delrome said.

'Who?' both Raj and Jenkins asked in unison.

'Brown *Sahib*. Only a superhuman could have done what he did, bringing that little baby girl to this place. At that time, the villagers were very edgy. They used to kill at the slightest pretext. Brown *Sahib* practically tamed them. He made them promise that they would take care of the baby girl. He assured them continued protection from his department.'

'Does he still come here?' Jenkins asked, perplexed at how his deputy had pulled off such a clandestine operation.

'He used to come regularly when he was younger. He had a bevy of Santali beauties here waiting for him. He may look gruff now, but he was once a colourful character,' Dr Delrome said with a loud laugh.

'He became a part of this society?' Raj queried, wondering how the brawny forester could have mingled so easily with the villagers.

'Yes, he grew up in the district of Santal Pargana in the state of Behar. His Australian missionary father worked amongst the Santali people of the region. In fact, his father wanted him to become a missionary like him. Brown *Sahib* studied in the local missionary school along with other Santali kids. That's how he learnt the language. The villagers accepted him because he could speak the language.'

'Let's not put our old friend through the trouble of trekking through miles of forest from Kachugaon. Let's instead call on him in Kachugaon and discuss everything in detail. My daughter has lived here for twenty-four years. She can stay a few more days,' Dr Delrome said. They had reached the edge of the forest. The tall dark trees stood as sentinels. Raj knew walking any further would take them to the wall of sal logs.

'Let's go back to the village.' Dr Delrome said. 'It isn't safe to venture any further.'

The trio started walking back towards the centre of the village. As they approached the dancing crowd, a few drunk girls came over to them and pulled Jenkins towards the dance area. Soon a tall white man was dancing in the circle amongst a group of Santali girls. He was drinking from a pitcher that was being passed from one hand to another.

Raj also partook of the fermented rice alcohol. There were meat dishes of various unidentifiable animals. There were also a few rice dishes cooked with vegetables grown around the houses or picked from the forest. The food was simple, much like the joy of the villagers dancing under the moonlight. They were oblivious to the changes that might be coming their way, under the administration of the Assam forest department.

Raj realised that Dr Delrome had consumed more rice alcohol than his old body could tolerate. The fermented rice liquor, with the aid of yeast and various assorted plant products, was a very potent drink.

The doctor gulped down one last cup and licked his fingers dipped in a chutney of tamarind, chilli and salt.

Jenkins joined them, sweating and smelling of alcohol. He didn't hold back and did justice to the platter laid before them.

The dancing and the drums stopped. The drunken villagers broke into spontaneous songs while returning to their homes.

'Are we telling Indira Devi about her daughter?' Raj asked Dr Delrome.

'She has lost her husband. If I break the news to her, she will feel cheated all over again. Will that make things easy for my daughter? How will she feel when she comes to learn her mother was a queen and yet she had to lead her life in the forest?' Dr Delrome said.

'Will Indira Devi refuse to accept her?' Raj persisted.

'No. She will be devastated if she comes to know of it. But she is a mother.' Raj didn't say anything. 'You were maybe nine or ten when we came to the palace. We would have felt like intruders to you. You have seen Indira through the eyes of a hurt child, whose mother's place was taken by this new woman. Maybe when you were growing up, you began to feel she was responsible for your mother's death. I can tell you that the *Maharaja* and your family's good health was the only thing I always had in mind. I was in a dilemma. I had just left a government job to take up the offer in the palace and my employer was trying to seduce the girl I wanted to marry. Later when I saw the feelings were mutual, I gave her up. But I didn't give up on my pledge to look after the health and wellbeing of those entrusted to my care.' Dr Delrome's voice choked up.

'I couldn't save your mother despite my best efforts. I wanted to take her to Calcutta. If I had, she might have been alive today. She had typhoid, which she might have gotten during the hunting trip. But your father ignored me. I know he is dead now, but you should know certain things. Your mother would be crying out for water, and the nurse, who was supposed to be looking after her, was kept busy by the *Maharaja* for his own pleasure. Your father, in fact, wanted your mother to die sooner so that he could attend the Delhi Durbar with a young *Maharani.*'

Raj didn't say anything. He thought of his father's portly shape and round jovial face. Could he have been so heartless? And to the woman, he supposedly loved and was married to for years? He thought of the night in the forest and the journey again to meet the girl.

'Anything is possible,' he murmured.

'On the other hand, let me tell you, Indira had no ill intention. She didn't even realise that the *Maharaja* wished to get rid of his wife. Her only fault was that she reciprocated his advances. But I ask you, did she have any choice?'

Raj realised his stepmother had never really acted in an offensive manner to him or to his brothers, even after she bore three boys of her own. Had he been harsh on her due to prejudices carried from childhood?

'She was actually quite thankful that you accepted her into the family, in the early days of her marriage. She knew she could not take your mother's place, but she never wished to cross swords with you. You are the one amongst all the children who she holds in the highest regard.'

Raj's thoughts shifted to what her daughter was doing at that time. Was she spending the night with someone? Raj couldn't hold his curiosity. 'Does your daughter stay in the temple?'

'No, she stays with the chief's father who treats her as his daughter.'

It was well past midnight. All the villagers had left except a few who were too drunk and had fallen asleep under the night sky. They reached the cottage they had been allocated. As they entered, Raj wasn't sure whether they would get any sleep.

What if I had never taken the train trip that day? What if I had not seen the old man getting down from the train? What if I didn't have that story session with Gethela? What if Baruah didn't challenge me to take the train ride to find out for myself? Would she have remained here, like this?

The thought horrified him, making him shudder and he made up his mind. He would do whatever was needed to rescue his stepsister.

Chapter 41

It was only four in the morning, but the whole village was bathed in the glorious light of dawn. The archers were already waiting outside the cottage to take them to the river. The village was still asleep after a long night of feasting, dancing and drinking. They crossed the first stream on the dinghies and walked across the river island. It was a slow and laboured walk for the three sleep-deprived bodies. Even the whistle of the fishing eagle seemed piercing to Raj.

By the time they reached the other side of the island, it was almost six. Tapash and the boatman were waiting to take them to Kumargram. The stop at Kumargram was brief and soon they were on the road to Kachugaon. Raj leaned back in the car seat and closed his eyes, enjoying the warmth of the sun.

They reached Kachugaon in under three hours.

A surprised Brown *Sahib* greeted them at *Lal Bungalow*. A quick 'Welcome back' was all he could manage to say to Raj. But he was visibly pleased to see Dr Delrome and they hugged each other like long lost brothers. Raj was amazed to witness the affection of two men he not long ago, would have thought were strangers to each other.

Raj noticed there was a difference in Brown *Sahib*. In just a week's time, it seemed he had mellowed somewhat and was more at ease. He looked happier — as if some load had been lifted off his shoulders.

'I was about to start for Dhubri,' he said to Jenkins. 'I hope you had a good trip to Paschim Behar.'

'Yes, it was a very eventful trip. Why are you going to Dhubri?' Jenkins enquired. 'Luckily, we managed to reach you early. Otherwise, it would have been a wasted trip for all of us. We need to talk.' He didn't mention Santhalbari.

'We do indeed have a lot to catch up on — both work-related and personal. Most importantly, I have some new insights into Rajah *Sahib's* murder. I have the murderer here in Kachugaon. Now that His Highness and our friend Dr Delrome are here, we can see if he has any connection to the palace,' Brown *Sahib* said.

Raj and Dr Delrome looked puzzled. Brown *Sahib* gestured with a wave of his hand. 'I will explain but first, let me arrange for your accommodation.' He clasped his hands together and shouted out to his orderlies, giving them instructions.

Raj and Jenkins were allotted the IB. Tapash and the drivers were to be accommodated in the cook's quarters.

'You will stay with me,' he said to Dr Delrome. 'Let's meet at the IB dining room for lunch after you settle in.'

Raj hadn't seen Brown *Sahib* so hospitable. He and Jenkins proceeded to the IB. To his delight, he found he had been allotted the same room as last time.

All three met in the dining hall at noon. Raj felt refreshed after getting some rest. Brown *Sahib* was seated at the head of the table, which had already been laid. The cooks arrived with dishes one by one, all Raj's favourites. Raj couldn't contain his curiosity any longer. 'Did you by any chance ask anyone at the palace about my food preferences?' He looked at Jenkins who shook his head.

'Your Highness, the cooks know your choices by heart,' Brown *Sahib* said.

Raj wasn't sure whether or not he was joking. He picked up a succulent piece of kabab.

'Your Highness, we have your attacker in our custody. He made two attempts on your life. God knows how many more he would have made if you hadn't left suddenly. He says he was sent from your palace,' Brown *Sahib* gestured to a guard to get the man.

'Has he admitted to his crimes?' Dr Delrome asked, speaking for the first time. 'Was he also involved in Rajah *Sahib's* murder?'

'Let's finish our lunch. Then we will meet the bastard,' Brown *Sahib* said through a large mouthful of rice and chicken curry. Everyone at the table devoured the food hungrily. They had not realised how famished they were.

As Brown *Sahib* struggled to stand up, he released a

series of burps. A few morsels of food clung to his moustache.

'Have you got him?' He thundered from the hall.

As they went outside, Raj saw the guards dragging in a man in very a poor condition.

'That bastard is from your palace,' Brown *Sahib* said.

Raj didn't recognise him. He looked like any of the hundreds of people who worked at the palace.

'Maharaja, please save me,' the man pleaded, meeting Raj's eyes as he tottered towards him with folded hands. He prostrated and tried to touch Raj's feet and suddenly began to wail.

'Who is he? What has he done?' Raj scrutinized the man.

'Well if he had his way, you wouldn't be standing here, Your Highness,' Brown *Sahib* said. 'Do you remember the party I threw in your honour? This scoundrel tried to mix your drink with a lethal poison he brought all the way from Calcutta. He knows a lot about elephants too. He was the one who let that elephant loose on you. And he was the one who...' Brown *Sahib* paused, choked with emotion. He bent over and picked the man up from the ground and gave him a thunderous slap. 'He was the man who poisoned Rajah *Sahib*. Don't be deceived by his wretched look. This contemptible man is a murderer.' He trembled with rage, now grabbing the man by the hair.

'Your Highness, I know this man. He used to work in our elephant stable as a labourer. He also used to dabble with marijuana and other stuff.' It was Tapash who spoke. 'He used to supply marijuana to Prince Indra,' he murmured to Raj. 'If you ask him who sent him here, he would surely say the *Maharani*. Your brother was a very smart man. He must have employed a middle man to engage this man, and have told the middle man to convey that he was acting on the *Maharani's* behest.'

Raj went over to the man who was standing in a hunched position. 'Who sent you here?'

The man looked at Raj. Then flicking his glance at Tapash he said, 'A man from the palace told me that I had to come to Kachugaon and do certain things for the *Maharani*.'

'Did I not tell you, Your Highness? He was sent by someone from your brother's camp. But they have made him believe that he was carrying out orders at the behest of the *Maharani*.' Tapash said.

'So, it was Indra after all,' Raj's voice was heavy. He looked at Dr Delrome. 'There is no point grilling him any more as Indra is dead. What do we do with him?'

'I am not going to let him go easily. He has not yet admitted to Rajah *Sahib's* murder,' Brown *Sahib* said grabbing the man by the neck and shaking him. 'Enough of lies! Tell us today why you killed Rajah *Sahib*. Who ordered you to kill Rajah *Sahib*?'

'I didn't kill Rajah *Sahib*. Believe me,' the man cried, folding his hands and looking around imploringly.

Raj didn't feel like spending any more time looking at the wailing man.

'Brown *Sahib*, hand him over to the police or take him wherever you like. I don't want to see this man again.' His voice broke as he thought of the betrayal.

'Don't worry, I have it all lined up for him. He will go to Raimona. A black panther is stalking the villagers. He will save the village from the beast,' Brown *Sahib* said with a menacing tone. He gave a kick to the bundle of a man, who had slumped to the ground. 'Lock this goat up. Feed him properly. We will despatch him to number sixteen tomorrow.' The guards dragged the man away with Tapash following behind.

'Did he have an accomplice here?' Dr Delrome asked.

Brown *Sahib* looked at Jenkins. 'This is somewhat sensitive. It's why I wanted to go to Dhubri. Can we go inside and discuss?' Brown *Sahib* spoke with a new seriousness.

Once they were all inside, Brown *Sahib* closed the door. 'I think he has a local master. Someone who ensured you stayed here long enough for that man to complete his task.'

'Who is it?' Dr Delrome asked. Raj knew who it could be.

Brown *Sahib* didn't say anything. He stood up and took a folded piece of paper from his pocket. He handed it to Dr Delrome. 'This is what we found in one of our ranger's quarters. It looks like a letter from the Paschim Behar palace.' Dr Delrome read the letter and then handed it to Raj.

Raj read it.

Dear Amaresh,

Greetings for old time's sake!

As you may know, my elder brother Prince Raj Narayan will be visiting your forest. May I request you to take good care of him during his stay? On the other side of the page, based on the information provided by the palace cooks, I have listed his favourite foods.

Hope to see you soon.

Your friend

Indra Narayan

By the way, I have already requested our treasury to transfer Rs. 50,000 to your estate

Jenkins was confused. 'Who are we talking about?'

'Sir, it is Ranger Baruah,' Brown *Sahib* clarified. 'It seems he received fifty thousand from the palace.'

Raj read the letter again and then turned it over to see the list of his favourite foods. He handed it to Jenkins.

'Why doesn't it say anything? Why would he write such a general letter to his friend unless he needed specific help?' Jenkins said.

Dr Delrome took the letter again and showed to Raj. 'I thought Indra's handwriting was elaborate.'

Raj looked at it critically, studying the handwriting. Indra used to write to him regularly when he was in London and he had seen Indra's handwriting many times on official documents.

'More than the handwriting, the food list-- anyone could obtain a list of my favourites from the palace cooks.' Raj said, still mulling it over.

'Maybe the letter is far more cryptic than it seems. By 'good care' did he mean finishing you off? Remember they are friends from college days. They may have some code language between them. And the fund transfer was a reward to his friend for taking 'good care' of you,' Dr Delrome said, looking around at the others to see their reactions.

'Have you asked Baruah about the letter?' Jenkins asked.

'What's the use? He will lie,' Brown *Sahib* said.

'Are you going to ask?' Jenkins snapped.

'We picked it up from his house without his knowledge.' 'Where is Baruah now?' Jenkins asked.

'He is in his quarters. He is under house arrest.' Brown *Sahib* declared.

'Under house arrest? Are you a police officer? No, Mr. Brown, you don't have the authority to arrest a departmental colleague,' Jenkins shouted, pushing the door open. 'Why have you arrested him?' He turned to Brown *Sahib*, confronting him like he had never done before.

'He is under arrest for murdering Paritosh Baruah, *zamindar* of Parbatipur.' Brown *Sahib* said, looking his superior straight in the eye.

Chapter 42

Dr Delrome took his friend aside and asked, 'How can you be so sure about Rajah *Sahib*? That letter doesn't say anything about Rajah *Sahib*.'

'It doesn't say anything about Rajah *Sahib* because the letter doesn't have anything to do with Rajah *Sahib*. But it says one thing about Baruah. He is a greedy man. A bad man,' Brown *Sahib* said through gritted teeth, his face red with uncontrolled rage.

'It is because of his greed that he killed Rajah *Sahib*, using that girl from Calcutta. The girl goes to his place at ten after spending the evening with Rajah *Sahib*. She spends the night with Baruah and Rajah *Sahib* dies the same night. Was I born yesterday to not see what's going on?' Brown *Sahib* thundered.

Dr Delrome led his friend further away and said something that seemed to pacify him. After some time, he returned to Raj and Jenkins. 'We are going to Rajah *Sahib's* tent.'

It was a short drive to the elephant camp. The massive wooden gate of the camp was closed. Brown *Sahib* shouted and honked a few times. A few workers came running and opened the gate. The camp looked like a different place. There were fewer men and no elephants.

'Where are the men?' Jenkins said. 'What have you done with the elephants?'

Brown *Sahib* parked the car near the entrance and shouted to a man sitting outside a tent.

'I told you about Baruah. They are a greedy family,' he said.

'What has this to do with Baruah?' Jenkins practically growled.

'Most of the men were uncertain about their future. I assured them that our department would look after them, but many felt there were better opportunities outside. They have moved to the Manikpur estate where Baruah's father is the *zamindar*.'

'And what have you done with the elephants?' Jenkins asked with mounting trepidation.

'They remain the property of the forest department.'

'But, where are they? The last time we were here, the place was full of them.'

People had started to gather around them, including few forest department personnel. Raj noticed the ranger who had escorted him on the train trip.

'I will explain everything,' Brown *Sahib* said to Jenkins and then turned to the ranger. 'How are things here, Das? Whose truck is that?' he asked, pointed to a large truck parked behind a fig tree.

'Sir, police personnel from Dhubri are here,' Ranger Das said.

Brown *Sahib's* eyes nearly popped out of his head. 'The police are here, and no one informed me?'

'No, sir, they came this morning. They didn't allow anyone to leave the camp.'

'Let's go to the camp office,' Brown *Sahib* said.

A policeman stepped out just as they reached the office tent. 'Hello, Bert, good to see you.' It was Baker, Dhubri's police chief.

'Hello Baker! So, the police have reached the crime scene,' Jenkins said.

'We had to. Pressure has been mounting from Shillong to solve the murder of Rajah *Sahib*. I tried contacting you in Dhubri. They said you had gone to the *Maharaja's* ceremony.'

'What have you found out?' Raj asked.

The police chief was surprised by the query but before he could respond, Jenkins announced, 'His Highness, *Maharaja* Raj Narayan.'

'Apologies, Your Highness, I didn't recognise you. You look quite different from the other day. Let's all go inside, and we can talk directly to the CID personnel from Gauhati.' They were all ushered into the big tent. An attendant came with tea and biscuits. All of them including the two CID sleuths sat around a large circular table.

'We have come to a conclusive finding regarding Rajah *Sahib's* unnatural death. Our friends from Gauhati have found many empty bottles of barbital, which is often taken as a sleeping aid. Their conclusion was that the death was caused by excessive consumption of barbital while heavily under the influence of alcohol.' Baker pronounced. The CID men nodded.

'Rajah *Sahib* came from your bungalow that day, didn't he? Was he drunk?' Dr Delrome asked Brown *Sahib*.

'Yes, he was quite drunk. I asked him to stay at my place. But he wouldn't listen.'

'We also arrested the girl who stayed with him before his death,' Baker said. 'She was passing on messages to a person working at the camp. We understand that person has been apprehended by your department. But we had to let her go as she had no other information to divulge. She received money for her services from her pimp in Dhubri, who was the conduit for passing on the information coming from Paschim Behar. Our men have arrested the pimp also. But the girl didn't have any role. She was here in Kachugaon on business and earned extra money for acting as a courier.'

'But she went to one of my ranger's houses that night,' Brown *Sahib* said.

'Yes, we know she went to stay at Ranger Baruah's place. That doesn't mean anything,' Baker said.

'Sir,' Choudhury, who was standing with Das, interjected. 'Rajah *Sahib* had asked me to keep Champa reserved for the night he was returning from Paschim Behar. But he returned a day early. That night Champa was meant to stay at Baruah *Babu's* house. I knew Rajah *Sahib* would be mad at me, so I asked her to stay in the camp for him and then go to Baruah Babu's place later on.'

By now Brown *Sahib* was shaking his head. 'Do you do any other useful work in this camp?'

'While talking to the girl, we found out that Rajah *Sahib* was already in very bad shape. According to her, he had already taken quite a few tablets before she left him,' one of the CID men said.

'We couldn't find this Baruah. Do you know where he is?' Baker asked Jenkins.

Jenkins looked at Brown *Sahib*.

'He is in Kachugaon,' Brown *Sahib* said, his head hung low. He looked at Baker and said, 'He is not feeling very well. He is resting to recover.'

Baker looked at the senior CID sleuth and asked, 'Do we really need to talk to him? I don't see any need. I think we have what we needed.'

Brown *Sahib* heaved a sigh of relief. 'He isn't going anywhere. We can always send him to Dhubri if needed.'

The officers nodded.

'What we need to confirm is whether he took barbital only on that night or whether he was a habitual user. I think we will have to go to his estate to talk to his personal physician,' said the senior CID official.

'There is no need for that. I knew him more than his family doctor did, if he even had one. He had been on barbital for a long time. I told him many times to reduce his dependency. But that night I think it was a combination of too much alcohol, barbital, mental anguish, exhaustion and maybe sex. How much can an old man take? He was in his seventies. Quite a few years older than me,' Dr Delrome said. 'By the way,' he turned to the CID officials, 'did you ask that girl Champa whether they were physically intimate that night?'

'We did. She said he wasn't capable of lifting his *dhoti*, leave aside do anything. The camp attendants who went to serve him the evening meal confirmed his inebriated state.'

Baker stood up. 'I suggest let's not drag this out for long. He had a good life. We'll pray for the peace of the departed soul. I will close the case with the help of these two gentlemen.'

The three policemen left with due permission and headed outside to board their waiting police truck.

Dr Delrome looked at Choudhury. 'I want to see Rajah *Sahib's* tent.'

As they entered the tent, a stale smell hit them. It was very different from the last time when the aroma of women's perfume and incense had greeted them. The tent looked exactly as it had before but was very hot and stuffy. Raj came out quickly, followed by Jenkins. Brown *Sahib* and Dr Delrome remained inside.

Raj looked around. It was a hot afternoon. There was anxiety on the faces in the crowd that had gathered. They were fanning themselves with small hand towels. Ranger Das was urging them to get back to work.

With all the elephants gone, what will they do? Raj wondered.

Dr Delrome and Brown *Sahib* came out of the tent. Dr Delrome showed them a small brown glass bottle. 'He had dozens of these stacked insides. This was his own doing. Nobody had to give him anything more. He also had enough alcohol in there to drown an entire garrison.'

'Now that we know what happened to Rajah *Sahib*,' Jenkins looked at Brown *Sahib*, 'can we please have Baruah released?'

'It was just a precaution. He was never officially under arrest,' Brown *Sahib* muttered. 'Hey, Das!' He quickly called. The unfriendly ranger came running and went away reluctantly after hearing Brown *Sahib's* instructions.

'Where are all the elephants?' Jenkins asked again.

Brown *Sahib* took a deep breath. 'After Rajah *Sahib's* death, this place was a riot of high emotions. There were rumours he had died because of a curse. Many *mahouts* and elephant catchers were afraid to work here anymore. Then talk started that they would be better off working in an estate than for the forest department. They were concerned about their rations; who would feed them now that Rajah *Sahib* was gone. He was a rich man. We struggle to pay our employees every month. Many of them left to work with contractors and others have gone to Manikpur in the hope that the estate will be doing the elephant catching from next year. We ended up with many elephants but few men.'

'What did you do then?' There was tension in Jenkins' face.

'I released all the uncontrollable beasts to the Kachugaon reserve. Broke a section of the log wall,' Brown *Sahib* said pointing to the far side of the camp. 'The elephants slowly disappeared. They were the property of the forest department and they remain property of the forest department, but imagine the cost we would have had to incur to feed them and their men in the camp.'

Jenkins listened quietly. In the end, he said, 'You released them all?'

'No, the trained elephants have been sent to different ranges for patrolling purposes. I have also sent twenty elephants to the timber depot. They can be useful there.'

'This camp was Rajah *Sahib's* lifeblood. He managed it for decades. And you dismantled it in days,' Dr Delrome said, bemused.

'If something is generating revenue, I am all for maintaining it. But this camp would have been a huge liability. We have already received the money for this year's catch from Rajah *Sahib*. But we have released the elephants. Someone will bid for the contract to catch them again. We will receive payment again for the same elephants.'

'What about the people in Rajah *Sahib's* estate?' Jenkins asked.

'He doesn't have anyone. That's why no one will question our actions. The estate is run by useless people like him,' Brown *Sahib* pointed to Choudhury who didn't seem to take any offence. 'All these people are too old and lazy. We too will have to revamp our department. We need young rangers.'

'Young rangers like Baruah?' Jenkins smiled.

Brown *Sahib* smiled back. Raj realised he had started to like the burly man.

Chapter 43

The dinner laid out on the table troubled Raj: everything from sweet corn soup to tangy mustard oil onion salad, to fine cut potato fries to mutton chops to peas and minced meat to red hot chicken curry, all his favourites from childhood, all there. Even the custard was pink with glazed cherries and no banana. It seemed, thanks to the letter menu, everything was made for Raj with no consideration for the preferences of others.

There was a knock at the door. 'Yes, come in,' Brown *Sahib* said. The door opened and a dishevelled man with an unkempt beard stood in the doorway.

'Ranger Baruah!' Raj exclaimed.

Baruah offered his salutations to Raj and then said to Brown *Sahib*, 'Sir, Das told me you wanted to see me.'

'It wasn't urgent. You could have come tomorrow,' Brown *Sahib* said, totally unprepared to be receiving the ranger in that state.

'Are you all right Baruah?' Jenkins asked with concern.

'I am all right. The lack of sunlight made me sick. I was relieved to report for duty.' He managed a faint smile.

Jenkins stood up. 'There is nothing to worry about now. The mystery of Rajah *Sahib's* death has been solved. There was a misunderstanding. I am sorry for that. I apologise on behalf of the department,' he said placing a hand on the ranger's shoulder.

'I hope those bastards treated you well,' Brown *Sahib* said as if his rangers had acted on their own. Then he said something unexpected. 'I am sorry to have put you through this.'

Baruah looked at his senior. He didn't say anything.

Dr Delrome nudged Raj. 'Ask him about the letter.'

Yes, the case of Rajah *Sahib's* death had been solved. But Indra's letter was still puzzling.

'You never mentioned to me that you were a friend of Indra's,' Raj looked at Baruah's tired face. 'And what does this letter mean?' He handed the letter to him.

'Indra was a good friend of mine in ranger college. Letter or no letter, I tried to take good care of you. I apologise that due to departmental order I couldn't accompany you on the train trips,' He looked at Brown *Sahib* who pretended to be looking the other way.

'You were very helpful to His Highness. But this letter

from Indra is confusing us. What is this about fifty thousand?' Dr Delrome interjected.

'I don't know about any fifty thousand.'

Dr Delrome didn't look satisfied. 'Why didn't you tell His Highness that you knew his brother?'

'Why should I? I am a ranger on official duty. I did not wish to flaunt my personal connections. But then there were these letters...' Digging into his pockets, he took out two more papers and threw them on the table, almost in Dr Delrome's face.

'Read them. I know Indra, he wouldn't have done this. One letter said, don't tell my brother you know me. I had suddenly started receiving letters from a friend who I had not heard from in years. I still don't know who sent these letters. The only thing I found useful was His Highness's food preferences, which I passed on to the cooks. In fact, I wrote a letter back to Indra asking him about the letters, but I don't know whether he received it.' Ranger Baruah's tone was no longer subdued.

'So, you think those letters were written by someone other than Indra?' Dr Delrome asked.

'They had the seal of Paschim Behar. They were signed in Indra's name. Whether he wrote them or not, I don't know,' the ranger said impatiently. The house arrest and now the questioning over the letters were taking a toll on him.

'Do you know Indra is dead? He died under unfortunate circumstances,' Raj said.

'What? No! How did it happen, Your Highness?' Baruah shook his head in disbelief.

'Yes, it is very unfortunate. And you being just a little more cooperative regarding the letters would help us in unravelling the mystery of his death,' Dr Delrome said as kindly as he could.

'What more do you want from me? I have given you the letters. Indra was a caring man, but he wouldn't write to tell me to do the obvious,' Baruah said. 'Frankly speaking, after reading the last letter regarding that fifty thousand rupee transfer, I thought it was a joke.'

Baruah paused for a moment, lost in thought, and then continued, 'All I can see is that somebody is trying to implicate me and Indra in some wrongdoing. These letters, particularly the third one was sent to give the impression that Indra was paying me for some favour.'

'As you can imagine, these letters are causing us some amount of grief as there were two attempts on His Highness's life,' Dr Delrome said slowly, his steel blue eyes piercing through Baruah.

'How does that involve me? Why would I try to kill anyone even if someone gave me a hundred thousand? Just because I am working as a ranger doesn't mean I am short of money.' Raj never imagined the friendly young ranger could fly into such a rage. His tone had lost all subservience and now he spoke in confidence that bordered on arrogance.

'I love nature. I wanted to be independent. That's why I am here. Not for money. Excuse me for saying this but I can assure you my estate could employ all the people of the Kachugaon division with double the salary.'

Raj realised it was no longer Ranger Baruah, but the scion of the Manikpur zamindari Amaresh Baruah speaking. 'There is a limit to my patience. I could have it conveyed through Shillong that I should be given the respect I deserve and not treated the way I have been so far.'

Jenkins put an arm around the young ranger and took him outside.

Brown *Sahib* gave a sheepish look and said, 'I think he is totally innocent.'

'You old bastard,' Dr Delrome muttered under his breath. Both Raj and Dr Delrome couldn't contain their laughter.

'Your Highness, I think you should be going back to the IB. It's been a long day for you all,' Brown *Sahib* said to Raj. 'You, my friend, are not going anywhere,' he said turning to Dr Delrome. 'We have got a lot to talk about.'

'Rajah *Sahib's* spirit is angry with you for letting all his elephants escape,' Dr Delrome said with a chuckle.

Suddenly, the head cook Bhola appeared near the door and whispered something to Brown *Sahib*.

'You get lost and tell them to keep an eye on him,' Brown *Sahib* said to the cook.

'Everything all right?' Raj asked.

Brown *Sahib* paused, then said, 'Why don't you rest? We can discuss it tomorrow.'

'Something is not right. Is the captured man causing trouble?' Dr Delrome asked. Jenkins and Baruah joined them. Baruah had regained his composure.

'Now that all of you are here and His Highness is not yet ready to retire for the day, let's get this sorted,' Brown *Sahib* said.

'What has happened now?' A frown appeared on Jenkin's face.

'It is regarding the attendant who came with His Highness,' Brown *Sahib* said. 'Your Highness,' Brown *Sahib* turned to Raj. 'How long have you known this attendant of yours?'

'Who? Tapash?'

'Yes.'

'Why, what has he done?'

'My man reported that he has been talking to that man from Paschim Behar.'

'So?' Dr Delrome said. 'They come from the same place. Maybe Tapash knows him.'

'No, they are more than acquaintances. My people know what they are saying. They heard the two of them having a long discussion.'

'How can Tapash be in collusion with any such person?' Raj queried. 'He is my most trusted aide.'

'Since when, Your Highness, if I may ask?' Brown *Sahib* asked as if he was the investigative authority.

'Well, he has been with me since my return from London. Maybe since the last three years.'

'Three years? That's all?'

Raj looked at Dr Delrome and asked, 'Anything about Tapash that I need to know?'

'Your Highness, one incident, medical though. He was admitted to the hospital I was working at, around four years ago,' Dr Delrome said.

'What is unusual about that?'

'It was a case of rectal prolapse. He was sodomised by someone in the palace. Then his silence was bought with money. And when you came back from London, he was given the non-demanding task of looking after your needs.'

'Who did it? Surely not Indra?' Raj asked.

'No, it was done by someone whose preference is not women. Indra was quite fond of women,' Dr Delrome said.

It was then Raj knew who he was referring to.

'Can we discuss Tapash's medical conditions tomorrow?' Jenkins said. He looked disapprovingly at Brown *Sahib*.

'Gentleman, I seriously think His Highness should retire. You too doctor. You didn't sleep last night.'

'I am not that tired, I'm not the one who danced with the Santali beauties the whole night,' Dr Delrome said. Brown *Sahib* looked quizzically at Jenkins.

'Even so, let's pick this up in the morning,' Jenkins said, turning to Raj. 'Let's return to the IB for tonight, Your Highness.'

Raj relented. As he was walking back to the IB with Jenkins, he remembered Tapash's whisper in his ear. Tapash had urged him to ask the man who had sent him. He had said that the man would say the *Maharani* because Indra was very smart as if he wanted Raj to believe that everything had been orchestrated by Indra. This was the first time Raj had sensed something in his tone.

Could Tapash and Pran be lovers?

Chapter 44

The night collapsed on itself at Kachugaon, and Raj fell into an exhausted sleep as soon as he hit the bed. In his dreams, he saw Indra's eyes momentarily wide open, his punctured chest rising and falling. Pran looked straight into Raj's eyes as if taunting him to come and save his favourite brother. Raj couldn't move however hard he tried. With his eyes still locked on Raj's, Pran plunged the serrated dagger into Indra's chest and blood gushed out from his body like a torrid river.

Raj woke up crying. The tightness in his chest was so bad he thought his heart would burst. He got up and rushed to the bathroom to splash water on his face. He came back and sat in the bedside chair. Thinking back he remembered, on that fateful night, Indra had said he wanted to discuss something the next day. He shook his head; he would never know what his brother wanted to tell him. As Dr Delrome said, his brother died with many secrets buried in his heart.

He drifted off to sleep sitting in the chair thinking of his brother.

When he awoke in the morning, he could hear a lot of people talking outside. He came out of the room to see Jenkins and Dr Delrome already in the lounge room. Brown *Sahib* was standing outside in the courtyard in his full official khaki uniform. The buckle on his thick brown leather belt glistened in the morning sun. Ranger Baruah was standing with Brown *Sahib*. He had shaved and looked quite handsome. Raj joined Jenkins and the doctor and they all headed outside.

'I can send him to number sixteen along with that wretched creature from your elephant stable. The beast will get a double treat,' Raj heard Brown *Sahib* saying gleefully.

'Not so fast. We need to interrogate him. We can't act in haste,' Dr Delrome said worriedly.

'Discussing Tapash?' Raj asked. 'Yes, we do need to clarify a few things.'

'If I may, I can make that rascal spill the beans in minutes. Please allow me, Your Highness?' Brown *Sahib* requested, highly confident in his extra judicial measures. Raj looked at Dr Delrome who nodded. 'Leave it to me now,' Brown *Sahib* immediately signalled to two forest guards who rushed over. Now that he had gotten the green signal, he would stop at nothing. The guards ran off with their instructions.

'I have asked the guards to bring the rogue to the IB. They should be here shortly,' Brown *Sahib* said. 'In the meantime, may I request Your Highness to join us for breakfast?' Turning back, he yelled after the guards, 'Make sure the bastard is brought to the backyard! I don't want a spectacle for everyone to watch.'

After breakfast, Raj, Jenkins, and Dr Delrome went out to the backyard. Under the watchful eyes of Brown *Sahib*, two guards were tying a sobbing Tapash to a fig tree. Raj knew Tapash's game was up when he saw Brown *Sahib* walk over to Tapash wielding a cane stick.

'Wait, sir, don't hit me! I will tell you everything,' Tapash cried.

'Not so soon! Don't say anything yet,' Brown *Sahib* said. He seemed irritated with Tapash for breaking down even before the thrashing began. He threw the stick to the ground and rolled up his sleeve, and before anyone could guess what was happening, he threw a solid punch at Tapash's face, shattering his nose. Then he yanked his head back. Tapash let out a cry of pain, blinking his eyes and staring at Raj who himself was shocked by Brown *Sahib's* brutality.

Brown *Sahib* called out to Raj. 'I have made things easy for you. Just ask him anything.' He let out a proud laugh. 'He will clarify all your doubts about who was behind the plot to kill you.'

'Tapash! What's going on?' Raj's voice carried the pain of betrayal.

'Your Highness, please spare me. It was all plotted by your brother Pran *Sahib*. He had me trapped. Your brother is sick! He loves men and not women. I had to pleasure him regularly or he said he would have had me killed.'

Brown *Sahib* shoved the cane stick into his crotch. 'How did you pleasure him, you bastard?' Brown *Sahib* pursed his mouth in a self-satisfied smirk.

Raj looked at Brown *Sahib*, silently imploring him to spare the man so that he could clarify his doubts.

'Who killed father?' Raj demanded.

'Pran *Sahib* killed the *Maharaja*. He smothered him with a pillow. And then he tried to put the blame on Prince Indra. He asked me to send Ramu to Kachugaon to kill you. He was sent here as soon as we came to know of your Kachugaon trip.'

'That man is Ramu? You know him?'

'Yes, I know him.'

'When I was in Kachugaon, did Pran try to kill Indra also?' Raj asked, recalling the attack on Indra when he was camping near the Bengal border.

'Yes, Your Highness, Pran *Sahib* bribed some villagers to kill Prince Indra by setting his tent on fire while he was asleep. But some of his attendants saved him.'

'What about that letter to Ranger Baruah? Did Pran send it under Indra's name?'

'That was written by Pran *Sahib*. He knew Ranger Baruah was Prince Indra's friend. I posted those letters at regular intervals.'

'What about the fifty thousand?'

'I don't know about any fifty thousand,' Tapash said, crying and spluttering.

'I think as Baruah said there was no money involved. Your brother Pran knew these letters would be discovered. He just included it to give the impression that Prince Indra was paying his friend to get rid of you,' Dr Delrome clarified.

'This means that letter to *Diwan Sahib* was also forged.'

'I don't know about any more letters. But I can tell you Pran *Sahib* made me steal a lot of documents, letters, seals, and stamps from Prince Indra's office. He was always up to something.'

'And why did you not say anything to His Highness?' Brown *Sahib* growled again even though he was confused by all the confessions. He couldn't resist giving Tapash a smack in his already bloodied face.'What about Rajah *Sahib*, why did you kill him?' Brown *Sahib* wanted to remove any nagging doubts he had about Rajah *Sahib's* death.

'I have absolutely no idea what you are asking me about. I don't know any Rajah *Sahib*!' Tapash was sobbing loudly.

Raj looked at Brown *Sahib* assuring him that it was most likely the truth.

'Why did you do all this? You could have come to me,' Raj asked.

'How could I?' he broke into a sob again. 'Pran *Sahib* abused me both physically and mentally. He made me sleep with him. He assured me that my old father would be killed if I said anything about it to anyone. Even during the mourning period, he made me do a lot of terrible things.'

'Does the *Maharani* know anything about Pran and you? Is she in league with you?' Raj raised his voice surprising the others.

'No, she doesn't know anything. She is not involved. She loves you a lot,' Tapash said in one breath.

'And did you leak any information about my Kachugaon trip to Indra so that I wonder how he came to know about it?'

Tapash nodded his head.

'Wait,' Dr Delrome intervened. 'I have something to check. Were you in contact with the attendant looking after Princess Divya?' Dr Delrome demanded, pinning Tapash down with his steel blue eyes like a tiger.

'Yes,' Tapash nodded.

A shiver ran down Raj's spine.

Was he responsible for Divya's state when he found her?

'What did you do?' Dr Delrome had real menace in his voice.

'Dr Roy asked me to give some homeopathic medicine to Princess Divya's attendant. She was supposed to mix a small amount into the Princess' porridge without her knowledge. Dr Roy told me it was a bitter medicine and hence, the Princess shouldn't know. I was...'

Before Tapash could finish what he was saying, a stick came flying out of nowhere and hit him across the eye.

'Poisoning an innocent Princess, you bastard!' Brown *Sahib* shook the cane in his face.

This time, Brown *Sahib's* rage felt justifiable to Raj.

'Dr Roy is Pran's drinking partner. He must be in league with Pran. They must have been poisoning her slowly to avoid suspicion. Her exit saved her,' Dr Delrome said with relief.

'But it was he who arranged her trip to Calcutta,' Raj blurted at the doctor.

'Don't worry. I've talked to her doctor over the phone. She is alright,' Dr Delrome said.

Brown *Sahib* poked Tapash in his good eye with one finger. 'Good, you will be able to see the black panther with one eye.' Then he turned to the guards. 'Send this man and his accomplice to number sixteen at once.'

'Your Highness, let's go inside. There is no point in wasting any more time with this traitor,' Brown *Sahib* said. He then looked at the guards. 'You two know what to do with him. Don't give him anything to eat or drink. He has been sufficiently fed in the palace. Panthers don't like very fat men.'

A short while later, all of them were sitting in the lounge drinking cool tamarind juice. Nobody spoke, each bewildered with the revelations and the discoveries in the past hour.

'Is there a nearby river? Can I get a priest?' Raj broke the silence.

Everyone looked surprised.

'Yes, the nearest river is three miles away,' Brown *Sahib* said.

'And a priest?' Raj asked.

'We have a priest in the local temple. But why do you need a priest to go to the river?'

Raj looked at Brown *Sahib*; he had started to thoroughly like the man.

'Today is the eleventh day of Indra's passing away,' Raj said. 'He deserves a decent send off. I want to perform his final rituals on the river bank. He was unmarried, and I am his only living relative, other than Pran, who we now know has been the utmost traitor. I will do what I did for our father two days ago. I will really be blessed if I am able to unite my father with his favourite son in the spirit world. We need a priest for that.' He smiled at Brown *Sahib*. 'Can you please send someone to get the priest?'

A few hours later they stood in a group on the bank of a small river that wound its way through the Ripu forest. The Bhutan mountains stood silently in the distant background. The riverbank was lined with red and yellow flowers. Raj picked a few and proceeded to the river. Bending down, he scooped up some water in his cupped palm and released it slowly back to the river saying a silent prayer.

Chapter 45

Six months later

The Goalpara DC's bungalow had been converted into a makeshift church and a pastor had been brought in from Gauhati. The cooks from IB and *Lal Bungalow* were also in Dhubri preparing the wedding feast. Some of the royal party had arrived the day before. The bride's parents were amongst them and were staying in the Dhubri Circuit House. The new *Maharaja* of Paschim Behar had arrived that morning to attend the ceremony.

Brown *Sahib* was also there to attend the wedding. He had aged considerably in the last six months, but in his face was contentment. He had retired from the Assam forest department after almost forty years of service. He had decided to return to Australia — the country from which his missionary parents came. It was a big decision. But staying in India would have been equally difficult as he felt he couldn't have adjusted to any life outside Kachugaon. And after retirement he couldn't stay in Kachugaon, as not residing in the prestigious *Lal Bungalow* to him was tantamount to the ultimate humiliation. Jenkins wanted his retired deputy to stay in Dhubri, and he had been willing to find a part-time role for him in the department. But Brown *Sahib* said that staying in the busy border town would make him feel like a fish out of water.

Amaresh Baruah became the new ACF of Kachugaon. He was getting ready for a trip to the Rangoon Forest Institute after taking up the post. He would be on the lookout for new rangers to fill the positions vacated by the recent retirees. He held no grudge against his senior for all the insinuations and suspicion. He was also in Dhubri for the wedding. He had been in continuous consultation with Brown *Sahib*; he wanted to pick up as many tips as he could from the veteran forester. Baruah's elevation to ACF was instigated by Raj who had suggested to Jenkins that he overlook seniority when deciding on the new ACF for his division. Jenkins happily complied, but to strengthen the case for Baruah's elevation bypassing more elderly rangers, he decided to send him to an advanced forestry course in Rangoon for six months.

Jenkins wanted to release Ranger Das because of his not insignificant ineptitude. But an act of exceptional bravery had saved the day for him. A few months ago, he had led an ambush party deep inside Ripu and apprehended the kingpin of the river bandits. The patrolling party shot dead eleven smugglers, seized three large boats of loot, and captured their leader. With the help of the police, the ambush led to further arrests and the backbone of the illegal boat-making industry was broken. Jenkins and Brown *Sahib* were very happy with this outcome.

Ranger Miri retired and returned to upper Assam. He would never be rid of the guilt of lethally shooting his long-time associate Gethela. Nobody knew till date why Gethela disappeared after his meeting with Raj. He perhaps regretted implicating Brown *Sahib* and Rajah *Sahib* in the elephant girl trickery and feared the consequences. Nobody knew what he was doing in the timber depot that night when he was shot dead by Miri. Brown *Sahib* engaged one of his children to replace him.

Another casualty was Ghosh *Babu,* the head clerk of the forest department office in Kachugaon. He wielded considerable influence due to his intermediary position between Brown *Sahib* and all the other employees of the department. However, Baruah and Jenkins couldn't ignore the fact that no file in the office moved without his palms being greased. There were numerous complaints from the forest contractors, timber merchants and Kachugaon residents. Baruah forced him to take an early retirement with no benefits.

Tapash and his accomplice Ramu were transported to a remote location of the Ripu forest by Brown *Sahib.* There were speculations that they were used as live bait in the Big Cage. Some believed that Brown *Sahib* just let them loose in the deep forest. But the black panther terrorising the villagers was captured, which made many believe that some live enticement had been used. After Raj Narayan had returned from London, Tapash had been like his shadow. But since that day in Kachugaon, Raj never gave him another thought. The next time he saw Brown *Sahib*, he didn't even bother to ask what he had done with his one-time assistant.

Pran Narayan was arrested for double murder and criminal conspiracy. In consultation with the *Maharani, Diwan Sahib,* and Dr Delrome, Raj didn't press for a trial. They believed it would be embarrassing for the royal family. After a few weeks of incarceration, Pran Narayan committed suicide in his cell by consuming poison. It was said that the jailor in charge had facilitated the act and was secretly applauded for getting rid of the royal filth.

Dr Delrome retired from the Paschim Behar Royal Hospital and decided to join a Christian missionary hospital group based in Dhubri. He helped to organise various health camps in the numerous forest villages of Kachugaon including forest village twenty-two, Santhalbari's official name. This would also allow him to stay near his daughter and soon-to-be son-in-law. He had regularly visited his daughter for the past six months to check on her progress in rehabilitation. Each visit made the doctor prouder of his daughter and thankful to the Jenkins family.

Dr Delrome's assistant Dr Roy would not confess to his complicity with Pran Narayan, but he was removed from his post anyway.

Jenkins had been busy. It was a much more involved process than he initially realised to regularise Santhalbari as a forest village. There were endless meetings with superiors in Shillong. The biggest obstacle was that it wasn't a normal forest village that had been set up by the department based on manual labour needs. It stood as an alien civilisation in the forest of Ripu with a culture that revolved around bows and arrows. Jenkins and his superiors in Shillong realised that it would take a monumental effort to sanitise the community of its dependence on the archers. It was decided to set up an armed border police post in the village and recruit twenty young Santali men as forest guards.

Fortunately, Jenkins was successful in shielding Brown *Sahib* from departmental enquiry and possible criminal prosecution. He wrote to his mother that he had found out how his father was killed and where he was buried. He thought of exhuming the remains of the naturalists but later gave up the idea as it would generate too much publicity and could again implicate Brown *Sahib*. Instead, he erected a memorial stone at the site deep in the heart of Ripu. He had wanted to bring his mother to India and they would go there together as a family to pay homage. The wedding provided the perfect opportunity. His mother had arrived a week ago to attend the ceremony and to visit her husband's memorial. She later told him she was thinking of staying in India for a few months.

Jenkins' sister Janet had also had a busy few months. She extended her stay in India to care for the new guest in their house. She had thoroughly enjoyed rehabilitating the elephant girl as it had been so easy. The girl was intelligent and picked things up quickly. Janet taught her English and Police Superintendent Baker taught her the local language. Jenkins wasn't sure whether his sister would go back to England. She had become extremely attached to Teesta and he knew he wouldn't really mind if his sister stayed in India with him. He had also noticed her becoming quite fond of the police superintendent.

Divya seemed to recover from her sickness in the Calcutta hospital. But when she was taken to Bombay, her condition deteriorated. It seemed the slow poison, in the guise of homeopathic medicine being administered by Dr Roy ultimately took effect and Divya became seriously ill. Though she delivered a healthy baby girl, her health remained precarious. Raj blamed himself for Divya's condition. He moved to the Gwalior palace to stay with his wife until she recovered. Raj named his little Princess Narmada as he believed she had been conceived when they were on a camping trip on the bank of the Narmada River, in the state of his father-in-law. Divya didn't agree with the story though.

And that was when Raj decided that he would be a responsible husband and a good father. They both agreed to raise their daughter in Darjeeling, away from the palace with its never-ending secrets. Raj chose to look after the family's plantation business there. Divya wholeheartedly supported her husband's decision. Dr Delrome assured Raj that the salubrious climate of Darjeeling would be conducive to Divya's recovery.

Raj Narayan abdicated in favour of his half-brother Deep Narayan and made a promise to himself — he would never ride the Goalpara Forest Tramway again.

Indira Devi received the news about her daughter with mixed feelings. She was relieved as well as sad. Dr Delrome made a pact with her that they would let Teesta know the truth about her mother when the time was right. Indira didn't hold any grudges against Dr Delrome as she understood the circumstances in which he had acted to hide their daughter from the world. She also went to Parbatipur to organise a ceremony to liberate Rajah *Sahib* from his earthly connections, the sister, at last, embracing her roots. She set up an institute of higher education in Rajah *Sahib's* memory. The bloodline of Paschim Behar descended from her womb, but instead of distancing herself from her brother she took the young king to the Parbatipur mausoleum of her brother to seek his blessings.

Bert Jenkins looked handsome in his black suit. As Bert and Teesta entered the makeshift church through the doorway adorned with Frangipani, Raj noticed an emotional Dr Delrome standing near the doorway gazing lovingly at his daughter.

The bride's half-brother, *Maharaja* Deep Narayan, was sitting next to his mother. Deep looked proud and happy while Indira Devi shed many tears of pain and relief.

Soon afterwards, the priest declared them Mrs and Mr Jenkins. Raj wondered if Jenkins' new wife would ultimately tell her husband what had happened that one night in the forest. Or maybe then she had been a different girl — the elephant girl. The one who was standing today at the altar was his stepsister Teesta.

Glossary

ACF: Assistant Conservator of Forest, an intermediate post between ranger and a DFO (Divisional Forest Officer)

Almirah: A free-standing cupboard or wardrobe

Bandhani: A type of saree popular in the Western part of India

Bhaji: Indian finger food made of vegetables and spices and deep-fried

Beedi: An Indian cigarette which uses a leaf instead of paper for rolling the tobacco

Beel: Term for water body in the North East of India

Circuit House: An accommodation for Indian government officers to stay when they go on field trips

Dada: Older brother (Eastern India)

Dao: A type of Indian sword

DC: Deputy Commissioner, the administrative head of a district in the Eastern part of India

Devadasi: Meaning "servant of God", devadasi is a woman who dedicates her life to God in the temples of India under an ancient practice that has now been abolished

DFO: Divisional Forest Officer, a rank in the Indian Forest department heading a forest division and generally reporting to a conservator

Dhoti: A single piece cloth worn by Indian males that is tied around the waist.

Diya: Indian oil lamp

Durbar: Assembly

Goad: A tool used in the training of elephants

Golmohur: Native flame tree of India

Howdah: Seat on top of an elephant

IB: Inspection Bungalow-an accommodation for Indian officers to stay when they go on field trips

Koonkie: Tame elephant used to capture wild elephant

Lal Bungalow: Red Bungalow

Mahout: Elephant driver

Maidan: An open green area in the heart of city of Calcutta (Kolkata)

Makaibari: A type of white tea. Highly valued.

Mela Shikar: A type of elephant catching technique in north east India whereby a wild elephant is captured by throwing a noose from a domestic elephant

Musth: A state of heightened sexual arousal of male elephants

Pagli: Indian word for mad girl

Pakora: Vegetables deep-fried in a chickpea batter

Pandal: Temporary structure erected for functions

Poori: *Unleavened deep-fried bread popular in India*

Ranger: *A post in Indian Forest department in charge of a forest range*

Sahan: *Term for herd of elephant used in the lower region of Assam*

Sahib: *A polite formal address for a man*

Sal: *A type of tree native to India*

Shraddha: *A religious ceremony and feasting for close relatives of the departed*

Temporin: *A gland secretion from elephants in heat*

Terai: *Foothill region of the Himalayas in Nepal and India*

Zamindar: *Feudal landlord in Eastern India*